A BAD DAY AT THE OFFICE

After the third time I knocked and got no response, I tried the doorknob. The door was unlocked so I stuck my head in. "Stephanie?"

Standing in the open doorway, facing Stephanie's desk, I couldn't quite grasp what I was looking at. I mean, Stephanie was there, all right. She was slumped forward on her desk, arms hanging limply at her sides, head turned to her left, her right cheek pressed against the desk blotter. The icy blue light of the computer screen seemed to give an unnatural glow to her blond hair.

"Stephanie, are you asleep?" I whispered. If I woke her up, she'd yell at me for sure.

I tiptoed closer, trying to make as little noise as possible on the plush carpet. Halfway there, I froze. Even from where I stood, I could see the dark clotted blood on the underside of Stephanie's head, soaking into the blotter.

You'd think when you see something like that, you'd immediately start screaming your head off. The way they do in the movies. You don't, though. You take a couple of uncertain steps forward, and you stare at the small, dark hole at the base of your boss's skull.

*   *   *

Praise for the Bert and Nan Tatum mysteries:

"Deftly plotted and wickedly amusing."—Joan Hess

"Sheer fun. As enjoyable as mysteries get."—*Cleveland Plain Dealer*

"An engaging pair of sleu[ths] [from start to] finish."—Dorothy Cannell

"Most engaging."—*Bookli[st]*

"Easy, breezy fun."—*Publ[ishers Weekly]*

BOOK YOUR PLACE ON OUR WEBSITE AND MAKE THE READING CONNECTION!

We've created a customized website just for our very special readers, where you can get the inside scoop on everything that's going on with Zebra, Pinnacle and Kensington books.

When you come online, you'll have the exciting opportunity to:

- View covers of upcoming books
- Read sample chapters
- Learn about our future publishing schedule (listed by publication month *and author*)
- Find out when your favorite authors will be visiting a city near you
- Search for and order backlist books from our online catalog
- Check out author bios and background information
- Send e-mail to your favorite authors
- Meet the Kensington staff online
- Join us in weekly chats with authors, readers and other guests
- Get writing guidelines
- AND MUCH MORE!

**Visit our website at
http://www.kensingtonbooks.com**

A Bert and Nan Tatum Mystery

Double Cross

Barbara Taylor McCafferty
and Beverly Taylor Herald

Kensington Books
Kensington Publishing Corp.
http://www.kensingtonbooks.com

KENSINGTON BOOKS are published by

Kensington Publishing Corp.
850 Third Avenue
New York, NY 10022

Kensington and the K logo Reg. U.S. Pat. & TM Off.

First Kensington Hardcover Printing: October, 1998
First Kensington Paperback Printing: February, 2000
10 9 8 7 6 5 4 3 2 1

Printed in the United States of America

To our parents, Charles Allen and Marjorie Taylor
(who do not in any way, honest to God,
we promise—are we clear on this?—resemble Nan and
Bert's parents),
with much love and gratitude
for giving their own doubles
double helpings of love and guidance.

We'd like to acknowledge the following people who helped so much in the writing of this book:
Sandie Stutzenberger, who encouraged our identical murderous impulses by presenting us both with identical pens (with blades concealed inside); Rita Safranek, who helped us clean up Nan's language; and Lynn Hightower, who acted as our literary labor coach ("Push! Push!").

We'd also like to acknowledge the help of all the sets of twins who've shared with us their twice-told tales and twin facts, including Meredith and Melissa Cook. It has been wonderful talking and meeting all of you, and that goes double for both of us.

Chapter 1

●

BERT

I guess I should be happy. After a mere thirty-nine years, my twin sister Nan and I finally have the chance to do something that a lot of Baby Boomers like us have been wanting to do all their lives: *Blame it all on Mom.*

What's more, Nan and I can blame it all on Mom without the slightest fear of contradiction. Because, let's face it, if Mom had not gotten the job for me in the first place, if Mom had not been old friends with the mother of my new boss, *and* if Mom had not been the type to absolutely freak out if I were to play hooky from the aforementioned job, Nan and I would never have found ourselves hip-deep in another murder. It's as simple as that.

I guess, then, that I should be relishing the moment. The last time Nan and I had anything we could legitimately blame on Mom was, I believe, right after we were born. When she named us. Can you believe the woman actually named Nan and me after the older pair of Bobbsey twins? I mean, does the word *tacky* come to mind?

Mom didn't let a little thing like the Bobbseys being boy and girl twins stop her either. Oh, no, even after she found out that the boy and girl twins she'd thought she was expecting had in actuality turned out to be two identical little girls, she'd still used the two names she'd already picked out. That's Mom for you. Once she makes up her mind about something, she isn't about to change it for something as insignificant as the facts.

Right after Nan and I were born, Mom had simply lengthened the older Bobbsey boy's name, from Bert to *Bertrice*. She'd called me Bertrice just long enough to have it written on my birth certificate; then, from that point forward, she'd called me Bert, explaining to anybody who asked that Bert was my nickname.

Good thinking, Mom.

But then again, Mom is always thinking. Also, planning. And scheming. That was pretty much how Nan and I ended up in this mess in the first place. Nan, I admit, does not totally agree with my interpretation of events, but there's not a doubt in my mind how it all happened. This whole thing lies right at Mom's fuzzy-slippered feet. The only reason Nan refuses to blame it all on Mom is that my beloved twin sister is pretty much dead set on blaming a lot of it on *me*.

Apparently, I am somehow at fault just because I asked Nan to cover for me at my new job with Stephanie Whitman, J.D., P.S.C. Or, as Nan used to refer to Stephanie's initials: B.I., T.C.H. Before I'd worked for Stephanie, I'd always thought that Nan saying such a thing was a bit unkind. Now, of course, I think Nan was guilty of understatement.

She is also guilty of a slight distortion of the truth. The way Nan tells it, from that very first day, she'd known I was on the road to ruin, and in a rush of sisterly devotion, she'd tried to put up a detour.

That's not exactly the way I remember that first day. Or, rather, that first evening. It had been, as I recall, a Friday evening in late July. Even though it was dark outside,

Louisville was doing what it always did in the middle of summer—it was pretending it was a sauna. Inside, though, I had the AC set at "meat locker," and I was feeling cool, calm, and collected. My tone—no matter what anybody else might say to the contrary—was definitely congenial as I sat down on the couch next to Nan.

"Nan," I began, "can I talk to you a minute?"

Nan didn't even glance in my direction. She was doing what she always did around six o'clock on any Friday when she doesn't have a date. She was sitting on my couch, eating one of the Quarter Pounders I'd brought home, and reading the Louisville *Courier-Journal*. More specifically, she was reading the comics. That's right—Funky Winterbean, Rex Morgan M.D., and Charlie Brown—these are the sort of people that Nan likes to keep up with.

I just sat there for a moment, watching her dark eyes traveling over the page and trying to gauge just how absorbed she was in what she was reading. When you're looking at a face identical to your own, it's not exactly a stretch to pick up on nuances of expression.

Not to mention that lately I've had a lot of practice watching Nan read the comics. These days Nan is what I refer to as "between boyfriends," and what she refers to as "in No-Man's-Land," so she's been spending a lot of her Fridays over here. Of course, it's not as if she has to drive clear across the city or anything to get over here. I live right next door in the other half of Nan's duplex.

I started renting this apartment from Nan shortly after Jake, my husband of nineteen years, decided to up and leave me for his twenty-two-year-old secretary. Jake's affair with his secretary didn't last, but our divorce has been hanging in there for almost two years now. Our divorce has lasted even though Jake started coming around a few months ago, trying to talk me into taking him back.

Nan's eyes were now looking a little glazed. A good sign, if I ever saw one. If I timed it just right, there was every chance that Nan might not hear one word that I was saying. I might get her to agree without having the slightest idea what she was agreeing to. "Nan?" I said. "I've got a favor to ask."

Once again, Nan didn't even look in my direction. She'd spread several sections of the newspaper all around her, and I tried not to notice that the newsprint was making direct contact with the tailored cushions of my pale blue chintz sofa. Mind you, I've pointed out to Nan more than once that if handling the *Courier* causes your hands to turn gray; then the same thing would probably happen to just about anything that touched the paper. Like oh, say, my pale blue chintz sofa cushions, for example. I'm not sure what kind of ink the *Courier-Journal* uses to print its newspaper, but I do believe it could not possibly smear any worse if it printed the thing in black chalk.

I didn't say a word, but I think Nan might've picked up on my air of disapproval—or she might even have dimly recalled the four or five hundred times that I've asked her not to put newspapers on my couch—because she gave the comic section a vehement little shake, almost daring me to complain, as she reached for her glass of Coke. It was sitting right next to mine, in front of us on my Ethan Allen maple coffee table.

I reached for mine and took a long, long sip. Nan and I have not lived together since high school, but ever since we started living right next door to each other, we've discovered more and more things that we do just alike. For example, both of us always order the exact same thing from Mickey D's. A Quarter Pounder without the pickles, a medium Coke, and large fries.

Nan was now munching on a large fry and smiling to herself as she continued her scan of the comics.

This looked like as good a time as any. "Listen Nan," I said as fast as I could, "I need you to cover for me at the law office. It'll just be tomorrow, just the one day, and—"

Uh-oh. Nan was paying more attention to me than I thought. She stopped eating the french fry, and her dark head jerked in my direction. "What?"

I began to talk even faster. "—the job is really easy, you'll have no trouble at all—"

Nan cut me off, responding with the kind of empathy you'd expect from somebody who'd once been your womb mate. "Are you freaking nuts?"

I took another long sip of Coke. *Freaking* is a word that Nan says a lot these days. It is a definite improvement over the F-word she used to say. In fact, it's an improvement over the S-word, the A-word, and the assorted other letter words that she still uses quite a bit. She's been trying to tone her language down ever since a mutual acquaintance referred to her as "the potty-mouth twin."

Nan tells me that talking like this is an occupational hazard. Nan, you see, is a disc jockey. She's on WCKI, one of Louisville's several country-music stations, doing the afternoon shift from ten to three. According to Nan, if you spend your entire day being very careful what you say on the air, lest the FCC take away your license, you've got a whole lot of curse words saved up by the end of the day.

In my opinion, if you've managed to hold them all day,

you should have the holding thing mastered by the time you get off work.

"I can't believe you'd ask me to do such a shitty—"

OK, so self-control was not one of Nan's strong suits. I interrupted her. "Look, all I'm asking is that you just substitute for me tomorrow while—"

Nan's large eyes got even larger. "You can't be talking about switching," Nan said.

It was a statement, not a question. "I can't be?" I said. I was pretty sure I not only could be, I was.

Nan glared at me. "I can *not* believe you'd even consider doing such a thing again," she said. "After we freakin' *agreed*. Never, ever again. Not in our mutual lifetimes."

Nan gave the paper in her hand another little shake for emphasis.

"Come on, Nan," I said. "I've got a job interview tomorrow. All you have to do is fill in for me while I'm at the interview. *Please.* I wouldn't even have to ask you if Stephanie the Hun wasn't making me work overtime—wouldn't you know, she'd make me come in on a Saturday?"

"But this will never work. This is a desk job, for God's sake. Surely, Stephanie would notice that you're suddenly writing left-handed," Nan said.

Nan had a point. She and I are what is called mirror twins, which means that instead of being exact duplicates like most identical twins, Nan and I are a even more rare subtype of identicals—mirror images. What it means to us on a more practical level is that Nan's natural hair part is on the left, mine is on the right, she starts off on her left foot, I start off on my right, and she is left-handed while I am right-handed. What it also means, in this particular instance, was that Nan was grasping at straws.

"Not a problem," I said. "Because Stephanie's going to be out of town herself. In fact, that's why she wants me to work Saturday anyway—to cover the office. Come on, Nan, you gotta help me out here. It's not like you'd have to take off work to do it for God's sake."

Nan does do the weekend shift, but she only has to do it every other Saturday. Tomorrow was a Saturday she had off.

Nan lowered the paper and just stared at me. "Bert, the last time we switched, somebody *died.*"

I gave her a level-eyed stare of my own. True, the last time we'd done this, there had been a slight problem concerning a dead person on the premises, but Nan was making it sound as if our switching had been so traumatic for some poor soul it had killed him. "Nan, our switching places didn't have anything to do with it." I shrugged. "It was just a coincidence."

Once again, Nan didn't blink. "Somebody *died.*"

"Yeah, well, I'm dying now," I said. "Every single day I have to work for that woman, I am absolutely shriveling up and blowing away. I have got to find another job. And soon."

The truth was I'd started looking through the want ads right after my first day on the job. The problem was I couldn't just take any old job. It had to be something pretty outstanding, or else Mom would never understand why I'd want to quit.

"Really, Nan," I said "I have *got* to get out of there."

Nan's response was somewhat less than sympathetic. She snorted. A truly disgusting sound.

So much for twins being able to feel each other's pain.

Nan followed up the snort with a head shake. From to side to side. "No, no, a thousand times no."

I tried not to get irritated, but it wasn't easy. After all, none of this was exactly news. I'd been complaining to Nan ever since I'd consented to taking the job Stephanie's secretary had so unceremoniously vacated. My predecessor's abrupt departure should've told me something right there. I mean, who would quit a perfectly good job with no notice, no resignation, no nothing?

I believe "perfectly good" is the questionable phrase here.

I'd taken the job in the first place, as I mentioned earlier, under maternal duress. Without checking with me or anything, Mom had up and given my name to her friend Lydia Whitman to give to Lydia's daughter, Stephanie-The-Attorney. Over the years Mom had never said Stephanie's name by itself—she always added those other two words— so after a while, I'd begun to think of Stephanie-The-Attorney as one of those hyphenated names. Like Julia Louis-Dreyfus. Or Jean-Claude Van Damme. Or Rikki-Tikki-Tavi. According to Mom, Stephanie-The-Attorney needed a Girl Friday right away.

I'd had my reservations right from the beginning. For one thing, I've always hated the term Girl Friday. I mean, sure, Friday had no doubt been a godsend to Robinson Crusoe, but, as I recall, old Rob had the poor guy doing everything but spoon-feeding him. As a job title, I've always felt that it invariably led to unreasonable expectations.

"It'll be so cute, having my daughter work for Lydia's daughter," Mom had cooed, smiling at me. She'd actually shown up on my doorstep one evening to do the hard sell in person. "Why, it'll be almost like working for family, Bert."

Uh-oh. Which family was she talking about? Our family? Or the Manson family? I'd cleared my throat. "I wonder why the other girl left so quickly," I said. "I mean, without giving notice or anything."

Mama took a long drag off her cigarette. "Now, Bert, Stephanie-The-Attorney is a lovely, lovely, lovely girl."

I just looked at her. Oh God. Three lovelys. The last time Mom used three lovely's, she'd been trying to talk me into going out with the son of a friend of hers. The lovely, lovely, lovely boy had not been all that lovely. In fact, all he'd needed was a bell to ring and he could've given Quasimodo a run for his money.

"This is a wonderful opportunity, Bert," Mom added, giving me a piercing look over the top of her wire rims. "A wonderful, wonderful, wonderful opportunity."

Oh dear God in Heaven.

Unlike the moms of all our friends, Mama has always been taller than Nan and me—about an inch taller than our own five-six. She also outweighs our 125 pounds by about twenty pounds. We have brown eyes, Mom has blue. And while our hair is a dark, chestnut brown, nobody knows exactly what color Mom's hair really is these days. Her hair color is pretty much whatever shade it turns out to be when she finally comes out of the bathroom. Over the years Mom has been a blonde, a brunette, and a redhead, sometimes all in the same month. Fortunately, once she hit her sixties, she realized she really ought to lighten up on the shades somewhat. Or else people were going to start confusing her with Morticia from the *Addams Family*.

On this particular week, however, Mom had apparently

lightened up a little too much, and whatever box she'd picked out had gone a little too red. Her short-cropped curls bore a distinct resemblance to a Brillo pad.

"I really don't think, at this point, Bert, honey, that you can afford to be picky," Mama went on. Two exclamation points had formed between her brows. "I mean, it's not like you already have a job."

Mama was slightly in error there. I'd been working steadily as an office temporary for almost two years now, at one assignment after another—but apparently, if the job title has the word temporary in it, it just doesn't qualify as steady employment in Mama's book. "And, sweetie," she said, pointing at me with her cigarette, "I don't want to make you feel bad or anything, but I have gone to an awful lot of trouble here just to make sure that you get this opportunity."

Have I mentioned that, as a proper Southern lady, Mama talks very slowly? In a soft, lazy drawl? She talks so slowly that more likely than not, when she leaves me a message on my answering machine, it gets cut off. So that a lot of her messages go like this. "Bert? Are. You. There? No? O. K. Well. Then. This. Is—" If I didn't always recognize the lazy drawl, I'd never have any idea who it was.

"I should think you'd be thrilled," Mama was going on.

Oh God. Mom was now doing her injured "after-all-I've-done-for-you-this-is-the-thanks-I-get" tone. I suspect that if there was a Mother school somewhere, where all the new moms could go to learn how to perfect their mothering techniques, Mom could teach the Injured-Tone class.

I knew when I was beaten. "Mom," I said, "I'm thrilled."

Mama's face immediately brightened. "You're going to love Stephanie-The-Attorney," she said, beaming at me. "She's a lovely, lovely, lovely girl!"

Oh God.

The first day I reported to work, the lovely, lovely, lovely girl was sitting at the desk in the receptionist area—where I would be working. As I walked in the door, Stephanie got to her feet, and—without so much as giving me a cursory glance—picked up a stack of papers from the top of the desk and stared pointedly at her watch.

I was five minutes early, I'll have you know.

While Stephanie stared at her watch, I stared at Stephanie. Even though our mothers were good friends, I'd never actually met Stephanie before.

In all honesty, she was most definitely lovely. In fact, she was gorgeous. From Mom, I knew that she was thirty-five, but she could easily pass for late twenties. Tall, willowy, with a chest that might've gotten her a part on *Baywatch*. And as if that wasn't enough, short, wavy, golden blond hair, a perfect nose, big blue eyes, and a full red mouth. In a navy blue suit with a white draped-neck blouse that was draped just a tad too low and a tight skirt that was just a tad too short, Stephanie reminded me of Marilyn Monroe in *Niagara*.

I wouldn't want anybody thinking, however, that Stephanie looking the way she did made me feel like chopped liver, and that this was the real reason I didn't want to work for her anymore. True, I did feel, standing next to her, that chopped liver and I had quite a lot in common, but the real reason I wanted to quit is, I believe, pretty much evident from our first conversation. "Stephanie, it's so nice to finally meet you," I said, smiling. "Mom and Lydia have told me so many wonderful things about you." I stuck out my hand.

Stephanie glanced at it, stretched her mouth in what she

must've thought was a smile, and, instead of shaking my hand, put the stack of papers in it.

"These need to be retyped for court in one hour," she said. "I've penciled in all the corrections. One full copy to the file, of course—and all documents are to be filed with the most recent correspondence on top, punched one-half of an inch from the top. Not one-fourth of an inch, not three-fourths of an inch, but exactly one-half of an inch. Please measure if you're unsure. Everything else you need, I'm sure you can find."

With that, Miss Congeniality turned on her stiletto heels and marched into the inner office, closing the door behind her with a little slam. "Nice to meet you, too," I said to the door.

And then, of course, I sat down and began to type.

Before Stephanie left for her hearing, she gave me still more typing, and instructions on exactly what to say when particular clients called, depending upon whom she was avoiding, whom she was wooing for more business, and who still owed her money. She rattled the names off so fast, I was sure I'd ask some deadbeat to meet her for lunch. I had to ask her to repeat the names.

Stephanie gave me a look that could frost an iron. "Bertrice, I'm really not accustomed to repeating myself. Mother told me you were fully trained. That is correct, isn't it? You do take shorthand, or speedwriting, or something of that ilk, don't you?" As Stephanie spoke, she waved a manicured hand in the air. As if to indicate that all these mundane details were really too, too beneath her to even think about.

I was thinking about a few mundane details myself. Like how nice it would feel to get to my feet and walk right out of there without looking back.

Except that Mom would kill me.

"Of course I take shorthand," I heard myself say.

Stephanie heaved a huge sigh and rolled her eyes. "Well, then, please," she said, "*use* it." Then, continuing to sigh and roll her baby blues, she went over all the names and the accompanying messages again. Even though she wasn't a mother, Stephanie had apparently taken Mom's Injured-Tone class. It was my guess she'd gotten an A.

When Stephanie came back from court, though, the injured tone was history, and she was all smiles. This, I soon learned, was a very bad sign. Stephanie's smiles were much like a crocodile's smiles. Only, in the case of the crocodile, the smile would've been significantly more sincere.

"Look what I've got!" Stephanie said. "I dropped into that computer store a block or so from the courthouse, and, on impulse, I bought a Newton!"

I stared at the box she held in her hand. The only Newtons I was familiar with were Fig and Isaac. "A Newton," I repeated vaguely.

Stephanie nodded, her blond curls dancing around her face. "I'll be able to keep track of appointments and look up client phone numbers and make notes even when I'm out of the office!"

I was now looking at the box even more closely. It had a multicolored Apple logo prominently displayed and the words MAC OS printed on all four sides.

I cleared my throat. "This is a Macintosh machine. Our desktops are PCs." I knew almost nothing about computers, but I did know this: the Macintosh and the PC had two very different operating systems, and much like me and my ex, they were totally incompatible.

Stephanie waved her hand again. Yet another insignificant detail beneath her notice. "Oh, I know that," she said, her tone implying that everyone in the Western Hemisphere also knew it. "The salesman tried to sell me a software program that would convert all the contact information on my desktop into something or another that the Newton could read, but I told him, what did I need to spend the money to get that for? I've got *you!*"

Oh my, yes, she had me all right. In fact, from that point forward, she had me typing in every one of her clients, business associates, and family members' home addresses, work addresses, and assorted phone numbers. She also had me adding little notes to each contact, detailing telephone conversations she'd had with every one of them. Some of the names in her contact file had as many as fifty little notes to add.

I'd been working for Stephanie for almost a month, and I was still trying to finish the stupid thing. I saw absolutely no reason to mention this little detail to Nan, however. I also saw no reason to tell her that working on a few of the documents in the PC had been a little tricky for me, and that a couple of times I'd hit the wrong key and obliterated a few of the files I'd typed in for the last hour and a half. I'm still not sure how I did this. All I know was that I eventually had to phone my son Brian and have him perform a rescue mission.

Brian is taking a couple of computer science courses at the University of Kentucky this summer, temporarily sharing an apartment with his sister Emily. Both of them continue to assure each other it's just for the summer—God forbid they'd have to put up with each other for more than three months at a time. However, it was a good thing he was within driving distance, because he showed up only a couple of hours after my distress call. Of course, I did have to put up with Brian's continual small talk during the whole thing. Small talk that began, "Jeez, Mom, I cannot believe you did this."

Horror was clearly in his voice. Which kind of hurt. Considering that this was the kid who used to brag about how cool I was to his friends, back when all I needed to do to wow him was throw a strike in softball. Back then, he called me Dead-Eye. Now it was Brain-Dead.

At any rate, the Newton still needed completing. But it wasn't as if I was asking Nan to work for Stephanie for the rest of her life or anything. All I was asking was one tiny, little, infinitesimal day. And, when you thought about it, spending the day typing contact information into Stephanie's Newton might even make the day go faster.

"Nan," I said, putting my hands together in a gesture of total supplication, "come on, I just can't miss this interview."

The job I was supposed to interview for did sound like just what I was looking for. Actually, what I was looking for was anything that did not have Stephanie within a five-mile radius, but I knew full well if I just went back to doing temporary work again, I'd have some tall explaining to do to Mom—and to Lydia.

The only way to avoid that little scenario was to find a job that was too good to pass up. This one, according to the ad in last Sunday's *Courier*, was a secretarial position at the Kentucky Derby Festival. It offered better benefits than Stephanie, and it paid three thousand dollars a year more. After I saw the ad, my heart actually started pounding. I typed out my résumé, and traveled to the only post office in Louisville that is open on a Sunday—the one on Crittenden Drive—just so I would be among the very first résumés the

Festival received. Even still, I was surprised when they called me for an interview.

"Nan," I added, "please. I'm begging here."

Nan was rolling her eyes again. "You and I made a solemn vow that—"

"Solemn, schmolem." I hate to admit it, but I really did say that. "Look, Nan, if it weren't for Stephanie, I would be off tomorrow like normal people, and switching wouldn't even be necessary. It's not my fault. I don't want to switch. I have no choice."

I tried to explain. How I'd already scheduled the interview at the Festival before Stephanie had asked—no, told—me that I'd be working on Saturday this week. How I was tempted to just quit, but I knew if I did, Stephanie would complain to Lydia. And then Lydia would tell Mom. And Mom would jump from Injured-Tone class to Historic-References class, listing all the ways I've disappointed her over the years up to and including the agony of delivery. "Nan, you've got to switch with me."

Can you believe, after all that, Nan still said, "Bert, the last time we switched, somebody died."

Oh for God's sake. Wasn't this where I came in? I was suddenly reminded of something else about that last time we switched. "And who exactly found that dead person, Nan? Who was switching with whom, and who found the body? Who had to walk in and stumble over an actual honest-to-God dead person?"

Nan just looked at me without saying anything. Apparently, she needed her memory refreshed.

"That would be me, Nan," I said. "I ran into a dead person because of you." I hated to admit it, but I was beginning to sound as if I'd taken Mom's Injured-Tone class. "The way I see it, you owe me," I said.

Nan rolled her eyes.

"You owe me big-time," I added.

Nan rolled her eyes one more time, and ran her hand through her dark hair. But this time she did not shake her head.

I suppressed a smile. Guilt can be a powerful thing.

Chapter 2

•

NAN

I cannot believe I actually agreed to do this. Without a gun being held to my head or anything.

I actually stood there in Bert's apartment at 8 A.M. on a Saturday morning—a Saturday morning that I had off, for God's sake—and I said nothing while Bert handed me several sheets of handwritten instructions and blithely told me to "do the best I could."

Man, I must really adore my sister.

Of course, no matter how much I adored her, I probably would never have agreed had Bert's new boss not been out of town. For some reason, knowing that Stephanie-The-Attorney wouldn't be in the office to stare at me oddly when I began to act as if I had no idea what the hell I was doing actually gave me the ridiculous notion that I could pull this whole thing off without a hitch.

Then, too, Bert assured me that she herself acted as if she had no idea what she was doing every single day that she was on the job, so my stumbling around looking bewildered would only make my impersonation that much more convincing. "Everything will be fine," Bert said.

I can't believe I believed her. I also can't believe I actually put on one of her Corporate-Bert suits. Bert has a blue million of these little suits, all crisp and tailored, all in varying shades of blue and gray and brown.

One of the things that I've always loved about being on the radio is that nobody can see me. I can stagger into work wearing no makeup, torn jeans, a discolored T-shirt, and boots that look as if a dog has been chewing on them, and nobody is the wiser. As long as my voice sounds sexy, I am lookin' good.

Becoming Corporate-Nan, in fact, was one of my nightmares. But here I was, in a nightmare come true, wearing a brown, double-breasted Liz Claiborne suit, a brown print Liz scarf, Liz gold door-knocker earrings—and, of all things, Liz Claiborne panty hose. I myself didn't have any panty hose without runs in them, so Bert had insisted on giving me a pair of hers. I would've thought that Bert was being terribly generous, except that I knew full well that since I was being Bert all day today, she just didn't want people thinking that she was the sort of woman who'd go out in public with zebra legs.

Unfortunately, the only type of panty hose Bert owns is control top, meaning evidently that the panty part of the panty hose is so tight that it controls the blood flow to your head. I was feeling a little dizzy as I drove Bert's Camry down Bardstown Road, heading toward Broadway and downtown Louisville. In the interest of authenticity, Bert and I had switched cars.

It made me a little uneasy to realize that Bert was, at this very moment, driving my dent-free Neon to her interview. Particularly since she'd totaled her other car— a turquoise Festiva—only a few months ago. Of course, the accident had not been her fault—unless, of course, you count causing someone to want to murder you as something that would be your fault.

The thought that someone had actually tried to end Bert's life still makes me feel a little ill. I try to concentrate on the fact that the guilty party is now behind bars, and that luckily the only casualty was the turquoise roller skate that Bert called a car. With the insurance money she got for the Festiva as a down payment, Bert bought herself the 1989 silver Camry I was now driving, a car which she calls Hi Ho. She seems to think that this is a great name for a car, but I've noticed that she's had to explain it to people more than once: "Uh, you know, *Hi Ho Silver?* As in what the Lone Ranger called his horse? Since, you know, in order to get this car, I had to deal with a, you know, *Loan Arranger,* I thought that ..."

Sometimes, I worry about Bert.

Hi Ho has a mere 86,000 miles to its credit. It also has a small dent near the gas tank, and a pretty big dent in the front fender, but according to Bert, a dented car was exactly what she was looking for. So that the next time she backs into a parking meter or collides with a tree, she won't feel bad.

This is something I've always admired about Bert. She may give her car a name she has to explain to people, but she's always planning ahead. As proof of this last, in addition to the pages of instructions, Bert had given me her parking garage security card. "You'll need to have it," she said, "to get in and out of the office parking garage."

Sure enough, when I pulled in at the address on Liberty Street that Bert had given me, there was a yellow-striped bar blocking the entrance. There was also a metal boxlike contraption with a slit the width of Bert's garage card. In case a visitor didn't immediately make the connection, printed in all caps above the slit were the words INSERT CARD HERE.

I'd put the card on the seat beside me, right on top of Bert's handwritten instructions, and what do you know, the card was actually still there. It hadn't fallen into a crack in the seat, or slid off onto the floor, or any of a number of things that always seem to happen to things I put on the seat beside me.

Heartened by how well things seemed to be going, I deftly inserted the card. After which, I just sat there, waiting for the bar to lift so that I could drive right in.

The bar didn't move.

I knew it. Nothing could be this easy. I yanked the card out and stuck the damn thing in again, wiggling it a little this time. I have found, when dealing with machinery of any sort, that wiggling can work wonders.

This time, however, must've been the exception that proved the rule. Wiggling didn't do a thing. The arm barring my way remained motionless.

I took a deep breath and tried to remain calm. Across the way, I could see the parking garage attendant's head turning in my direction. He was in a glass cage about twenty feet ahead of me, near the bank of elevators into the building. I shifted the car in reverse, intending to back out of the garage, and go somewhere to figure out what was wrong with the card. Just as I was shifting, however, a red Honda pulled in behind me. Blocking me in.

OK, back to the original plan. I shoved the card in again, jiggling it this time. Jiggling is a lot like wiggling, only you do it with more force.

Jiggling didn't work either.

Apparently, the guy in the Honda behind me took this turn of events even worse than I did. He honked. I briefly considered giving the guy the finger, but I decided against it. Bert would never give anybody the finger. And today I was being Bert.

Even as Bert, however, I could not believe that anyone in Louisville could possibly be in that big a hurry to get to work on a Saturday morning. The guy behind me actually honked again. I was rethinking the finger issue when I noticed the garage attendant was now opening the door to his little cage and looking this way.

Damn. Or, as Bert would say, *Darn.* The third time is supposed to be the charm, so I stuck the card in the slot one more time. Wiggling and jiggling and ramming and jamming. A combination I have found to be extremely powerful in the past.

All this powerful combination did, however, was prove that the third time in some cases is not charming at all.

Behind me the Honda honked again. The attendant was now walking toward me, a frown on his face.

I knew that I was being ridiculous, but my heart actually started to pound even as I was telling myself: *For God's sake, Nan, even if they found out you weren't who you were pretending to be, what could they do? Arrest you for impersonating a Bert?*

Bert would be the one who was in trouble. Not me. Stephanie-The-Attorney would, no doubt, fire her. That thought was a splash of cold water. Oh my, yes, if anybody noticed that I was not really Bert, Stephanie would probably fire the woman who still owed me this month's rent.

It was a sobering thought.

There were now three cars behind me, all honking in a

cacophony of sound. They were making so much noise that if I hadn't been looking right at him, I might not have noticed the parking attendant walk up to my car. Having spotted him, however, I finished rolling the Camry's window down all the way and gave him one of my most winning smiles, if I do say so myself.

The parking attendant, apparently, was not won over. About twenty-five or so, black, tall, muscular, and handsome in a Denzel Washington kind of way, the attendant folded his arms across his chest and did not return my smile. "You put in your code?" As he spoke, his black eyes scanned the inside of my car, like maybe he thought I was trying to bring in explosives.

"Code?" I said. I glanced down at Bert's instructions, still lying on the seat beside me. It probably would've been a good idea to actually read those pages before I got here. On the top page, in Bert's neat round handwriting, were several numbers under a heading: GARAGE CODE. The two words had been underlined three times.

Hey, who knew? I guess the keypad to the left of the card slot should've tipped me off, but WCKI, the radio station where I work, has an open parking lot. I never have to worry about this kind of shit. Of course, I do have to worry about stolen car radios, boosted hubcaps, and missing automobile batteries, but special codes? That would be a no.

I gave the parking attendant another winning smile—which incidentally felt pasted on—and then I reached over and punched in the numbers on the keypad. All the while the attendant just stood there, frowning and—I don't think this was my imagination—looking more and more suspicious.

I smacked the *enter* key on the keypad, and, slowly, the arm lifted. Behind me, the driver applauded.

I briefly rethought the finger issue, but once again I concluded that it was a bad idea considering I was still being Bert, of non-finger fame. Not to mention, Denzel was still standing right there. He might misinterpret my finger, and think I meant it for him. I gave him yet another smile, as he shook his dark head. "You know," he said, "I can't understand your not remembering your code."

I just looked at him, my mouth going dry. Did he suspect that I really wasn't Bert, after all? Oh God. I took a deep breath, wondering if I should try to explain why I hadn't remembered the dumb garage code. Maybe, oh, say that I had a drug problem which had unfortunately resulted in short-term memory loss. Saying such a thing would, no doubt, serve Bert right for getting me into this mess in the first place. Before I could say anything, though, Denzel hurried on, "So, how many times have you forgotten your code so far this month, Miss Tatum?"

I blinked at that one, and then grinned in earnest. Well, what do you know, I'd been doing Bert perfectly, after all. "I'll get it right the next time," I said. "Sorry." Then, fighting the impulse to lay rubber, I drove slowly and cautiously—just like Bert would have—into the darkened garage.

Stephanie's office was located on the fifth floor of the stone, Victorian-era building adjacent to the parking garage. These lovely, old buildings are rapidly disappearing from downtown Louisville, being replaced in the name of progress by many-storied high-rises with a lot more glass and a lot less charm. Stephanie's building at Third and Liberty was one of the few that had been preserved. It had, in fact, just been renovated. Stephanie's must've been one of the first offices to locate here after the building was reopened for tenants, because there seemed to be no other tenants on her floor. The other offices I passed after I got out of the elevator and headed toward Stephanie's still had *this-space-for-rent* signs on their front doors.

Getting into Stephanie's office just took a key, thank God. No code, no secret handshake, just one simple twist of a key. What's more, I hadn't had any trouble finding the office key either. It had been Scotch-taped to one of Bert's instructions. I have mentioned, have I not, that I do love my sister? Bert is nothing if not thorough.

Stephanie's front door wasn't hard to find either. It was, in fact, hard not to notice. At the far end of the hall, her door was extra wide, natural oak, and polished to a mirrorlike sheen, with a large engraved brass plaque that read: *Stephanie L. Whitman, J.D., P.S.C.* Just walking through a door like this, you knew it was going to cost you.

I inserted Bert's key into Stephanie's office door, unlocked the door, reached for the doorknob—and the door suddenly jerked inward, right out of my grasp.

I was so surprised, I just stood there with my mouth open, as some guy came rushing out the door and ran right into me. If I'd known what was coming, I might've braced myself. As it was, the impact sent me staggering backward as the guy bounced off me and darted down the hall. I tried to regain my balance, failed miserably, and ended up falling with a soft thud right in the middle of the carpeted hallway.

Fortunately, the hall carpet was thickly padded—as was, coincidentally, the part of my anatomy that I landed on. I believe, in fact, it was the first time in my life I have ever felt glad that this particular part of my anatomy was as well padded as it is.

I also felt glad I was being Bert. Because, let me make this abundantly clear, it was *her* skirt, not mine, that hiked up to her upper thighs when she fell. And it was one of *her* heels, not mine, that snapped off and went bouncing softly along the carpet.

As I got to my feet, I could see the lowlife who'd just knocked Bert on her derriere tearing off down the hall. I stared after him. For a lowlife, he didn't look bad. Oddly enough. He was tall, with graying temples, wearing a well-cut, dark gray, pin-striped suit, wire-rimmed glasses, leather gloves, and carrying a brown leather briefcase. He looked for all the world as if he'd just stepped out of the pages of *GQ*.

With a broken heel, there wasn't a chance in hell that I could catch him, so instead, I contented myself with just standing there in the middle of the hall, yelling "Stop!" As if I actually expected the guy to hear that one word and immediately come to a screeching halt.

Talk about your delusions of grandeur. The guy didn't even slow down.

I yelled again. "Stop! NOW!"

Oh yeah, that was all the *GQ* Bandit needed to hear. He fully intended to stop, sure he did, he just needed somebody to tell him *when* to do it.

After I yelled that last time, the *GQ* Bandit did, however, slow his pace a little as he turned to give me a look. Apparently, he was trying to fix in his mind exactly what a person looked like who could yell something in public that was as dumb as "Stop!" Smirking a little, he yanked open the door to the emergency exit and hurried out. Right away I heard his shoes clattering down the steps.

I did have the comfort of knowing that the guy had five flights to run down before he got to the ground floor.

I went over, picked up the broken heel to my shoe, and hobbled into Stephanie's office. I went straight to the first phone I saw—the one on the small receptionist's desk to the left of the front door—and I dialed 911. "I want to report a—a—" I glanced around the office, not sure what to call it. Robbery? Had the intruder been robbing the place? Of course, it was going to be a little difficult to figure out if anything had been taken when I didn't know what had been there in the first place. "—a break-in," I finished. That was noncommittal enough.

I gave the address, was told that the police would be there shortly, and that was pretty much that. Except that when I hung up the phone, it occurred to me that since the police were going to be dropping by shortly, I really ought to take a look around so that I and Louisville's Finest could have something to chat about.

Not to mention, if I was supposed to show them around the office, I'd better acquaint myself with it first. I was now standing in a small outer office, carpeted in a muted gray and painted a pale mauve. There was a small couch upholstered in a gray-and-mauve print against the left wall, two office chairs, one mauve, one gray, on either side of the couch, and a dark mahogany coffee table in front of it. A large oil painting featuring varying shades of mauve and gray hung above the couch. The painting was of the "trip-and-spill" school—it looked as if someone carrying several open jars of oil paint had tripped and fallen again and again and again, each time splashing the contents of his jars all over the canvas.

Across from the receptionist's desk, a door stood ajar. Inside I could see several shoulder-high, natural oak file cabinets lining the far wall. Several of the drawers in various file cabinets were not quite shut. In a couple of them, a few papers were sticking out at odd angles. As if, oh, maybe somebody had opened them, looked inside, then hurriedly shut them again.

Of course, for all I knew, this might've been just the way Bert filed. Although I had to admit it was a lot more likely that I would file this way, rather than Bert. As far back as I could remember, Bert has always been referred to as the "neat twin." At one time I'd thought people were saying that Bert was a lot cooler than I was. I'd been relieved to discover that all they meant was that I was a slob.

I moved from the file room to the next door down the hallway. This turned out to be Stephanie's office, if you could believe the ceramic nameplate on her desk. Stephanie's office didn't look bad. Unless, of course, you had an aversion to an Indian motif.

In that case, Stephanie's office looked terrible. She'd done the whole thing in austere Native American. Pure white walls resembling fake peeling stucco, black-and-chrome desk, black-and-chrome chair, black filing cabinets. Prints of doe-eyed Indian women holding papooses hung on both sides of a woven patterned rug in pastel pinks, blues, and yellows behind her desk, and Native American figurines stood on glass and chrome shelving in one corner.

I just stood there in the doorway for a second, taking it all in. If a real Native American saw this place, they'd have probably cried more than that guy on those antilittering commercials that used to air on T.V. all the time.

Stephanie herself might've cried if she'd seen the drawers of her desk. Every one of them had been pulled open; a few papers littered the floor. There were gouge marks on the lower drawers, as if the *GQ* Bandit had been trying to force them open. The doors to the metal cabinet just to the left of Stephanie's desk were open, too, but inside it looked as if nothing had been touched. This must've been where the *GQ* Bandit was a when he'd heard me opening the front door and immediately decided that vacating the premises was a good idea.

So the question was, what had he been looking for? Not to mention, was a gray suit and tie what all the best-dressed burglars were wearing this year? Of course, maybe the guy had a date after the break-in. I suppose even felons had to have a personal life.

The two police officers showed up a lot faster than I had expected. I'd just finished my tour of the office and was taking a good look at the lock on the front door. Now I knew why they called it breaking and entering. The lock had most certainly been broken. The *GQ* Bandit had simply cracked the old lock to let himself into the office. I bent to take a closer look at the splinters in the wood, when a deep voice sounded behind me. "You call in a burglary?"

I jumped at the sound. Turning, I saw two policemen standing behind me, one already taking out the notebook that I guess is standard equipment with the boys in blue. One was short, fat, and round-faced, the other tall, thin and frowning. Oh boy. It was the Abbott and Costello of crime fighting.

As it turned out, the part of Abbott was being played by Officer Maury Thompson, and Costello was Officer John Crandall. We all moved inside to sit on the mauve-and-gray couch, and right away Detective Thompson gave me a smile that dimpled his round cheeks and asked me a question that totally rattled me.

"What's your name?"

I just stared at him. Should I say who I really was? If I did, it would probably cost Bert her job. From what I'd heard about her, Stephanie was not the type to let bygones be bygones. Not until after she's said bye, and you're clearly gone.

Not to mention, if I told them I was Nan Tatum from WCKI, I'd probably have the same credibility problem I'd enjoyed so much in the past. Can you believe the police have actually accused me and the radio station of staging crimes just to drum up publicity? There wasn't a doubt in my mind that they'd do it again.

Besides, let's be reasonable here, I didn't think this particular crime was all that felonious. Nothing appeared to be taken. It wasn't likely that Stephanie had kept anything of value in any of the unlocked file drawers. And the ones that were locked were still locked.

Nothing was even messed up very much. From what I'd heard about Stephanie and how drop-dead gorgeous she was, this burglar could be some suitor she'd dumped who was looking for the jewelry he'd given her. Or a client she'd shafted who wanted his check back. Hell, for all I knew, he was working for Stephanie herself, who needed something from her office and didn't want anyone to know she was really in town. OK, I admit it, that last one was a bit far-fetched.

The point was, though, this whole thing was going to be one of those deals where these guys just take your name and number, talk to you a little, then they go away and you never hear from them again. Sort of like the men you meet in bars.

These two guys were not going to spend a whole lot of time investigating who broke into Stephanie's office and probably didn't take anything. They were going to make a report. And file it.

"Miss? Your name?" Costello prompted.

I cleared my throat. "*Bert* Tatum," I said. "Bert is short for Bertrice."

The things I do for my sister.

Chapter 3

●

BERT

I cannot believe Nan didn't tell me about the break-in the second she walked in my door late that Saturday afternoon. She'd had a chance to tell me even earlier than that, too, but she hadn't said a word. Not a word. I'd called her at Stephanie's office right after I'd gotten back from the interview at the Kentucky Derby Festival to ask her over for dinner, and she hadn't even hinted that anything unusual had happened.

I'd like to say that the only reason I'd wanted to ask Nan over was that I was determined to make it up to her for insisting that she switch with me. The truth was, though, I also didn't want to spend this particular Saturday night alone.

Not that I hadn't gotten pretty accustomed to spending Saturday nights alone back when I was married to Jake. Toward the last of our marriage, he'd told me again and again that he had to work on Saturday nights, and, like an idiot, I'd actually believed him. Until, of course, the day I was doing the laundry and I'd found in Jake's trousers a credit-card receipt for a dinner for two on the previous Saturday night when he was supposed to have been working. That would've been bad enough, but in that same pocket there had also been another credit-card receipt for a few items from Victoria's Secret. Needless to say, the lingerie for his girlfriend had been Jake's Secret, too.

What a generous guy.

Oh, yes, thanks to Jake, I can't say being alone on a Saturday night was a new sensation or anything. Even after Jake and my divorce, my Saturday night dance card had not exactly been filled—in fact, I could've counted on one hand the number of dates I'd had up until about four months ago. Then everything had changed. That, of course, was when I'd started going out with Hank Goetzmann. Ever since then, I'd had my own personal police escort on Friday nights, Saturday nights, and assorted other nights during the week.

Hank is a homicide detective with the Louisville Police Department. That, in fact, was how I met him. He'd been the big, adorable teddy bear of a man that Nan and I had ended up talking to after the murder of an acquaintance. He'd also been the big, adorable teddy bear of a man who'd almost immediately asked *Nan* out.

That's right, Hank had dated Nan almost as long as he'd now dated me. I wasn't quite clear on why Nan had decided to call it quits—I can't believe any woman would not be perfectly happy to look into Hank's clear blue eyes for the rest of her life—but I was sure on one thing. It had been her decision. Not his. He'd even phoned her several times after she broke up with him, but Nan was dating somebody else by then.

I was also sure about something else. Nan and Hank had slept together.

Something that Hank and I haven't quite gotten around to yet.

I don't think it's exactly a stretch to understand why I

might've been hesitating a little about this. For one thing, up to now the only person I'd ever slept with was Jake. After nineteen years of only going to bed with one person, you don't just hop into bed with somebody else. Without thinking twice. For another thing, OK, I admit it, knowing Hank had slept with Nan didn't exactly make me anxious to set up a situation in which Nan and I could be compared. I mean, let's face it, it stands to reason that the person who has the most experience doing something would be the best at it.

And, in this case, the person with the most experience certainly would not be me.

I'd been under the impression, though, that Hank was pretty understanding about all this. He'd always try to persuade me, of course, which I always thought was terribly flattering, but when I said I needed more time, he always smiled and backed away. Have I mentioned that this man is one of the most incredibly sweet guys I've ever met?

That is, he was incredibly sweet right up until last night. After Nan and I had finished our Quarter Pounders, and she'd finally caught up with the comics and headed on home, Hank had phoned. He'd suggested coming over to my apartment to watch a video rental, and it wasn't even our regular date night.

Generally, Hank and I see each other at least every Thursday night—we'd tried Friday nights at first, but, apparently, that's the day when a number of people in Louisville choose to kill each other. Hank was constantly being called away for a shooting or stabbing emergency.

When Hank phoned to watch a movie, like an idiot, I'd suggested *The English Patient*. This, I soon found out, was a particularly bad choice if you didn't want to get romantic.

Shortly after the first love scene in which Kristin Scott Thomas had the indecency to appear totally naked, Hank and I had ended up in each other's arms. I'd felt myself sinking into the warmth of Hank's kisses. His hands had moved up under my sweater, and for once, I'd actually relaxed, enjoying how wonderful his hands felt against my bare skin.

My heart was pounding. My breath was coming in short gasps. And then he'd whispered, "Let's go back to your bedroom."

And I, of course, had stiffened immediately, and whispered back, "Let's not."

Hank had pulled away so fast, you might've thought I'd slapped him. He'd sat there on the couch, shaking his head, as if waking from a dream. When he turned to look at me, his eyes had been unreadable. "Bert, you're driving me crazy," he said. His voice had been ragged.

That, of course, was when he'd launched into The Talk.

My mouth had actually gone dry, listening to him. The upshot of The Talk was that he thought we ought to spend some time apart. To give me a chance to think about things.

I guess I didn't react to that idea particularly well. "Are you telling me you're not going out with me anymore if I don't sleep with you? Is that what you're saying? Are we back in high school?"

Hank had just looked at me, his blue eyes growing darker. "High school?" he repeated.

"High school, Hank," I said. "In high school, some of the guys would never ask you out again if you didn't put out."

A red flush had slowly crept up Hank's neck. "This isn't high school, Bert," Hank had said, getting to his feet. "And *putting out* was not what I would've called it."

"Oh?" I got up off the couch myself then, straightening my sweater, smoothing my skirt. "Well," I said, glaring at him, "what would *you* call it then?"

Hank had just looked at me, his blue eyes never leaving my face. "Making love, Bert," he said quietly. "I want to make love to you."

My throat went dry again.

Hank had moved toward me, and pulled me into his arms. "Bert, if you don't feel the same way about me as I feel about you, I need to know that." He bent to kiss me, just once, ever so gently, "I need to know that pretty damn quick."

With his sweet face so close to mine, I actually felt dizzy. He started to kiss me again, and then abruptly, stepped back.

"Bert, I'm going to give you some time to think about everything, OK?" he said. "I'm not going to call you or see you or anything until Thursday night, OK? I guess I'll see you then."

And, with that, my police escort was gone.

I just stood there, blinking back tears. He *guesses* he'll see me then?

I didn't actually cry about it, though. Lord knows, I'd done enough crying over Jake. I wasn't about to do that again. Besides, there had been the interview at the Kentucky Derby Festival the very next day to think about, but once that was over, I knew that all I'd do for the rest of the evening was sit and go over everything in my mind.

And get more and more depressed.

That was why I phoned Nan at Stephanie's office. Well, one of the reasons anyway. I knew that Nan didn't have a date tonight either, so having her over would be a welcome distraction for us both.

And I did want to make it up to her for the switch. I really did.

To show you just how desperate I was to make sure she came over and kept me company, though, I even promised Nan that dinner would be slow food. As opposed to fast food, like we usually get when we eat together. "You pick it, Nan," I said. "What sounds good?"

We must've talked another ten minutes after that, trying to decide between barbecued chicken, pork chops, or pot roast, and finally going with the pot roast. During all that time, Nan didn't even hint that anything out of the ordinary had happened at Stephanie's office earlier that day.

Apparently, according to Nan, oven-baked potatoes, a garden salad, Italian dressing, dinner rolls, and green beans almondine—those were worth mentioning, but a little thing like a burglary where I work? Not on your life.

True to my word, my entire apartment smelled like pot roast and onions by the time Nan was coming through my front door.

Like I said earlier, guilt can be a truly powerful thing.

I think Nan had an idea just exactly how powerful guilt could be, too, because she hadn't so much as put one foot inside my front door when she said, "Boy oh boy, Bert, *what* a fun job you got me into. I'd been hoping that one day I'd be able to sit for hours on end and type about a million names and addresses and phone numbers into a computer, and now, at last, I finally got to do it. And, if I got tired of that, I got to type legal documents. How riveting. I mean, golly gee, Bert, you've helped me fulfill the dream of a life-time. I don't know how to thank you."

Sarcasm can be a truly ugly thing.

"Now, Nan, don't you think you're exaggerating just a—"

Nan apparently knew where I was going with this, because she interrupted me. "I mean, wow, what fun. Typing my fingers to the bone. And, every once in a while, I got to go into Stephanie's very own office and check to see that what I'd just typed in had downloaded to Stephanie's desktop! Thank God my heart could stand the excitement."

What Nan was talking about was on page two of the instructions I'd left her. Stephanie didn't trust that the computer would actually do its job—much like, now that I thought of it, she didn't trust me—so she wanted me to check to see that the software she'd bought was working properly. It was supposed to automatically send any new entry to the receptionist's computer to her desktop, and vice versa, so that both machines would have the latest and most up-to-date information. When Nan downloaded her updated contact file to the receptionist's desktop, it was supposed to also download to Stephanie's.

"OK, Nan," I said, "I'm sorry. Is that what you want to hear? I really am sorry."

It was pretty obvious that Nan was deeply moved by my apology. She shrugged, rolled her eyes, and started across the living room toward my sofa.

Well, if good old guilt could work for Nan, it could also work for me. "By the way, Nan," I said, "thank *you* for asking about how the interview at the Kentucky Derby Festival went. I'm a little nervous about the whole thing—" In fact, it had been one of those interviews where you have no idea how you were doing. The guy who'd interviewed me had just sat there the entire time, looking at me with a totally unreadable expression on his face. He could've been mentally thanking God that I'd answered his ad, or he could've been counting the minutes until he could get me out of his office. "—so, Nan, it really means a lot that you asked me right away how the interview went, because—"

That, of course, was when I noticed the way Nan was walking. Like maybe one leg was shorter than the other. I broke off what I was saying to ask, "Did you do something to your leg?"

For an answer, Nan came to an abrupt halt, gave me a quick smile, and handed me the heel of one of the shoes she was wearing. One of a pair of Pappagallo pumps that incidentally cost seventy entire dollars regularly, but which I'd found on sale for thirty-two. "Nope," Nan said, moving on to drop like deadweight onto my sofa, "I didn't do anything to my leg. I did something to your shoe." Nan reached down to rub her now stocking-clad foot. "Actually," she went on, "now that I think about, I had help."

I had no idea what in the world she was talking about. "You had help?"

"I certainly did," Nan said. She launched into it then, telling me all about the break-in, the *GQ* Bandit, and the lovely, little chat she'd had with Abbott and Costello of the police department.

All in all, I think I took it pretty well. Right at the beginning my knees got a little weak, but I just took a load off my feet by sitting down in one of the Queen Anne chairs flanking my sofa. I even managed to stop hyperventilating by the time Nan started describing the way the office file cabinets looked virtually untouched, and when Nan finally finished, I only had two questions. Both questions, I believe, were pretty predictable. The first was: "OK, what does he look like?"

Nan's answer was a little irritating. "What does *who* look like?"

I took a deep breath, and tried to act far more patient than I felt. "Your *GQ* Bandit, Nan. What does he look like?" It wasn't as if I was asking anything unusual here. Back when Nan and I were in high school, they'd put us in separate classes more than once, sometimes at opposite ends of the building. So that by the time we were heading home in the afternoon on the school bus, Nan and I would have no idea whom the other one had run into during the day.

This can be a real problem if you're trying to attract the attention of a certain high-school basketball player, and you want to make sure that the person he might mistake you for does nothing to discourage him. The opposite is also true—it can be a real problem if you're trying to discourage the attention of this geek who sits behind you in algebra class, and your twin doesn't know that she should be doing nothing to encourage him.

For both these reasons, one of the first things Nan and I would do after we got home was to describe for each other the different guys we'd met—the To-Be-Cultivated and the To-Be-Weeded-Out. What I believe I'm getting at here is that what I was now asking of Nan was clearly not a new concept. "Come on, Nan," I added, "Stephanie will want to know what your *GQ* Bandit looked like, and I'll need to tell her. So, describe him for me, OK? And go slow."

Nan had taken off the heel-less pump, and was rubbing her foot. "Bert, the cops aren't even looking for the guy. Nothing was stolen, so all this amounts to is loitering or something. No big deal." She indicated the dining room with a tilt of her head. "Let's eat."

I gave her a long, pointed, irritated stare that pretty much mutely said, *Fat chance.*

To which Nan responded with a long, pointed, irritated stare of her own. Followed by a fast description of the guy.

Which, of course, I wrote down. It took me a second to find a paper and pencil, but I made Nan wait until I got them.

Once I had the description down—wire rims, great-looking suit, briefcase, and a smirk—I asked my second question. It was, I do believe, every bit as predictable as the first. "So, Nan, do you think Hank will hear about the break-in?"

Nan rolled her eyes. "Bert, how many times do I have to tell you, it's small potatoes, understand? With nothing taken and no one killed, Goetzmann's *not* going to hear about it."

I might've believed her except that, about five minutes after she and I sat down at my dining-room table and prepared to dig into the pot roast, my phone rang.

It was Hank.

My heart did a little jump as soon as I heard his voice. "Hey, Bert?" Hank said. "I know I said I wouldn't call you until Thursday, but I had to make sure you were OK. I mean, after what happened today."

Like an idiot, I had to clear my throat a little before I spoke. "I'm OK, Hank. It was no big deal. Just a little break-in."

There was a long pause. I had no idea what was going through his mind, but I could feel Nan's curious eyes. I turned my back on her.

"Well," Hank said. "I just wanted to make sure you were OK."

My mouth was getting dry yet again. "I'm fine, really. Nothing seemed to be taken, so it was—it was—" My brain was spinning. I scrambled in my mind for what to say next. "—small potatoes."

"Small potatoes," Hank repeated. "Yeah." There was a long silence then while he, no doubt, marveled at the masterful way I could draw an analogy between criminal activity and a starchy vegetable. Then he said, "Well, um, I'm glad you're, um, OK, Bert."

"I'm just peachy," I said.

"Great," Hank said. "Just great. Glad to hear it." There was another long pause, and he said curtly, "Well. Talk to you later."

After which the dial tone sounded in my ear.

I actually felt a little sick. What was even worse, I had to turn around and face Nan. Who knew the second she saw my face that I was not exactly a happy camper.

"You guys having problems?" she asked, as she helped herself to another dinner roll.

I shook my head. "Not really," I said. I returned to sit down opposite Nan, and I didn't even glance her way as I busied myself pouring Italian dressing on my salad.

Nan took a bite of her roll, chewed, swallowed, then said, "OK, what's the deal?"

I tried to give her the wide-eyed innocent look that always used to work with Jake. "The deal?" I said. "There's no deal. Everything's fine."

Nan smirked. "Yeah, right," she said. "So what's the matter?"

This is one of the downsides to having a twin. Somebody who knows your face as well as her own—mainly because it *is* her own—is almost impossible to fool. I also knew Nan was sort of like Arnold Schwarzenegger in that *Terminator* movie. She would never give up. Never. She would pester you to death until you told her what she wanted to know.

I knew when I was beaten.

So I told her.

The part about my not having slept with Hank yet wasn't exactly news. I'd already told her some time ago that I hadn't decided to go to bed with him just yet. The part, however, about The Talk and how Hank was giving me time to think was a late-breaking bulletin.

Nan's appetite certainly did not appear to be spoiled by my news flash. She sat there, feeding her face the entire time I was talking. When I finally wound down, she had a mouthful of pot roast which she chewed and swallowed before she spoke. "So why don't you just go to bed with him? You know you want to."

I just looked at her. She was, of course, right. I really did want to. Being near Hank actually made my knees feel weak. And yet, how could I possibly sleep with somebody who'd also slept with Nan? How could I ever be anything other than just a rerun? And a bad rerun at that?

Not to mention, did I really want to go to bed with somebody who'd preferred Nan over me in the first place?

I shook my head. "I don't know, Nan," I said. "Do you think that this is all that's going on here? I mean, maybe Hank is just looking for a reason to break up with me."

Nan had been about to put a forkful of green beans into her mouth, but she stopped and just looked at me.

I met her look head-on. "I mean, really, Nan, do you think that the only thing that Hank is upset about is that I won't go to bed with him? Do you really think that's *it?*"

Nan's reaction was slightly less sympathetic than I might've hoped.

She laughed.

Chapter 4

●

NAN

Right away I was sorry I laughed.

Because Bert looked a little hurt.

To be honest, though, I'm not sure I could've stopped myself. Bert sometimes asks the most naive questions. I'm sure her being so naive has something to do with the way she'd been at home raising her children for all of nineteen years.

I've only just recently realized how very much I envy Bert's getting to stay home and do this. She's gotten to watch her son Brian and her daughter Emily grow up, and then she's gotten to send them off to college. Getting to stay home with kids was most certainly a privilege, and yet, I suppose it did have a downside. It pretty effectively kept Bert in a cocoon, sheltering her from the rest of the world for a good chunk of her life.

On the other hand, maybe some of her naïveté is just Bert herself. She is just such a sweet person herself, she can't quite imagine people behaving badly on purpose. Can you believe she actually asked me just this last week, after she'd given a panhandler in downtown Louisville a five-dollar bill, "Do you think he's just going to spend that on booze?"

I watched the panhandler shuffling off down the street, already smacking his lips together in anticipation, and my answer, of course, was: "No, no, of course not, Bert, he's probably going to the bank right now to put your money in an IRA to save for his retirement."

And now, Bert had managed to come up with yet another unbelievably naive question. Was Hank just upset about her refusal to sleep with him?

Let me see now, Hank and I had gone to bed on our second date, for God's sake. And then we'd slept with each other almost every time we saw each other for the next three months. So, was Hank upset about Bert not going to bed with him after they'd been dating for *four* months?

I'd say that you could take that one to the bank. I cleared my throat, and tried to wipe the smile off my face. "Bert," I said, "in all seriousness, I think that your not wanting to go to bed with Hank might actually be the only problem that you two have."

I couldn't believe I was actually having to tell her such a thing. I mean, what did she think their problem could be? Halitosis?

"Well, my goodness," Bert said, buttering a roll now as if she had a grudge against it, "is sex all men think about?"

OK, if she was going to keep asking questions like this, I was going to have a real hard time keeping a straight face. To keep from outright guffawing again, I took a big, big bite of my own dinner roll. And chewed it very slowly to give my mouth something else to do besides stretch itself into a very large grin.

"Really, Nan," Bert was going on, "don't you sometimes wish things were the way they used to be? When all a man expected at the end of a date was a good-night kiss. And maybe a little necking. But nobody expected you to sleep with him until after you were married?"

I chewed my dinner roll and just looked at her. The way things used to be? When exactly was this? In the Eisenhower years?

Of course, I guess I should not have been surprised that Bert would have an attitude like this. I could still hardly believe it of someone who was supposed to be genetically identical to me, but Bert has told me—and there was no earthly reason why she would lie to me about a thing like this—that she'd been a virgin on her wedding night. She'd probably been the last virgin bride in America.

Actually, once I got over the shock, I'd thought that was kind of sweet.

It would've been even sweeter had she not been marrying Jake the Snake. Which is what I've been privately calling the man ever since he started carrying on right under poor Bert's nose with that bimbo child-woman he called a secretary.

I also had no doubt that Jake the Snake himself was most certainly not a virgin on his and Bert's wedding night, and the only reason he might've wanted Bert to be one was that he would not have wanted her to be able to make a comparison. In fact, in my opinion, this could possibly be the main reason a lot of men want their wives to be virgins in the first place. They want to make damn sure that the little woman really and truly believes that every other man in the world only takes thirty seconds, too.

I had finished chewing, and now I speared a big piece of pot roast. "Bert, I can't imagine committing yourself for a lifetime to somebody you hadn't even slept with," I said. "I mean, isn't that how you end up with some guy who wants to dress up in your underwear and maybe make you wear a chicken suit to bed?"

That seemed to me to be a valid point. Bert, however, clearly disagreed. She was shaking her head before I'd even mentioned the chicken.

"Well," she said, pointing her overbuttered roll in my direction, "maybe if I'd had the kind of experience that you've had, I'd feel the same way, but—"

I stiffened. Uh-oh, here it comes again. Once again Bert was going to make me sound as if maybe I'd gone to bed with the Marines. Every single one of them. That, in fact, I might've been personally responsible for their slogan. You know the one, about looking for a few good men? Only in my case, according to Bert, insert the word "hundred" after the word "few."

I don't know, maybe I'm sensitive, but this was getting old. True, I had without a doubt slept with more men than Bert. But, let's face it, nineteen years of monogamy—on *her* part anyway—had probably cut into Bert's average. Hey, I'll even admit that there was a time when I'd been sort of trying on personalities, and that one personality I'd tried on for a month or two had been somewhat on the promiscuous side. I would like to point out, however, that I had been quick to realize that this personality was not me at all. And that if it was, I was not only stupid, but I had some serious problems with self-esteem.

"Bullshit, Bert," I said, interrupting her, "I think all in all you've probably had sex more times than I have. After all, you were married all those years. Whereas, as a single woman, for me it was either feast or famine in the sex department. I was either dating somebody and sleeping with him all the time, or I was dating no one, like now, and sex was a distant memory."

For an answer, Bert shrugged and started buttering her roll again. That roll, let me tell you, was looking a little worse for wear.

"You know, Bert," I added, "if you don't want to sleep with Hank, you're not obligated to. I mean, there isn't some kind of hard-and-fast rule that, if you've dated somebody for so many months, you've got to hop in the sack with him."

Bert's head sort of jerked up at that one. "What makes you think I don't want to sleep with him? Of course, I *want* to. I mean, you know him. Hank is irresistible."

I just looked at her. Her dark brown eyes actually looked a little misty as she said Hank's name. Oh, yeah, she was in love all right. I didn't want to burst Bert's balloon or anything, but I was pretty sure that I would never use the word *irresistible* to describe Hank Goetzmann. True, when I first met him, I'd thought he was kind of cute, in a Brian Dennehy sort of way. Back then I probably would've said that he was heavyset. Now I'd just say he was heavy. About sixty pounds too heavy, as a matter of fact.

Square-jawed with short-cropped brown hair, he was not exactly the sort of man that draws every woman's eye whenever he walked into a bar. Unless they were looking for the bouncer. Cuddly was how I used to describe him. But now, unfortunately, after going out with him for three months, the descriptive phrase that most frequently came to mind when I thought of Hank was: fuddy duddy. Lord, Hank just had far too many rules in his head for my taste. In fact, a couple of times when I was driving some place with him beside me in the passenger seat, I'd actually gotten the feeling that he really wanted to pull me over and write me a ticket.

I'd tried to explain to Hank just how I felt about rules. "There aren't any rules, Hank. None. Zip. Zilch. There are no *shoulds*, understand? You know how it goes: You should do this, you should do that. All that is just bullshit."

Hank had blinked his baby bloodshots at that, so I'd thought I was finally hitting home.

"That's right, Hank, somebody just made all this stuff up. All that's really here is land and air and water. The rest of it—the names of the oceans, the names of the countries, the equator, for God's sake—somebody just made it up. It might've been made up an awfully long time ago, but somebody still just made it up."

Hank had blinked again. "And your point?" he said.

I'd actually felt encouraged. "My point is that, if continents and shit were all made up, then *everything* is made up. Out of the blue. Including all the rules we're supposed to live by. There aren't any real rules, except the ones you give yourself. Everything else is just shit."

Hank had been frowning by this time. "You know," he said quietly, "women really shouldn't use four-letter words. It's not very feminine."

Oh boy.

My reply, of course, was, "Oh. Then what I meant to say was: Everything else is just *bullshit*. That's not a four-letter word, is it?"

Hank's response, as I recall, had been a thin-lipped smile.

After a while, the only place Hank and I didn't argue was in bed. And, unfortunately, every once in a while, we actually did have to get out of bed and have a conversation. A thing which became more and more difficult.

Not to mention, although I didn't tell this to Hank, I may not have a whole bunch of rules that I follow, but I did have one prime directive. Sort of like the prime directive Captain Kirk and the others followed on *Star Trek*. Theirs was something like: Boldly go where no man has gone before, but don't make any changes in the civilizations you run into. Mine was even more simple: *Be kind.* In a world filled with pain, there was no reason to add to it.

I really didn't think it was kind of Hank to be constantly on my back about one thing or another. The day he gave me a lecture that could have been entitled, "Why Women Approaching Forty Should Not Wear Skirts Above Their Knees," I finally came up with my very first rule: Don't go out with Hank Goetzmann.

Of course, this was a rule that only applied to me. It certainly didn't apply to Bert. In fact, when Hank and Bert first started going out, I'd been delighted. Because, let's face it, these two were perfect for each other.

Bert still believed there were hard-and-fast rules to be followed, too. Hell, even now—even after her marriage to Jake had turned out the way it did—she was still trying to convince me that being a virgin on your wedding night was the way to go. I was pretty sure, in fact, that Bert fully believed today that her marriage didn't work out because of just one thing: Jake had not followed all the rules. The one rule he'd really not followed was, of course: "Thou shalt not commit adultery over and over again."

I speared another piece of meat. "Well, my goodness, Bert, if you think Hank is irresistible, what in the world is holding you back? I mean, why don't you take a tip from all those old Nike commercials, and just do it?"

Before Bert answered, she finally took a bite of her

extremely well buttered dinner roll. Thank goodness, I might add. "Well, for one thing," she said, after chewing far too long, "there's the whole taking-off-your-clothes issue."

I blinked. "The what?"

Bert shrugged. "Taking off your clothes in front of some guy may not be a big deal for you, but it is for me."

I just looked at her. "Oh yeah, that's right," I said, nodding, "I did join that nudist colony a while back. Thanks for reminding me. It had completely slipped my mind."

Bert ignored my sarcasm. "Besides, Nan," she said, actually lowering her voice, as though if she didn't, our neighbors next door might be able to hear her, "unlike you, I have"—at this point, she leaned across the table and whispered—"*stretch marks.*"

She made stretch marks sound like something unclean. Once again, I found myself suppressing a smile. I even tried to look sympathetic, but let's face it, if Hank cared anything at all for Bert, a few stretch marks would not exactly send him screaming from her bedroom.

"Of course," Bert was going on, "I had stretch marks when I was sleeping with Jake, but I always thought, well, he can't mind too much, after all, I got them having *his* kids. But, Nan"—here Bert leaned forward again—"Emily and Brian are not Hank's kids."

Bert actually said this as if it were news.

"Bert, I don't believe the first thing that Hank is going to notice, if you finally decide to go to bed with him, is that you have a few stretch marks." Once again I was trying not to laugh. "In fact, after him waiting for four whole months for you to say yes, he'll be so blind with ecstasy he wouldn't notice if you had scars from heel to toe. You might have to point your stretch marks out to him."

Bert frowned, clearly giving no thought whatsoever to what I'd just said. "But, Nan, you don't have any."

I just looked at her again. I wasn't sure what her point was exactly. "Yes," I said, "that's right. But I don't have any kids either."

It was Bert's turn, then, to just look at me. What the hell she was thinking, for once, was completely beyond me. Finally, she said, "Nan, really, wouldn't it bother you to go to bed with a guy who'd already gone to bed with me?"

I took a bite of potato, and thought that one over. Back in high school, when Bert and I first started dating, we'd both agreed that a prerequisite for any guy to go out with either one of us, was: he had better be able to tell us apart. Otherwise, he was just dating one of the Tatum twins. And, oddly enough, Bert and I both took it as a personal insult that anyone who was dating us might actually think we were interchangeable.

We'd also decided that if one of us had been going out with somebody, and she stopped, then she had to officially release the guy before the other twin could go out with him. There was one guy in high school—Johnny Brewer—that even though he and I broke up, I never officially released him. Somehow, I just couldn't stand the thought of Johnny going out with Bert instead of me.

I thought that all this was what Bert was talking about. "Bert, I don't think you have to worry about Hank thinking we're interchangeable. I mean, after four months, I think he can tell us apart." Bert still didn't look the least bit mollified. I hurried on. "And, I didn't realize that this was still necessary, but pay attention now—I officially release Hank." I waved my fork in the air like some kind of magic wand. "Presto. Chango. Hank is released. You can date him all you want. You can do anything you'd like with him. OK?"

Bert did not look the least bit cheered up. She just looked at me again in total silence, and if I didn't know better, I thought she might actually have tears in her eyes.

"Bert?" I said.

She quickly looked away. "You know, we need to go over the description of that guy who broke into Stephanie's office. Can you tell me again what he looked like?"

I speared some more pot roast and slowly chewed it. Well, that was an abrupt change of subject if I ever heard one.

"Bert," I said, "I think Hank really does care about you. From what I've seen, he looks at you like a man pretty much madly in love."

Bert now seemed to be totally preoccupied with trying to determine just how many green beans you could spear with a fork. She didn't even look up, as she said, "When you're describing the guy, try to picture him in your mind, OK? See if you can think of any details you left out before."

I took a deep breath. Oh, yes, the subject had been changed, all right. On a permanent basis. So, as a caring, devoted sister, what did I do? Obediently, I launched into yet another description of Stephanie's intruder.

Chapter 5

•

BERT

Sometimes, as much as Nan and I are alike, it is painfully obvious how very much we are different, too. A case in point was the whole discussion about Hank and me. It was clear Nan didn't get it at all. She really didn't seem to realize that what was bothering me most was the possibility of Hank comparing me to *her*.

And yet, how could he not?

Not to mention, how could I not end up the worse for the comparison?

Totally unperturbed, Nan just sat there, across the dining-room table from me, looking straight at me with big, brown eyes so much like my own, and describing the guy who broke into Stephanie's office almost word for word the exact way she'd done it before. To tell you the truth, after a while I was barely listening. I was too busy going over the Hank dilemma in my mind.

By the time Nan left, I was feeling pretty depressed.

I continued to drag myself around my apartment all day the next Sunday, too. A couple of times I started to pick up the phone to call Hank, and then almost immediately, I reconsidered. He'd said he'd call me.

I wasn't about to give him the satisfaction of knowing how much I missed him.

The following Monday I can't say my mood had improved. It didn't help to know that it was the beginning of yet another wonderful work week at the office of the she-devil.

The she-devil in question, of course, came waltzing in about an hour after I got to the office. Stephanie was dressed in a pink linen suit, with a brightly colored silk scarf flowing after her. I thought maybe she'd grown a few inches, until I realized she was wearing four-inch white heels. She even teetered forward a bit on the little skyscrapers when she stopped at my desk.

But then all she did was nod curtly, toss her plane tickets and receipts at me, and order me to log them into her computer program as business expenses. No "good morning," no "how was your weekend," no nothing.

"Be sure you enter every single bit of the information on those receipts, too—including numbers, dates, and times," she called over her shoulder as she sailed into her office, closing the door firmly behind her.

What a wonderful boss. The woman could make Mussolini look like a humanitarian.

But, hey, hadn't I put one over on her? Whether Stephanie knew it or not, I had outsmarted her. I'd gotten to go to my job interview, and she was none the wiser.

That thought alone kept me smiling as I typed my way through stacks of receipts and even taller stacks of legal documents which Stephanie—with a skill surpassing that of David Copperfield—seemed to produce out of thin air. The second time Stephanie appeared from her office, laden with still more work for me, it occurred to me that I hadn't even told Stephanie about the break-in on Saturday.

Of course—Stephanie being Stephanie—she interrupted me. "I *know*, Bertrice, I know," she said, waving a manicured hand in the air to shut me up. "The police phoned me at home on Sunday asking me some trifle about the office locks. Nothing was taken, and the locks have been changed, so I can't see why we need to talk about it. I really hate to be told things twice, don't you?"

Stephanie had a habit of making little pronouncements like that—as if her way of doing things was the only way that made any sense. And she often asked questions like that last one—questions that did not require an answer, and which would've irritated her if you'd tried.

She went back to her office, and I went back to typing. I guess I was making so much noise, I didn't hear the front door open. It was about noon, and I'd already been eyeing the clock across from me on the wall, ready to make my getaway for lunch. When I turned back toward my typewriter and glimpsed the persons who'd entered, I nearly shrieked.

What had startled me were the two men standing there. And not just any men. *Police*men.

"Sorry to startle you, Miss Tatum," one of them—the short, fat one—said.

Miss Tatum? How did this cop know my name?

I stared at them, willing my heart to quit trying to leap out of my chest. What was this about? Was it my kids? Had something happened to one of my children? Both Brian and Emily were away at college—they'd both decided to attend UK summer school so they could graduate early—so I wasn't in touch with them every day. Oh God, could there've been an automobile accident? As soon as all this flashed through my mind, my mouth was so dry I couldn't speak.

Then the skinny tall one said, "We've got some good news to report."

I blinked at him. That probably let out the whole car accident scenario.

"We think we've found the man," the fat one added, nodding proudly.

Naturally, I blurted out the first thing that popped in my head. "The man?" I asked. "What man?" Of course, right about then it hit me—even before he spoke again. I mean, here was a fat cop and a skinny cop. Abbott and Costello—wasn't that what Nan had called them? Lord, I just hoped they didn't expect me to remember their names.

And they'd found the man. *Ohmigoodness.*

Naturally, I started doing what I always do when I'm at a loss for words. I babble. "Oh, *that* man. Well, of course. Well, well, well. I mean, that's great. The *Man.* Well. That's wonderful. Really. Uh, terrific." I finally shut up and smiled at them, still wondering why they were coming to tell me about it. Shouldn't they be off filling out forms and locking the criminal up or something? The next thing they said made me wish I was still wondering.

"All we need you to do is to come to the police station and ID the guy," the skinny one said, his Kentucky drawl making *ID* sound like *idea.*

"Now?" I asked. "You want me to come now?"

Just the thought of going down to the station was enough to make my stomach hurt. That was, after all, where Hank worked. I really did not particularly want to run into him, with things the way they were between us. I don't even want to talk about how I felt about going there to identify a man I'd never seen.

"Don't worry about it—shouldn't take very long," Abbott said. "Your identification will wrap it up for us. You know, cross the t and dot the i. Fact is, we think you're probably the only person who's actually seen this guy."

I just looked at him. Actually, officer, you are mistaken in this regard. I would be part of the group who's never laid eyes on him.

"There's been a series of break-ins in this area, mostly in the doctors' offices around here," Abbott, the skinny one, added. " 'Course we didn't know on Saturday when we talked to you that there had been a pattern."

"Really," I said, trying to think. My heart was speeding up so fast, I was a little surprised that Abbott and Costello couldn't hear it.

"Yep," Costello, the fat cop said. "Not till one of our fellow officers mentioned that there'd been these other break-ins. That's when we realized there'd been several burglaries in this particular area of downtown. Put two and two together and we realized it had to be the same guy."

"Wow," I said without enthusiasm.

From the way Abbott and Costello acted, you might've thought I'd applauded. They grinned first at each other, and then at me. "It's kind of a lucky break, too, that you actually ran into the guy," the skinny cop added.

"Really," I said, again without enthusiasm. What on earth was I going to do? Could I possibly identify the guy? I had a vague picture of the way the guy looked, based on Nan's description, but I was pretty sure it wasn't enough to point a finger at somebody in a lineup. Unless he was the only one up there wearing wire rims, I really wouldn't feel good about it.

And Nan—the one person who really could identify the crook—was on the air until three. She couldn't exactly talk on the radio and be at the police station at the same time.

If only she could go to the station with me.

"So if you'll just get your handbag," Abbott was saying, "we'll drive you—"

"I wonder," I interrupted, holding up one finger, "if I might take a rain check on this trip. I mean, I could come down to the station later—say about five o'clock or so? You see, I've got all this work to do, and I—"

"Don't be silly, Bert!" From behind me, the shrill voice made me jump. The shrill voice belonged, of course, to Stephanie, who'd apparently overheard my conversation with Abbott and Costello. Their heads, naturally, swiveled toward the sound, and I watched their jaws drop as they took in Stephanie's total gorgeousness. Costello even tried to suck in his gut, but he merely succeeded in looking like his lower half had suddenly deflated. The skinny one merely looked transfixed.

Stephanie had to have noticed the cops' reaction, but she gave no outward sign of it. I knew she noticed, though. Now that I'd spent a couple of weeks with her, I'd have to say that there was a definite difference in the way she acted with each sex. With men—even the teenager delivering office supplies—Stephanie seemed to radiate a little extra heat. Like maybe she had some kind of inner thermostat that she could turn up in the presence of anyone producing testosterone.

Watching Stephanie in action was a little like watching Marilyn Monroe on the big screen. She seemed to draw every eye.

You can imagine how much old Steph really got on my nerves.

"Well, of course, Bert," Stephanie was saying as she moved toward us, her hips swaying quite a bit more than they did when it was just her and me in the office, "you can be excused from your duties to accompany these two nice gentlemen to the police station." She gave Abbott and Costello a quick smile. In return, the two policemen gave her grins so wide, they seemed to wrap around their faces a couple of times.

"And take all the time you want, Bert. I know *I'd* certainly like to put whoever it was who broke in here behind bars. I'm sure you feel the same way." She pushed a blond strand of hair out of her big blue eyes, and I thought Abbott's eyes might actually roll right out of his head as he watched her.

"Oh my, yes," I said. "I want to get that guy, that's for sure. But, Stephanie, if you don't mind, I'd like to wait and go to the police station with my sister."

With some reluctance, both cops tore their eyes away from Stephanie and focused on me. "Your sister?" Costello repeated.

"You want your sister along?" Abbott asked.

"Well, yes. For her moral support," I added. "I mean, identifying a criminal is nerve-wracking enough. My sister just being there with me would help me through the whole gruesome ordeal." OK, now I was sounding ridiculous even to myself.

At this point, Stephanie snorted. "You want your sister to come with you? Gracious, your mother told my mother that you two were close, but I think this is taking closeness a bit too far, don't you?" She glanced over at Abbott and

Costello, as if expecting them to back her up on this. "I mean, goodness, that's almost *sick*."

I guess decking your boss in front of two policemen wouldn't be such a good idea. It was tempting, though.

Faced with the choice of behaving as if I were emotionally unstable and unnaturally dependent on my sister, or heading on downtown to identify a guy I'd never seen before, oddly enough, I found myself choosing the latter.

In the backseat of the police car—which is really not as clean as you might think—I actually thought about confessing to the cops that I wasn't really at the office on Saturday. Let's face it, I didn't relish the idea of letting a crook go free, but how could I possibly finger some poor schmuck as the guilty party and take the chance of being wrong about it? Goodness, I'd rather let a guilty guy go free then put someone who was actually innocent in jail.

What I should do, then, was tell these cops the truth— that was obvious. After all, Nan and I hadn't exactly broken the law. Yet.

I finally opened my mouth to confess, when Costello looked around at me. "Tatum," he said, tapping his chin. "Tatum. Hmmm. Wait a minute—you're not one of those twins who's dating Detective Goetzmann, are you?"

Oh, God. I'd thought it couldn't get any worse, but it seems that there is always another depth to sink to. I sighed. "You know Hank Goetzmann?"

"Sure thing, he lives right down the street from me," Costello said. "Of course, we run in to each other all the time downtown." He looked me up and down, his eyes finally resting on my knees. "So you're the twins dating Goetzmann." He eyed me like I was some kind of side show exhibit.

"No, Officer," I said, and, yeah, probably a little irritation leaked into my tone. "I'm the *only* twin who's dating Detective Goetzmann."

He blinked a couple of times. When my meaning finally sank in, he grinned. And then he actually winked at me. "Sure, sure, that's right. You're the one he's dating now. How about that?" the tub of lard said, elbowing his partner and winking. "Old Hank dating *twins*. Who'd've thought?"

His partner grinned like an idiot, and Costello, apparently encouraged, hurried on. "Good old Hank—howzabout that rascal? He's really been keeping you two secret, you know. Wait till I tell the rest of the guys downtown that we finally met you all."

I smiled weakly. The bottom line here was that this guy actually knew Hank. And if I confessed to switching with Nan, Hank would probably hear all about it before I'd even left the building.

I was really hoping to make up my own mind about Hank and how important he was to me—before he broke up with me for being a liar and a fraud.

Of course, Hank had obviously been keeping secrets, too. He'd never ever once mentioned the ribbing he must've been taking from his friends and coworkers after dating first one twin and then the other. He'd probably been teased unmercifully, especially since, apparently, the entire Louisville police force seemed to think he was dating both of us.

The whole thing was just too awful.

All this was running through my mind at breakneck speed, even as the cops up front chatted with each other. Or, at least, Costello tried to chat. Abbott, driving the car, kept leaning away from Costello and turning his head away from him to avoid eye contact. Watching the skinny cop's body language, I decided that he did not like the fat one any more than the real Abbott seemed to like the real Costello sometimes.

Watching the two of them actually gave me an idea. I'd read somewhere that eyewitness testimony was actually the least accurate because the witness is so easily influenced by the policemen who already know whom they've arrested for the crime. Maybe these two policemen could clue me in on which guy it was if I just watched them closely. I've also read that twins are supposed to be able to pick up on that kind of thing better than most; because, let's face it, we've been reading another person's body language since birth.

Body language, that was the key. I'd just have to study these two cops when they bring out the guys in the lineup. Maybe their body language would tell me who the culprit was.

At the downtown police station, the officers deposited me in a wooden chair, outside an office on the second floor, and I sat there patiently waiting for them to get the guys I was supposed to look at in the lineup ready. Or, at least, that's what I thought I was doing. The two cops actually didn't tell me much of anything. They just gestured toward the chair and told me to have a seat.

I was a nervous wreck. Particularly after a while. It was bad enough, worrying if Hank was going to walk by any minute, but all around me, cops kept parading criminals in handcuffs in and out of doors. Every one of the crooks looked like they'd committed mass murder at the very least. As they passed me, the orange of their prison jumpsuits glowed brightly in the black linoleum on the floor beneath their feet.

I couldn't help staring. Where in the world were all these policemen going with all these criminals? Why didn't they just lock them up already?

Each time they passed me, the cops would glance at me, but the crooks always eyed me like a dog eyes meat. I tried to pull my skirt down over my knees; but, wouldn't you know it, the skirt I wore today was one of the shorter ones I owned. If I'd known I was going to be gawked at by assorted criminals, I'd have certainly worn slacks.

And, instead of starting to relax, I only got more and more scared that Hank would walk by any minute. I mean, when he wasn't out investigating a homicide, he had to come back to his office, didn't he?

I happened to know, from having met him down here at the station a couple of times, that his office was one left turn, down the steps, and then right down the hall—not thirty seconds from the very spot where I was now sitting, trying to pull my skirt down to my ankles.

I almost leaped up and kissed Abbott and Costello when they finally came back. If I hadn't been so happy to see them, I'd have probably noticed that they didn't seem so happy to see me.

The fat one was actually shaking his head as they came up to me. "All right, Miss Tatum, you're free to go. We'll have an officer drive you back to your office." He was actually looking kind of disgusted with me.

I stared at him. "Excuse me?" I looked back and forth at the two policemen. "I can go? Really?" I couldn't imagine what he was talking about. I wouldn't have to do the lineup, after all?

"What happened? Did the crook get away?" I asked. I

believe I'd seen this happen in the movies, and it was the only explanation I could think of.

Costello made this really unpleasant noise in the back of his throat, but Abbott jumped in before his fat partner could say what was on his mind. "You didn't ID our man," Abbott drawled.

I stared at him again. "But I haven't had a chance to," I said. "I haven't been to the lineup."

I was thinking that these policemen really don't coordinate things very well with each other, when Abbott went on. "We did a walk-by with the perp—more than once, in fact—and you didn't recognize him."

I was starting to get the picture. "A walk-by?" I said weakly. I thought of all those cops marching by with their criminals in tow. They were walking these crooks by me to see if I recognized anyone. OK, that pretty much explained where they were all going. "But," I stammered, "what about the lineup, like on TV?"

Costello made another really disgusting noise, but Abbott merely smiled tolerantly at me. "On these lesser cases," Abbott said, "we sometimes just walk the perp by the victim—if he's recognized, that's all we need. Needless to say, you didn't even blink."

"So we had to let him go," the fat one said, his tone angry. "Damn!—pardon my French—but I was sure that creepo was the one."

He might have been, I thought, feeling very, very guilty right about then. "I'm really sorry," I mumbled, but the tub was already moving away.

"Not your fault," Abbott said. "We just got the wrong guy."

Not necessarily, I thought.

Abbott handed me off to another cop, who drove me back to Stephanie's office without saying two words to me.

Before I could even sit down at my desk, Stephanie came out of her ivory tower and asked me how it had gone. I shrugged. "Wrong guy," I said, lying through my teeth.

Stephanie frowned. "I really wish they'd caught the guy," she said, looking around the office. "I don't like the idea of someone in here looking at my things." She actually shivered a little.

I stared at her. This was the first time Stephanie had actually shown some vulnerability. I knew what she meant, too. I'd had a break-in myself in my apartment once upon a time, and the idea of a stranger going through your things feels like a terrible violation.

Of course, hearing what Stephanie had to say made me feel just that much worse if I'd let a guilty person go.

"I'm really sorry that—" I started to say, but Stephanie cut me off.

"You are so silly," she said. "It wasn't your fault they caught the wrong person." With that she swept into her office and closed the door.

I stared at the tightly closed door. OK, so I didn't feel quite so bad anymore. It's hard to feel bad about letting someone down who's just called you silly.

On the way home, I'd like to say that I thought about the injustice I might've done to all those people who could be burglarized in the future by the guy I'd let go. And how awful it was of me to let down Abbott and Costello, who'd gone out and done their part by apprehending a bad guy. I'd like to say that's all I thought about. But, to demonstrate how really shallow I am, my mind instead pretty much hovered around something far more important.

My love life.

What in the world was I going to do? How on earth could I go to bed with somebody who'd obviously preferred Nan first?

Chapter 6

●

NAN

I was a little distracted. Otherwise, I think the conversation I had with Bert after she got home from work on that Monday evening would've gone a little differently. At the very least, I would not have blabbed to Bert all the stuff I did.

Bert apparently was so rattled by everything that had gone on at work that day, she hadn't even gone home first. She'd just pulled her Camry into her driveway, marched right over here, unlocked my front door, and walked in.

It's things like this that make me question just how good an idea it was to give her a key to my apartment. Of course, being her landlord, I already had a key to hers, so it seemed only fair. Then, too, having spare keys has come in handy during those embarrassingly frequent occasions when one or the other of us has been identically scatterbrained and locked herself out.

Having let herself in, Bert plopped down next to me on my sofa, ignoring the fairly obvious fact that I was paying my monthly doles to the leeches I owe. I had spread out all around me my bills, my checkbook, envelopes, and the accordion file in which I keep paid invoices.

Bert didn't even give all that a glance. She was too busy telling me some long-winded tale about the two cops I'd met on Saturday dragging her down to police headquarters to identify some turkey she'd never seen before. Listening to her, I was tempted to laugh. Not that I didn't sympathize, but, really, it was kind of funny. That old saying, "Oh, what a dangerous web we weave, when first we practice to deceive" did leap to mind. I had no intention of rubbing it in, but if I recalled correctly, I do believe I had voted against the switch in the first place.

"You cannot imagine how awful it was," Bert was saying. She reached under her rear to pull out an envelope that she'd apparently sat on. "What's worse, I found out that one of those policemen actually knows Hank. Personally!" She tossed the envelope carelessly on the coffee table.

I tried to look stunned. "No kidding. Personally, huh?" I retrieved the envelope from the coffee table, glanced at it, and put in on my unpaid stack. "Bert, lighten up. You're making too much of all this."

"Are *you* kidding?" she said. "Hank tracks down criminals for a living! It's what he does!"

I just looked at her. She was making Hank sounds like James Bond, for God's sake. Now, who was kidding whom?

Bert was hurrying on. "What's Hank going to think when he finds out that I let one go?"

"It's not like you did it on purpose. Besides, how will Hank find out?"

"He could figure it out! He's not stupid, you know!"

I just looked at her, recalling the "Women Approaching Forty Should Not Wear Skirts Above Their Knees" lecture. I decided this would probably not be the best time to get into an extended conversation with Bert regarding Hank's intelligence or lack thereof. "Bert," I said, struggling for patience, "the only way Hank will find out that you deceived those cops is if you or I tell him. So, the way I see it, it's really very simple. *Don't*."

Instead of brightening, her face fell. "You mean, lie to Hank?"

"I'm not telling you to lie," I said. "I'm just telling you to keep your mouth shut."

Bert frowned. "But, Nan, don't you think personal relationships should be built on trust?"

I turned to stare at her. Surely, Bert and I had never been the same entity once upon a time. "Where did you hear that load of crap? Personally, I prefer relationships built on deceit. It takes you a lot longer to find out that the guy's a total jerk."

Bert must've thought I was serious. She gave me one of her looks. "For all I know, Hank's figured it out already. He knows I lied to those police officers." She ran her hand through her hair.

I shook my head. "He hasn't figured it out."

Bert asked the obvious question. "How do you know?"

I sighed, got up, and went out into my kitchen; and Bert, now looking more than a little curious, followed me. I got out two glasses and started filling them with ice cubes from my freezer. "Well, he called me a few minutes ago."

Next, I got out a two-liter bottle from the fridge and poured Bert and me a large Coke each. As far as I'm concerned, there's absolutely nothing that a little Classic Coke can't make all better.

Judging from the expression on Bert's face, her glass of Coke had its job cut out for it. "Hank called *you?*"

"He sure did." I took a long healing sip of Coke and headed back to my sofa and my assortment of bills.

Like I said, I was a little distracted. Paying bills is always so painful that it takes up a lot of my concentration. Otherwise, I'm sure I would've really looked at the expression on Bert's face and realized that she wasn't taking the news about Hank calling me any too well.

"What did he want?"

I should've picked up on the change in Bert's tone, too. By then, though, I was seated once again on my couch, and I was looking at my latest electric bill, trying to figure out why in hell the stupid thing was thirty dollars higher than last month. It was July, for God's sake—surely a little bit of air-conditioning wouldn't add that much.

"What did Hank want?" Bert asked again.

I shrugged. "To talk about you, naturally. Really, Bert, you've got the guy completely bamboozled. Evidently, you've been blowing hot and cold so much, he can't decide whether you even like him—let alone, love him." The air-conditioning was definitely on my mind.

"Hot and cold," Bert said slowly, as if maybe she were thinking those two concepts over.

I didn't even glance at her. I'd decided there was no way of telling how my electric bill had gotten that high. For all I knew, I'd left my toaster plugged in too long. There wasn't anything I could do, though, so I might as well just pay the damn bill. I reached for my checkbook. "Yeah," I said, "Hank wanted to know how you feel about him."

On the phone, as a matter of fact, Hank's voice had actually been shaking a little. "Nan," he said, "you know Bert better than anybody. Do I even have a chance with her?"

I'd actually felt a little sorry for the big lug.

"Wait a second." Bert actually sounded a little put out. "Hank is asking you how *I* feel?"

I gave her a quick glance this time, and that's when I noticed how still her face now looked. Pale and still. Except for her eyes which had gone so dark, they almost looked black.

Uh-oh. Bert was steamed.

"Oh now, come on, Bert," I said. "Don't get mad. Hank was just trying to figure out where he stands with you, that's all."

"So he calls the woman he slept with before he started dating me?"

Uh-oh. It sounded as if Hank was in big trouble. "Well, now, Bert, this right here is no doubt why he told me not to tell you he'd called me. He must've known you'd take it like this." I started making out the check to the electric company.

"He told *you* not to tell me he'd called?" Something in her tone this time made me glance her way. She was still pale, but two bright red circles had appeared on each cheek.

"Well, Hank didn't want to upset you, I'm sure."

"What did you tell him?"

"I said, Bert cares about you very deeply. You are very important to her. *That's* what I said."

Bert shifted position on the couch and took another long, long sip of Coke. Finally, she took a deep breath, and said so fast, it was almost like one word, "You-know-Nan-if-you-wanted-to-go-out-with-Hank-again-it-would-be-OK-with-me."

As I believe I mentioned, I was writing a check. Otherwise, I would have been stunned at the very idea. Instead, I just laughed. She was making some kind of joke, right? I didn't even think before I said, "Well, it isn't OK with me. Bert, Hank and I are over. Kaput. Put a fork in us, we're done. Understand?"

I wasn't sure she did. She just sat there, looking almost as sad as the day she'd discovered that Jake was running around on her.

I reached over and touched her hand. "Bert, the guy's crazy about you."

Her answer was succinct.

"Hmm," she said.

Chapter 7
●
BERT

Hank was still on my mind as I drove in to work the next morning. Of course, this was nothing new. He'd pretty much been on my mind ever since Nan and I had had our little chat about him the night before. I'd even dreamed about the man. In my dream, he'd been dancing with Nan, while I sat alone at a table in the darkness, glumly watching the two of them.

I'd call that a nightmare.

I couldn't help wondering exactly why Hank had called Nan. I know, I know. Nan had said that he'd just wanted to talk about me. But had that really been the reason he'd called her? Maybe Hank had just been using me as an excuse to talk to Nan again.

When you come right down to it, Nan could even have been the reason he'd gone out with me in the first place. If he couldn't have Nan herself, I was clearly the next closest thing. Let's not forget, it had been Nan who'd ended their relationship. Not Hank. For all I knew, Hank had been pining away for Nan all these months.

My stomach was beginning to hurt.

Even so, I probably would've continued along this pretty horrible line of thinking the entire time I was driving into downtown Louisville, except that, thankfully, the trip took me down Bardstown Road. If ever you want to have your mind diverted from something that's troubling you, you should immediately travel to Louisville, Kentucky, and drive down Bardstown Road. This particular street in the Highlands neighborhood is pretty narrow, and it has a lot of traffic—both of which provide significant diversions all by themselves.

Bardstown Road, however, does one more truly inspired thing to take your mind off your problems. It's got three lanes, and depending on what time of the day it is, the middle lane changes direction. In the morning, the street has two lanes going toward downtown Louisville; in the afternoon, it has two lanes going away from downtown.

I believe the city fathers have done this because they are under the impression that we Louisvillians never really know whether we're coming or going. So they're going to help us out. By simply counting the number of lanes on Bardstown Road heading in the same direction as we are, we'll always be able to figure this one out. No doubt, then, this whole direction-change concept is just a terribly considerate thing to do. Instead of what I'd always thought it to be: a head-on collision waiting to happen.

Bardstown Road also offers ample opportunity for rear-end collisions. For some reason, it seems to have more than its share of drivers over the age of sixty-five, all of whom drive about twenty miles an hour, no matter what the speed limit is, and all of whom seem to suddenly stop for no apparent reason.

On my way downtown, I must've braked at least five times behind this one white-haired elderly woman who kept slamming on her brakes apparently just to see if her pacemaker was still working. The jolts she was taking were a sure test for the thing.

Despite the annoyance, the last time I braked behind her I couldn't help it—while I waited for White Hair to decide to get moving again, my mind wandered to Hank once again. How on earth had I gotten so involved with him? And just exactly how involved was I?

Some of the time that I'd been with him, looking up into his hazel eyes, I'd had absolutely no doubt that I was in love with him. And yet, how could I possibly be in love with somebody who might be in love with my sister? Could I be that stupid?

The answer, of course, was yes. Let us not forget, at one time I'd been positive that I was in love with my ex-husband Jake. Today, of course, I had no idea how on earth I could've ever thought such a thing, but back then I'd been convinced that I was head over heels.

So exactly how does anybody ever know for sure if they really were in love?

White Hair up ahead had apparently remembered which pedal was the one she needed to step on to get going again, so traffic in the middle lane of Bardstown Road finally started moving again. By the time I was sitting at a stop light at Muhammad Ali Boulevard and Second Street, I'd pretty much made up my mind that what I really wanted was a *That Girl* kind of relationship. Like the one Marlo Thomas enjoyed with Don Hollinger on that old seventies sitcom. Marlo was free to pretty much do as she pleased, and Don was totally at her beck and call. Marlo called on Don to go to dinner, and to go to an occasional movie, and—I suppose—to go to bed. It being the seventies, this last, of course, was never overtly mentioned. I just pretty much assumed Marlo and Don did this sort of thing, it being highly unlikely in my opinion that a grown man and woman could date for the number of years that dumb show was on without ever going to bed together. Unless, of course, Don had a problem. Like, oh, say, women not being his type. Or it could be that he'd slept with Marlo's twin sister before he started dating Marlo.

OK, this line of thought had gotten depressing. It was, in fact, so depressing that as I finished my trip downtown, parked my car, and took the elevator to Stephanie's office, I actually found myself hurrying. At least, work would give me something else to think about. I unlocked the door to Stephanie's office, opened it, and was surprised—no, stunned—to see that Stephanie had actually arrived at the office before me. At least, I figured she must already be here, because the office lights were on.

I was stunned because Stephanie was not the early-riser type. In fact, she always seemed to take a particular delight in sailing in an hour to two after me. Stephanie always gave me a particularly triumphant look as she came in the door, too. A look which clearly said: *Yes, I do happen to be the Boss, free to sashay in any old time I feel like it; you, on the other hand, are the Flunky who'd better be here at nine on the dot.*

I walked to my desk, giving Stephanie's closed office door a quick glance. I stowed my purse in the usual place—the lower left desk drawer—and I looked around. The computer terminal on my desk and the spare one over on the walnut credenza were both turned on, a screen saver showing on both computers.

Screen savers generally involve some cutesy image that keeps blinking or hopping or moving in some way. The constant motion is supposed to keep text and pictures from burning themselves permanently into the screen.

The screen saver Stephanie had installed showed a tiny woman, dressed in a tiny business suit, carrying a very large mallet. The tiny woman marched around the screen like a wind-up toy and knocked out any unsuspecting tiny man who wandered haplessly onto the screen. Probably this thing had been marketed to women divorce lawers like Stephanie. Or maybe to just women in general who were in permanent bad moods. For some reason it was called "Hear Me Roar."

I hit a key on the keyboard, and the screen saver disappeared. In its place, my computer displayed a series of icons. Icon is the name the computer nerds give those little pictures that represent files on a computer screen. Before the nerds got hold of it, the word *icon* had meant a religious image, which pretty much gives you an idea of how the computer nerds feel about their work. Unfortunately, the presence of several new icons on my computer screen told me that quite a few new files had been created since I'd left work yesterday.

Great. Workaholic Stephanie had obviously been amassing more stuff for me to do. What a woman. She'd still been here when I'd left last night, so these new files were, no doubt, carryovers from what she'd been working on. Her new files had appeared on my computer because Stephanie—to make sure she didn't lose any time getting work to the hired help—had installed some kind of automatic program in her office network that would immediately transfer her rough drafts to my computer. Her files also went automatically to the spare computer on the credenza in my office. That way, I could begin typing her work in a final form on either computer without losing so much as a nanosecond.

Staring at these new icons, I wondered if Stephanie were

typing on something at that very moment. I'd found out the hard way that if I started typing on something that Stephanie was also working on, I could possibly lose a portion of Stephanie's current work as it was being transferred to me. I wasn't sure how this happened. What I was sure of, however, was that Stephanie had actually yelled at me last week when she'd had to transfer a file to my computer for the second time—because I'd messed up her first automatic transfer. And when I say yelled, I'm not exaggerating. Old Steph had stood in the doorway to her office and thrown a tantrum the likes of which I hadn't seen since my kids were in elementary school. Stomping her foot, clenching her fists, and screaming.

Recalling that poignant moment, I decided I really needed to find out if I could start typing on the work she'd left me from yesterday. I started to knock on Stephanie's door, then I hesitated. Stephanie didn't like to be interrupted when she was working. If I interrupted her, she might yell at me again.

And yet, if I didn't check with her first, I could get yelled at for causing her to lose some files. I took a deep breath. It looked to me as if, no matter what I did, I was going to be yelled at. I took a deep breath and rapped on Stephanie's door. "Stephanie?" I said, "Excuse me?"

There was no answer.

I knocked again. "Stephanie?"

After the third time I knocked and got no response, I tried the doorknob. The door was unlocked, so I stuck my head in. "Stephanie?"

Standing in the open doorway, facing Stephanie's desk, I froze. "Stephanie?"

At first, I couldn't quite grasp what I was looking at. I

mean, Stephanie was there, all right. She was slumped forward on her desk, arms hanging limply at her sides, head turned to the left, her right cheek pressed against the desk blotter in the center of her desk. The icy blue light of the computer screen seemed to give an unnatural glow to her blond hair. I could see only one of her eyes, and it was closed.

"Stephanie, are you asleep?" I whispered. If I woke her up, she'd yell at me for sure.

I tiptoed closer, trying to make as little noise as possible on the plush carpet. Halfway there, I froze. Even from where I stood, I could see the dark clotted blood on the underside of Stephanie's head, soaking into the blotter.

You'd think when you see something like that, you'd immediately start screaming your head off. The way they do in the movies. You don't, though. You take a couple uncertain steps forward, and you stare at the small, dark hole at the base of your boss's skull, getting this strange feeling of unreality. As if none of this could possibly be true.

I forced myself to reach out and feel for Stephanie's pulse, even though once I touched her cold, cold wrist, I knew it wasn't really necessary.

I jerked my hand away, and took a stumbling step backward. Oh God. I couldn't say that I'd liked Stephanie, but she'd certainly hadn't deserved this. Nobody deserved this.

Still feeling as if everything was strangely unreal, I went outside to my desk and dialed 911. My voice didn't even quaver as I gave the address to the operator and told her that there'd been a shooting. The operator told me not to hang up until the police officers got there, and I assured her that I wouldn't.

I was pretty amazed at how calm I felt. Of course, this wasn't the first time I'd ever been in this situation. I must have the worst luck of anybody on the planet, because I'd actually had to report this kind of thing before. So, more's the pity, I knew what you were supposed to do. First, call the police. Second, don't touch anything.

As this last crossed my mind, I couldn't help staring at the phone I was now holding.

Oh dear.

I guess I should've called the police from outside the office. After all, what if whoever had shot poor Stephanie had used this phone? Maybe I'd just smudged a killer's fingerprints. I snatched up a Kleenex from the tissue box on my desk, intending to use it to hold the receiver with. Naturally, the Kleenex got stuck in the stupid box. I gave the tissue a hard shake, and when the box finally fell away, it knocked my stapler off the edge of my desk.

Without thinking, I picked up the stapler and started to put it back. Then I stared at the stapler in my hand. What if the killer had touched this? I wasn't sure what he might've been wanting to staple, but having never killed anybody before, how would I know what a killer did under those circumstances?

I immediately dropped the stapler—and the Kleenex—as if both had suddenly become red-hot; and in so doing, knocked the Rolodex card file off my desk. I reached over, still holding the phone, trying to pick the card file up with still another tissue, and I managed to pull the entire phone off. The phone cord lassoed the in and out boxes, the tissue box, the stapler—*again*—and the small plastic desk calendar. Plus all the papers stacked next to the calendar. Everything was dragged onto the floor.

Good Lord. Maybe having done this once before wasn't

all that big a help, after all. I was making it look as if the killer had rifled my desk, and he probably hadn't even touched it.

But what if he had? What if I had just obliterated the only evidence that would identify Stephanie's killer? I stood there for a moment, getting more and more rattled, staring at everything on the floor, wondering if I should pick the things up or leave them be, still holding that stupid phone with my bare hand.

That was when I did what I probably should've done the second I laid eyes on Stephanie.

I turned tail and ran.

I kept my head enough to lay the receiver down on my desk—and then I made a beeline out of the office and toward one of the phone booths down the hall.

That's right, *booths*. Whoever had renovated this building had the good sense to keep the original wooden phone booths. So that every floor had a couple of these quaint booths that look for all the world as if Clark Kent might be changing clothes inside.

I headed straight for the nearest booth, closed the wooden folding door behind me, and dialed the number as fast as I could. When the phone was answered, I blurted, "Stephanie's been murdered, and I've touched everything on my desk!"

I have to hand it to Nan. She actually acted as if what I'd just said made sense. She didn't bother asking me a lot of questions, either. Either she could hear the genuine panic in my voice, or our twin vibes were working overtime. "Let me call the radio station and tell them I won't be in—and then I'll be right there, OK?" Nan said. "And Bert? Stay calm."

Stay calm? I was not the least bit calm anymore, so

staying calm was totally out of the question. I sat there in that phone booth, shaking like a leaf, until I heard the sound of the elevator arriving. Then I ran to greet whoever was arriving.

I'd just made it to the hall directly in front of the elevators when the elevator doors parted.

And out walked Hank.

I was so surprised to see him, for a moment I just looked at him. I don't know why it hadn't dawned on me that Hank might be one of the detectives that showed up. Afer all, he was a homicide detective, for God's sake.

"Hank," I finally said. My voice actually quavered.

"Bert, are you OK?" Hank said. I nodded silently, not trusting my voice again. Hank took a step toward me, looking so concerned, so genuinely upset, that I expected him to take me into his arms. But then he drew up short.

I thought that he'd remembered The Talk, and that was why he'd stopped himself. And then I saw, coming out of the elevator right in back of Hank, his partner, Barry Krahzinsky. At a half foot shorter than Hank's six-three and about one-sixty to Hank's two-thirty, Barry always looks like a teenager to me. The traces of acne on his cheeks and his flattop haircut add to the illusion. In fact, I'd actually been shocked when Hank had told me that Barry was almost thirty-five.

With Barry standing right there, looking from me to Hank and back again, his eyes clearly curious, Hank moved away from me, cleared his throat, and crossed his arms. "So what happened here?" he said.

I just looked at him. Hank's tone was now almost formal. Oh God, he was going to do Jack Webb with me. You know, the no-nonsense cop from the old fifties TV series, *Dragnet?*

I'd be lucky if Hank didn't say, *Just the facts, ma'am, nothing but the facts*.

I just stared at him, feeling the tears welling in my eyes. Which goes to show you the kind of person I am. I mean, I can find my boss murdered, for God's sake, and I'm as dry-eyed as anything. But have the guy I'm dating act distant with me? I'm choking back sobs.

I cleared my throat a couple times, but the only thing I could manage to get out was: "She's in there." I pointed toward Stephanie's office. "She's been—she's been—"

Fortunately, I didn't have to finish, because it was at that moment that the elevator doors opened again, and we all turned to see who was walking out.

It was Nan.

I don't know what it was about seeing her, but this time I couldn't help it. Tears began to stream silently down each cheek. Nan was great, though. She acted as if she didn't even notice the tears. She just put her arm around my shoulders, led me back inside the office, over to the couch opposite my desk, and made me sit down. "How are you doing, hon?" she said.

I'd say that question didn't really need an answer. Hank and Barry must've felt the same way, because they didn't wait around to hear what I said. They both headed into Stephanie's office. After a moment or so, I heard Barry say, "Man, what a waste. This broad was one beautiful chick."

Hank has told me that Barry has never been married. I was beginning to understand why.

"So, what happened?" Nan asked, getting a Kleenex out of her purse and handing it to me.

While I dabbed at my eyes—very lightly so that my eyeliner didn't smear and give me raccoon-eyes—I launched into it, telling her everything that had happened from the point when I'd walked into Stephanie's office. When Barry and Hank came out of Stephanie's office, of course, I had to tell it again. At least, I had to tell Hank. Barry immediately headed for the door. "I'm gonna go phone the lab guys," he said over his shoulder. On his way past my desk, he added, indicating the mess I'd made with a nod of his head in that direction, "The perp must've been looking for something."

I swallowed, really hating to point out the error in his logic.

As it turned out I didn't have to say anything, because Nan did it for me. "Oh no," she said, "Bert did that."

Thank you so much, Nan. Barry came to an abrupt stop on his way out the door, as both he and Hank turned to look at me. Hank's eyes looked pretty big.

I shrugged, gripping Nan's Kleenex a little tighter. "I got a little rattled."

Barry raised his eyebrows at that one, then went on out the door.

Hank, on the other hand, frowned. Then he moved toward me, and I waited for him to take me into his arms this time. Instead, when he got to my side, he glanced quickly toward the door, then reached out and squeezed my shoulder. "You sure you're OK?"

I just looked at him. His partner was no longer in the room, and this was the best he could do? A shoulder squeeze? I felt like tearing up all over again. Did he just not want to do anything in front of Nan? My voice shook again as I said, "I'm OK."

Hank didn't look as if he believed me. He gave me a long look, frowned again, then glanced over at Nan. "Is she really OK?"

That brought me up short. Wait a second. What was he doing, asking *Nan* how I felt? Was Nan the ultimate authority on me these days?

Nan didn't seem to find anything odd about this, though. She was already shaking her head. "Of course, she's not OK. She's just run into a dead person. How could she be OK?"

Hank actually looked as if he'd been reprimanded. He cleared his throat, and asked me, "Do you need some water or something?"

I just looked at him again. What I needed was a hug. Water was not going to get it. I shook my head. "No." As an afterthought, I added, "Thanks."

Hank was taking out the small, dog-eared notebook he always seems to have with him. Pulling up my desk chair, he sat down opposite me. "Well," he said, "I'm sorry to have to make you do this, but I need you to tell me what happened."

So I told him. Every single thing I'd already told Nan. Hank scribbled away, and when I was finally finished, he cleared his throat again. "While we're at it, you might as well tell me about the break-in on Saturday, too."

I just looked at him. "The break-in?" Oh God. I was supposed to tell him all about a break-in that had happened when I wasn't anywhere around?

"Why do you need to know about that?" Nan asked.

Hank gave Nan a look that said the answer to her question was pretty obvious. "A woman has her office broken into, and two days later, she's murdered? It could be just a coincidence, but then again, maybe it isn't."

Nan's eyes, I could see, had gotten a little bigger. "What do you mean?"

Hank gave her the same look he'd given her before. "The two things could be connected," he said slowly.

I had to swallow once before I could ask, "You think that the guy who broke in here could be the same guy who did this?"

Could it be true? Was Stephanie dead because we hadn't owned up to having switched? Had the guy who'd broken into the office, Nan's *GQ* Bandit—whom Nan could've identified but whom I had apparently set free—returned to murder Stephanie?

Oh my God.

Hank shrugged. "At this point I don't think anything. I just think I really need to hear about that break-in, that's all."

I tried, I really did. I did the best I could to remember exactly what Nan had told me, and what I missed Nan was able to jump in and clarify. She did it pretty well, too, acting as if she herself were simply remembering what I'd told *her* earlier.

By the time I'd gotten to the part where the *GQ* Bandit was running down the hall, Barry was back with several other policemen, some uniformed, some not, from the forensics lab and the Medical Examiner's Office. Barry had apparently waited downstairs in order to direct the others on how to get to the scene of the crime. When the new arrivals hurried past us, heading into Stephanie's office, Hank got up and followed them.

The second we were alone, Nan leaned close to me and whispered. "OK, I know what you're thinking."

I just looked at her. It didn't take a twin to figure that one out. "We let a murderer go, Nan."

Nan shook her head. "Not necessarily. Besides, he wasn't a murderer then," she whispered.

"My point exactly!" I hissed. "Stephanie might be alive today, but—"

Nan was still shaking her head. "Nonsense! Stephanie was a divorce attorney! And she was a royal bitch. She had to have made zillions of enemies."

I really hoped no one asked Nan to say a few words at the funeral. "Nan, zillions didn't break into her office a couple of days ago. Just one guy—"

I would've continued, except that Hank suddenly reappeared. As he came walking purposefully out of Stephanie's office, I stared at him, wondering how much he'd overheard. "I'll need the keys to the file cabinets in there, Bert," he said, indicating Stephanie's office with a nod of his head. If he'd heard anything Nan and I had said, he sure didn't act like it.

I got the keys out of the top drawer of my desk and handed them to him. When Hank took them, his fingers brushed mine. "You're doing OK, aren't you?" he asked. His eyes never left my face.

I didn't hesitate. Let me see now. I was probably in love with this man who was probably in love with my twin. I was no longer employed. And I might have caused the murder of my boss. "Oh, my, yes," I said, "I'm just fine."

Oddly enough, Hank didn't look convinced.

Chapter 8

•

NAN

If Bert was *just fine*, like she told Hank, I was the Queen of England.

Not feeling at all inclined to don some really frumpy-looking clothes and start waving at my loyal subjects, I decided that Bert was far from fine, and far too rattled to drive. I think Bert even knew it herself, because she didn't protest when I suggested that she leave her Camry in the parking garage and hitch a ride with me.

I made this suggestion right after Hank came out of Stephanie's office and told us finally that we were free to go. I guess by then Bert had reached sensory overload. When I told her that I'd drive her in tomorrow so that she could claim her car, she just looked at me for a second, as if trying to figure out what the hell I was talking about. Her tone was clearly distracted as she said, "Oh. Yes. Sure." Her eyes wandered to Hank.

Hank's eyes had never left Bert's face. "You take care," he said.

"I will," Bert said.

What can I say? It was a moment.

You'd have thought that once Bert and I were in my car and on our way that she would've relaxed a little. She didn't, though. She sat on the seat beside me, ramrod stiff, twisting and turning the Kleenex I'd given her until it began to fall apart. "Oh, Nan, what are we going to do?" she finally said. "What if we really are responsible for Stephanie being murdered?"

Oh, for the love of Pete.

I thought we'd already discussed this. But, hey, even though I saw no reason to go into it again, I believe I showed real understanding and compassion when I answered. "Don't start," I said.

Bert looked miserable. "But it's our fault. If we hadn't—"

"Look, Bert, I realize you've been through a lot. But I absolutely refuse to believe that you and I are responsible in any way for Stephanie's death. She was a *lawyer*. Need I say more? If you wanted to kill Stephanie, you probably needed to take a number."

Bert gave me a reproving look. "I really don't think lawyer jokes are appropriate right now," she said.

Oh brother. "I only meant that lawyers have a tendency to make enemies. Enemies such as, oh, opposing lawyers, opposing clients—hell, even their own clients, if they don't win big enough to suit them. Any one of these people could've killed Stephanie."

"But, what if it wasn't one of them? What if we really are responsible?" Bert asked. "Oh God, Nan, you and I set a killer free!"

She was making it sound as if we'd sneaked Charles Manson out of prison. I made the turn onto Third Street, heading toward the ramp to I-65 south, and tried not to raise my voice. "Bert, we don't know that the *GQ* Bandit is a killer, OK? And even if he was, how would we have stopped him? Even if we'd pointed him out, he'd have made bail and been out on the street, free to kill whomever he wanted, before we'd even finished our dinner."

My point, I do believe, was well taken. But was Bert swayed?

She was back to shredding her Kleenex. I was going to have to vacuum those little pieces up. "Nan, I just can't believe we let a killer go free! I knew we shouldn't have switched places."

Oh boy.

Patience, they say, is a virtue. It just doesn't happen to be one of mine. "Bert?" My tone implied that I could've been talking to a three-year-old. "We've switched before, and some people survived it."

Bert was not listening to a word I said. "You know, I wouldn't feel so bad if I'd liked Stephanie. But I couldn't stand her." A couple more pieces fell off her Kleenex. "Her getting killed like this makes me feel so—so guilty."

It was an effort not to roll my eyes. "Bert, sweetie, I'd like to point out that there are quite a few people you don't like, and every one of them is still healthy." I pulled onto the ramp to I-65 south, deftly dodging an oncoming semi.

Bert ignored me, looking at the exit signs we were passing. "Where are we going?"

I shrugged. "Lydia's, of course. Mom'll be with Lydia by now, don't you think? Maybe we can do something to help out."

Bert just looked at me for a moment, smiling a little. "You feel guilty, too."

I did not dignify that comment with a reply.

Lydia lived out in Okolona, a suburb south of Louisville, not terribly far from Valley Station where Mom and Dad lived. Although Bert and I had seen Lydia herself more times than we could count at Mom's, the number of times we'd been to Lydia's house I could count on one hand. It had been so long, in fact, since I'd been there, I was afraid I might not remember which house it was. Especially since Lydia's redbrick ranch-style house on Stonestreet Road looked almost exactly like every other house on the street— the only difference being the color of the shutters and front door. Each house featured the ubiquitous picture window of the fifties and a chain-link fence around the backyard. I drove slowly down Stonestreet, looking for something I could recognize, and what do you know, I spotted Mom's Pontiac in the driveway of the fourth house down on the right.

As I pulled in the driveway in back of Mom, I noticed a pair of women's gardening gloves and some garden snips lying next to a flower bed of marigolds, zinnias, and Shasta daisies in the side yard.

Bert saw the gloves, too. "I guess Lydia was out in her garden when she got the news." Her voice trailed off.

I couldn't help staring at those stupid gardening gloves. They looked so forlorn, somehow. "Yeah, after she got the call, she never went back." We knew that Stephanie had not been Lydia's only child; she had two sons who lived out West somewhere. But, to lose your only daughter? This way? I swallowed, blinked a couple times, then reached across Bert and threw open her door, before she and I both started bawling.

Even before we reached the sidewalk to the front of the house, Lydia, with Mom in tow, walked out. A cloud of blue smoke accompanied them—both women carried lit cigarettes and Kleenex tissues. At five-ten Lydia was a big enough woman that she could've carried twenty or thirty extra pounds, and you might not have noticed it. Unfortunately, she was carrying at least fifty extra pounds, and almost all of them had been packed into her chest and hips. Even more unfortunately, she was wearing a turquois double-knit sweat suit with gold metallic stripes down the legs which left little to the imagination exactly where all those extra pounds had gone.

She had unnaturally dark brown hair, and that nearly wrinkle-free, beautiful complexion that overweight women often have, with rosy cherubs' cheeks, which usually made her look younger than Mom. Today, though, poor Lydia looked as if she'd aged ten years. On each knee, there was a dark oval of caked dirt. Evidently, she'd been too distracted to remember to change out of her gardening clothes.

As she bore down on me and Bert, it occurred to me that there was something about Lydia that I'd completely forgotten up until that very moment. Lydia was a hugger. Meaning, Lydia hugged you whenever she saw you, regardless of the situation. She'd tackled me once coming up the aisle to find my seat in church. During the service. And, it was never any little around-the-shoulders type of hug, either. Boa constrictors hugged less tightly than Lydia did.

I hung back a little, but Bert must not have remembered this little detail about Lydia because she actually moved ahead of me on the sidewalk. When Lydia was within hugging range, she put her cigarette in her mouth and then threw both arms around Bert in a rib-cracking embrace. Bert threw me a pitiful "help me" look in the split second she realized her mistake—as she was engulfed by Lydia's plump arms. Lydia tried to snag me, too, but I managed to sidestep her, throwing an arm around Mom's shoulders instead.

"Lydia, I am so sorry," I said, reaching out and touching the hand Lydia was not holding the cigarette in. "I am so, so sorry."

Bert's condolences were muffled in Lydia's double-knit.

"It's good of you two girls to come," Mom said. She patted nervously at her red Brillo-hair, and took another drag off her cigarette. "It's real thoughtful." Her tone indicated that if we had not been this thoughtful, however, we'd have heard about it until the sun novaed.

Mom, like Lydia, was also wearing a sweat suit, but apparently, in deference to the solemnity of the occasion, Mom's sweat suit was black velour.

"My baby was only thirty-five!" Lydia was now saying, punctuating her words by jabbing her cigarette in the air, while maintaining a headlock on Bert—not an easy task. "And she was so beautiful. The sweetest little girl—so good to everyone she met. An angel, really. Loving and giving and generous. A saint on earth."

Over Lydia's shoulder, Bert gave me a look. It seemed to indicate that Bert might differ slightly with Lydia's character assessment of her daughter.

"Just the most unselfish, unassuming, sweetest young woman who ever lived," Lydia went on, loosening her grip at last on Bert so that she could dab at her eyes with a tissue. "Generous to a fault. Why, Stephanie'd do anything for anyone. Just anything. She never wanted to offend, never wanted to cause anyone any trouble. A saint, for sure, an absolute saint."

Next to me, Mom nodded. "A saint," she echoed, taking another drag off her cigarette. "An absolute saint."

"It's just such a shame," Bert said, rubbing her neck a little.

Lydia whomped Bert hard on the back and hugged her with both arms again. "God love you, sweetie pie!" she wailed. "I know you loved her, too! Well"—Lydia made the word sound as if it ended in a p: *Welp*—"Stephanie's up there with her daddy now, God rest his sorry soul." Stephanie's father and Lydia had been divorced for several years before he finally succumbed to a heart attack. The attack had been brought on, as Lydia told it, by his wanton excesses of food, drink, and unbridled sex with truck-stop waitresses.

"Welp, I just don't know what I'm going to do without her. I really just don't know," Lydia went on. "Not that she came to see her mama that often—but I understood. Stephanie was busy, you know. Always working for her clients or doing things for other people." With every third word, Lydia was giving Bert an extra little squeeze. I really don't know how she continued to breathe. "Stephanie was such a sweet, sweet, caring, giving girl."

Beside me, Mom sighed again and took a long draw off her cigarette. "You'll get by all right, Lydia," Mom said quietly, patting Lydia's back. "Because your friends are here. We'll all be right here with you to do anything you need."

I glanced at Mom. Had I heard her right? Was that a *we?* And an *anything?* I certainly did want to help Lydia. But the word *anything* seemed to leave a lot open to interpretation. And if Lydia was *anything* like her daughter, leaving things open-ended might not be a very good idea.

"Welp, what am I doing, standing out here in the yard?" Lydia said, giving Bert a final breath-robbing squeeze. "You two girls come on in the house. It's so good of you to come and see me," Lydia went on. "Come on in, and I'll get you some sweet tea."

Mom and her generation have apparently never discovered the healing qualities of Coca-Cola. Lydia released Bert, who could finally stand upright. I could hear Bert noisily sucking in air as we all went into the house.

The minute we went inside Lydia's house, I could smell vanilla. I looked around for some kind of potpourri, but all I saw were casserole dishes, Saran-wrapped bowls and covered dishes sitting all over the coffee table and end tables. As well as Tupper-wared cakes, cookies, and brownies.

It's always amazed me how quickly people are able to come up with something to bring when a friend dies—my God, do they have some prepared dish just sitting around? The only thing that qualified as food in my apartment was a six-pack of Coke, hardly appropriate as a condolence gift.

Lydia was already heading for the kitchen, but she noticed my look at the food. "Just look at all this—so sweet. My minister just left. And all the ladies from my church group. Just look how good everyone's been to me," Lydia said, looking around at all the food with an almost awed expression. "Somehow they've all heard."

"Probably it's already been on the radio," I said, realizing that I hadn't even thought about calling the news crew from my own station. I really must be upset about Stephanie's murder.

"Let's help bring these into the kitchen," Mom said to Bert and me, picking up some of the covered plastic containers and stacking them. Bert and I did the same.

"This meat loaf is from my Sunday school group," Lydia said, pointing at the dish in my hand. "And this casserole is from my Bible class and this German chocolate cakes's from my weight-loss clinic. Everyone's being so sweet—they all just loved Stephanie." Her voice broke then, and she kind of sank onto the sofa, covering her eyes with her hands as she began to sob.

Bert gave me a tortured look, as Mom rushed to sit next to Lydia, putting her arms around the woman's meaty shoulders. "Lydia, they all just love *you*," Mom whispered, while Bert and I just stood there. I knew Bert was feeling like I did—a little sick and a lot helpless, not knowing what to do. It didn't help that everywhere we looked, there seemed to be a framed portrait of Stephanie. On two walls in the living room, down the hall, and sitting here and there on end tables. A lot of the pictures had even been signed, "To Mom, Love, Stephanie," as if maybe her own mother needed a signature to remind her who exactly was in the picture. I tried not to look at the portraits as Bert and I picked up dishes and packed them into Lydia's refrigerator.

Luckily, just as we were out of dishes—and refrigerator space—the doorbell rang. We were so relieved that Bert and I both said it in unison. "I'll get it." We almost raced each other to the front door.

Bert's eyes widened when she saw who was standing there.

Hank Goetzmann stood on the front porch, his six-foot-five bulk dwarfing everything around him. He was already pulling his notebook out of his inside coat pocket as he turned toward the door. His eyes also widened a little as he looked first at Bert, then at me, and then over my shoulder to the woman still weeping behind us.

"You two really get around, don't you?" he said.

I wasn't sure what he meant by that, but Bert must've thought we needed to explain what we were doing here. "We thought we ought to pay our respects," she said. I could not believe it, but her tone sounded defensive.

Goetzmann nodded. Apparently, our visit had his approval. What a relief. "I need to ask Mrs. Whitman some questions about her daughter," Goetzmann said. "Do you think she's up to it?"

"I don't know," Bert said, "Lydia's pretty upset right now—"

We all turned toward the two women on the couch, just in time to see Mom whispering into Lydia's ear. Both women's eyes were now fixed on Goetzmann.

"The policeman? Him?" Lydia asked Mom, while she looked Goetzmann up and down and wiped her eyes. "Well, bring him on in here. You're telling me *this* is the cop who's been dating both—?"

Mom nudged Lydia, in an effort to get her to lower her voice, then leaned closer to Lydia, and whispered some more. Goetzmann had the good sense to look uncomfortable as he walked up to them. Lydia's tears evaporated as she all but dissected Goetzmann with her eyes. Mom always knew how to get Lydia's mind off her troubles.

I almost closed the door on Barry, Goetzmann's partner. He'd been standing behind Goetzmann, and I hadn't seen him. I watched him as he passed me, his eyes traveling from one framed portrait of Stephanie to another.

"Hello, Mrs. Tatum," Goetzmann said. He did his best to sound congenial, I guess, but Mom was having none of it. She just looked at him, unsmiling. Needless to say, Mom has not been pleased with a man "who dilly-dallied around" with her daughters, as she so eloquently put it. Evidently, Mom felt that first Hank dillied with me, and now he was intent upon dallying with Bert. While the introductions went around, Lydia continued to stare at Goetzmann like he was a bug on a pin. She barely gave Barry a glance.

"Mrs. Whitman?" Goetzmann plunged ahead. "I'm sorry to have to bother you at this difficult time, but there are some questions I need to ask you about your daughter. And time is very important this early in an investigation."

Lydia mutely nodded. Goetzmann proceeded to ask the usual—Stephanie's full name, age, place of business, etc., etc. . . . Finally, Goetzmann got to the part Bert and I wanted to know. We'd all taken chairs in the living room, nearest the couch, and Bert and I simultaneously leaned forward. "Did your daughter have any enemies?" Goetzmann asked.

"Of course not," Lydia sounded offended. "Of course not! Everyone loved Stephanie. She was a saint, an angel to everyone she met."

Goetzmann merely looked at her, his face portraying nothing of his thoughts. He glanced over at Bert briefly, and I realized that Bert had probably mentioned to him that Stephanie had not been so angelic in the past two weeks. Besides, it was readily apparent that *everyone* had not loved Stephanie. In fact, someone had *not* loved Stephanie to death.

The silence grew between Lydia and Goetzmann.

"Of course, if I absolutely *had* to think of an enemy, I guess you might count Stephanie's ex-husband," Lydia finally added. "Stephen Varner. They had kind of an ugly breakup. She really hated him, I know that. Although I have to admit she was crazy about him at the time they married. I used to think Stephanie had married Stephen just because she thought it would be cute to be known as Stephanie and Stephen. But she was wild about him—married him right out of high school—they both went to Pleasure Ridge Park back then."

It was the high school in the south of Louisville that to me always sounded like an erogenous zone. Sex education class must've been a dandy there. Across the room in a rocking chair, Barry smirked, probably thinking along the same lines. The possibility that Barry and I could be thinking similar thoughts was pretty scary, let me tell you.

"But Stephen was a brute, you know," Lydia was now going on, her eyes tearing again. She dabbed them with a tissue; and Mom took her hand and squeezed it. "Verbally abusive all through their marriage. When Stephanie finally told him she'd had enough, he actually hit her. Stephanie was only a kid herself back then. She absolutely fled—right back home to me where she belonged."

"But Stephanie hasn't seen her ex-husband in years," Mom added. "Isn't that right, Lydia?"

Lydia nodded. "She never mentioned it, if she had. The last I heard, Stephen moved out to California somewhere to join a commune or a cult or something. But his parents still live right here in Louisville."

"Any other boyfriends?" Barry asked.

Lydia jumped at the unexpected voice from across the room. She looked at Barry like a child who had spoken out of turn. "No, Stephanie didn't date much," she answered. "Stephanie had a very bad time going through that divorce, and she told me she really wasn't planning ever to marry any slimebag man ever again."

The two slimebag men in the room shifted position uneasily. "So how long were she and Varner married?" Goetzmann hurried on.

"Twelve, maybe thirteen years."

Goetzmann blinked. "Then their divorce was only about eight years ago—somehow I got the impression they split up when your daughter was still in her twenties."

"Oh, they did," Lydia said. "They just didn't make it

legal until she was almost thirty. And by that time, she'd set up her law practice. She just never got around to divorcing Stephen—she was just so busy, I guess, and he wasn't around, so it didn't seem that important to her. I kept telling her to do it, but she'd say she just didn't want to think about him."

Bert and I glanced at each other. This procrastination would, no doubt, come under the heading "Stupid Things Smart Women Do When It Comes to Men."

"She put him right out of her mind," Lydia went on. "That's what she always told me, but I think she was just getting over him. When she finally did get around to divorcing Stephen, he claimed he'd put her through law school, so the assets of her practice were half his. And he denied any abuse, and she didn't have proof. He hired himself this hotshot lawyer and absolutely stole half of what she'd earned since the time they married." Lydia dabbed her eyes again. "He was really not a nice person."

Bert and I glanced at each other again. It sounded as if Stephanie might have had a motive for murder, but not this Varner jerk.

Goetzmann was moving on to other topics. "Any close friends I could talk to about her?"

"She really didn't have any women friends. Stephanie was really beautiful, you know, and other women didn't like her much," Lydia said.

Being a bitch didn't exactly help her win women friends, either.

"Stephanie's work was her life," Lydia said. "She socialized with her clients, of course—they were women only, you know. But she really didn't have anything in her life but her work. A real stay-at-home."

If you could believe Lydia, Stephanie never saw anyone but her mother these days. Oh sure, that was believable. A woman who looked like Stephanie was living the life of a nun. If you believed that, I could get you the JFK Bridge over the Ohio at a good price.

Goetzmann finally thanked Lydia; and Bert and I saw him and Barry out. As soon as we were out on the porch again, Bert asked, "Hank, why are you asking about enemies?" She tried to keep the hopeful tone out of her voice, but I could hear it. "Wasn't Stephanie killed by a burglar?"

Goetzmann shrugged. "Could be, but Stephanie was shot only once. Point-blank range."

Barry made the sign of a gun with his left hand, placing it on the side of his head just under his left ear. "Bang," he said.

I gave him a look. Thank you so much, Bar, for the visual.

"Looks like someone came up behind her while she was seated, typing a document at her computer," Goetzmann went on. "What that means is, her killer was able to get very near Stephanie without her being alarmed."

"Then Stephanie's killer was someone she knew," Bert said.

"Or, at least, wasn't afraid of," Barry added.

"Or the guy was very good at being very, very quiet," Goetzmann added.

I remembered the guy who knocked me down, running from the office. Not exactly the strong, silent type.

"The medical examiner estimates that Stephanie was killed between 9:12 and 11:00 last night," Goetzmann added, glancing at his little notebook.

"But how can you be so sure? Nine-twelve? That's kind of precise, isn't it?" I asked.

"We got lucky," Goetzmann said, "that's how. Stephanie had last saved the file she was working on at 9:12 P.M."

Barry added, "I pulled up her list of files on the computer, and it's the last time listed. The computer logs the time she saves a file, and all we had to do was look. Nothing else is shown after that time, and she didn't have any kind of automatic save program on, so we at least know she was still alive at 9:12 P.M."

I knew a little about computers, just from working on the ones at the radio station. I knew that, sometimes, a computer can have a program that works in the background and automatically saves every few minutes or so any changes that are typed in. That way you didn't lose anything you'd typed if the power went off or the computer crashed or something. According to Barry, though, Stephanie didn't have one of these automatic save programs working. She was just keying in a command to save her changes as she typed.

"We're still going through Stephanie's office and her apartment; but so far, we've found nothing to indicate a motive for the break-in or the killing," Barry went on. "She was just your average drop-dead-gorgeous lady lawyer. I bet she won a lot of cases if she had a male judge. Hell, she probably didn't even have to go to court. The guys just caved."

Goetzmann frowned at him.

"OK, maybe *drop-dead* gorgeous wasn't a good choice of words," Barry said. "But, come on, did you get a good look at her?"

A change of subject seemed to be in order. "So what now?" I asked.

Goetzmann shrugged. "Maybe Stephanie's murder was

a random thing—a burglary gone bad, maybe—or maybe it was something else. I do have to admit that the previous break-in at her office makes me wonder if the two things are connected."

Next to me, Bert sagged a little. I felt a little deflated myself.

"You two let me know if you hear anything from the victim's mother that might be of help," Goetzmann said, looking at both of us but his eyes eventually resting on Bert. "And, if there's anything you can remember about that break-in, Bert, call me, OK?"

Bert nodded.

For a minute, Goetzmann seemed about to add something else, but then he seemed to think better of it.

I stood there, watching the two of them, wondering if I looked as depressed as Bert beside me. Surely, she and I had not let a killer go free. That really wasn't possible, was it?

Chapter 9

●

BERT

I was not going to be sick.

I was, however, going to get as close to actually being sick as one could possibly get without crossing over the line. The very idea that the burglar Nan and I had let go scot-free might've actually killed Stephanie really made me want to toss my cookies.

After Hank left, Nan and I stood on Lydia's porch for the longest time staring after him. Mute. Stunned. I finally said, "I can't believe this has happened because of us."

Nan stared at me. "Neither can I." Her tone indicated she meant it. But she must've had doubts, because the small areas around the edge of her mouth looked a little white. The same way mine does whenever I'm under a lot of stress.

Then we forced ourselves to go back inside. Actually, I forced Nan. She, for some reason, was pretty much ready to go home now. "We did *not* cause that woman's death," she whispered, as I dragged her through the front door.

"We could have," I whispered back.

"We did not—"

We shut up when we saw that Lydia had begun to cry again, poking at her eyes with the Kleenex tissue she'd been holding since we'd arrived. Mom sat with her, tight-lipped and silent. Mom actually looked relieved to see us as we came back into the living room, shaking her Brillo-head very slightly over Lydia's shoulder to show us that Lydia really wasn't doing very well at all.

I cannot remember when I felt so bad as we listened to that poor woman cry. "I'm sorry," Lydia finally muttered, dabbing at her eyes again. "I just can't seem to pull myself together."

"Well, of course you can't," Mom said, patting her arm. "You need some time, Lydia, that's all. And some rest. Why don't you go on and lie down in your bedroom and try to get some sleep?"

"But I can't," Lydia said. "There's so much to do. I have to arrange for the funeral and get the house ready for the boys."

Those boys were in their forties by now.

"They'll be coming in soon with their families," Lydia went on. "And I'll need to get all of Stephanie's things in order. Even Stephanie's second car, that old Thunderbird she's had ever since high school, is still at the shop. I was supposed to drive over and pick it up with her this afternoon." Lydia actually smiled a little, obviously remembering how things were just yesterday when her daughter was alive and things like car repair were the biggest problems they had.

"Stephanie just loved that car, you know," Lydia said, dabbing at her eyes. "She never let anyone else drive it, and she only drove it herself every once in a while. She'd left it for a tune-up while she was out of town this past weekend," Lydia went on. "Stephanie always kept the T-bird in my double-car garage, because she didn't have room for it in her own garage."

Now that was the Stephanie I knew—take up room in your mother's garage free of charge with a car you won't let her drive. Oh, sure, that was the Stephanie I remembered, all right.

"Lydia, we can pick the car up for you," I heard myself saying before I really knew I was going to offer. "We'll be happy to."

Nan turned to stare at me. She mouthed the question, *"Happy?"*

I gave her a twin-whammy. Which entails widening your eyes and making them kind of bug out. Not very pretty but really quite effective. My twin-whammy said: For goodness sake, we might've let the murderer of this woman's daughter go free—the least we can do is pick up her car. And be *happy* about it.

"Nan and Bert can help sort through Stephanie's business matters, too," Mom offered, while Nan turned to stare at her now. "Bert certainly knows what's going on at the office."

Oh, sure, I thought. Two weeks of full-time employment, and I was an expert. But I guess I did need to make certain all of Stephanie's clients were aware of her death. Stephanie's divorcee wanna-bes were going to have to find themselves another crusader.

"And Nan can certainly help Bert go through everything," Mom added. Nan was getting huffy, something that Mom either didn't notice or didn't care to notice. Apparently, Nan took offense at people volunteering her services without consulting her first. But, Mom and I both know that Nan might kick and scream about doing something, but she would still do it.

"And I can help you with the other things—talk to the

funeral home and make arrangements—at least until your boys get here," Mom added, still patting Lydia's arm.

It was shortly after that when Lydia's bingo group came by, bearing still more cakes and pies. With the house full, Nan and I decided it was time to leave. For one thing, we didn't want to stick around and see how they were going to store anything else in Lydia's refrigerator.

As Nan drove home, I had just one small question. "You know, Nan, do you think we ought to tell Hank that you could identify the burglar?"

Nan's reaction was a bit unexpected. She turned to stare at me, almost running off the ramp to I-65. When she pulled back onto the expressway, she said, "Let me see if I've got this straight. You think we should tell your boyfriend that somewhere in the city is a man I may or may not be able to recognize if I saw him again? Who may or may not have something to do with Stephanie's death?"

The answer to that question was obvious. "Yes."

Nan made this truly ugly noise in the back of her throat. "Bert, I got a pretty good look at the guy, but I can't guarantee I can recognize him. Not only that—there's nobody to recognize. The cops haven't arrested anyone. If and when they do, we can tell them if their guy turns out to be the same guy I saw. Otherwise, we're causing ourselves and this other guy a lot of trouble for nothing. OK? Does that satisfy you?"

All right, that sounded reasonable. Although I might add that she didn't have to sound so snippish about it.

Needless to say, I got hardly any sleep that night. What little I dozed, I either dreamed of Nan and Hank doing a Fred Astaire and Ginger Rogers, or I dreamed of a faceless killer stalking tiny women carrying tiny hammers. Have I ever mentioned that my dreams are so transparent that they could bore a psychiatrist to tears?

The next morning, about an hour before Nan was due to go on the air at the radio station, Nan and I drove over to Auto Heaven on Preston Street, where Stephanie's T-Bird awaited pickup. Auto Heaven was one of those mechanic shops in which twenty-year-old guys fix cars and treat the women who own them as imbeciles who don't know a spark cap from a distributor plug.

The young man at the back of the service desk had the name "Wes" embroidered on a tag sewn on the left pocket of his blue-chambray shirt. He wore a small diamond stud in his ear. This was the kind of boy who would grow up to wear gold chains and a shirt open to his beer belly and who would be convinced he looked sexy. When he handed Nan the bill, he also recited a list of things they'd found in the T-Bird that also needed fixing, all of which, according to him, were life-threatening. I've found that this is a common practice among oil-change and car-repair places—it's the "Sure-You-Fixed-This-But-You're-Going-To-Be-Killed-By-This-Other-Thing" ploy.

Nan started shaking her head even before he started on item two. "I don't think so," Nan said when he finished his laundry list. "We'll just take—"

"Yo, lady, you really ought to think about it—I'd hate for you to break down somewhere. Or you either." He glanced over at me for the first time and then back at Nan, then back to me, his eyes doing that tennis-match thing that people do when it finally occurs to them that the two women standing right in front of them look an awful lot alike.

"Wo, you guys twins?" he asked, grinning like maybe

he'd just discovered something that no one else had ever noticed.

"Twins, yes," Nan said, "Guys, no. And we'll just take the car as is, and just throw caution to the wind."

Nan can be so rude. I added, "But we'll let the real owner know what you said about the repairs."

Nan turned to look at me. "That's going to be kind of tough to do."

"I was talking about Lydia."

"Wo, you ain't the owner? Then no way, José. I cain't give you the car," the boy said.

Nan's face kind of imploded. "We're here as a favor to the owner," she said through her teeth, "and, yes, you can give us the car."

The boy was shaking his head. "Nope. Not without something in writing from that real owner you was talking about."

I could tell from the sudden tensing of all of Nan's muscles that she was forcing herself not to grab the boy by the front of his shirt and make him eat his name tag.

"Written authorization is going to be kind of hard to get," I said, jumping in to avoid bloodshed. "The owner is dead."

"*Mur-dered,*" Nan added ominously, her tone implying that he, too, could share that fate. The boy's eyes got sort of huge, and he took the money Lydia had given us and handed over the car keys without another peep.

We found the white T-bird in the parking lot and fitted the key into the lock. Nan got into the driver's seat and I in the passenger seat. The plan was for Nan to drive me to Nan's car. Nan started the T-bird right up. I could tell from the way she was looking around the leather-upholstered seats, the carpeted floors, the tape deck, that Nan shared Stephanie's appreciation of this car.

Nan changed the seat position several times, turned the radio and windshield wipers on and off, trying everything out. She reached over and popped open the glove compartment, revealing a small, black, zippered storage case.

"Nan, I don't think—" I began, but she was already unzipping the case. Inside were several tape cassettes, rubber-banded together. She took out one of them, reading the typed label. "Dalton A. Roark, III." She read. "7:30 P.M., Friday, October 26, 1996, The Cat's Meow."

Her eyebrows went up. The Cat's Meow was the name of a popular nightclub on Bardstown Road on Louisville's east side. But who was this Dalton Roark guy and why did Stephanie have a tape of him? Nan was already removing another cassette. It, too, was neatly labeled with the name of another man, along with a time, a date, and an address. The address was another popular nightspot in Louisville.

Nan popped the first cassette tape into the tape player. As soon as the tape began to play, I recognized the voice. "That's Stephanie," I said.

There was a man's voice on the tape, too; but him, I didn't recognize. The tape's background noises of clinking glasses and a hubbub of voices sounded as if Stephanie and the man were in a restaurant or a bar—no doubt, they were at The Cat's Meow, if the label was correct.

"So, tell me, beautiful lady, where have you been all my life?" the man was saying.

"Not a very original pickup line," commented Nan. Personally, I wouldn't know. As I believe I mentioned earlier, until I'd started dating Hank, I could count on one hand the number of dates I'd had. Nan, however, was a connoisseur of pickup lines.

On the tape, Stephanie laughed softly, as if the man had been extremely clever. "Unfortunately, at my apartment, all alone." Stephanie lingered over those last two words, making them sound like a tragedy of colossal proportions.

Beside me, Nan smiled.

"A pretty woman like you should never be alone—especially in your apartment." The man's voice dropped lower, but we could still hear what he said. Apparently, he was inviting Stephanie out, or rather, inviting himself over to that apartment of hers where she'd spent so much time alone. He also suggested a few things they could do to each other while they were there. Some of which involved whipped cream. And making Stephanie into something even more delectable. To my astonishment, Stephanie sounded delighted. "Ohhh," she said, "that sounds wonderful. Let's go. Right now. Shall we?" Her laughter was soft and inviting.

As my son Brian says, my flabber was gasted. *Stephanie* was picking up some guy in a bar? Lydia had said that Stephanie didn't even date.

"Why on earth would Stephanie be taping this conversation?" I asked.

Nan shrugged. "Maybe she likes to relive her sexual experiences, from start to finish. Or maybe she was doing a dissertation on pickup lines and obscene suggestions. Or maybe she had a few little kinks of her own, like having a verbal record of her conquests." Nan popped the tape out and examined it. "Dalton Roark," she mused. "The Third."

"You know, here's a name that sounds kind of familiar," I said, looking at another tape cassette.

Nan pulled it from the zippered case. She read the label,

"Judge Horace Bledsoe. With still another date and time and bar. My, my. Stephanie was a busy bee."

"I know where I've heard it," I said. "Judge Bledsoe has been on the news recently promoting some social cause or other."

"That's right. I remember now. I believe he spoke on the issue of sexually transmitted diseases," Nan said. "As I recall, he was for it."

I ignored her. "Isn't Bledsoe a superior court judge in Jefferson County?"

"More to the point, isn't he married with grown children?" Nan asked.

I started pulling out the other tapes. There were four different tapes in all, including a Dr. Bryce Hollister and a Reverend Burlington Loudon. "I don't know—all of these names sound kind of familiar."

Nan slapped the tapes into the player, playing little parts of them all. In all of the tapes, Stephanie was being propositioned. And, on every tape, Stephanie was saying yes.

"Well," Nan said. "So much for using *The Nun's Story* as the title of the movie version of Stephanie's life."

"But what on earth has she been doing?"

"The answer 'having a great time' comes to mind," said Nan.

"It almost sounds to me as if maybe she moonlighted as a prostitute."

"I don't think so, Bert," Nan said. "For one thing, no money seems to be changing hands. My guess is, she's giving away freebies. And loving it."

Nan can be so crude.

We sat in the parking lot, listening to the tapes until the windows began to steam up. I'm sure it was just from our breathing inside the car with the windows all rolled up, rather than what was being said on those tapes. After twenty minutes or so, the boy from the repair desk finally noticed our sitting in the T-bird with the motor running, not going anywhere. He was probably hoping we'd actually broken down right there in his lot, and he'd started out of the building toward us when Nan put the car in gear and pulled out, zipping right past him.

Nan drove us over to her own car, parked at the curb, with the plan being that I would follow her in her Neon back to Lydia's. Naturally, Nan was the one who got to drive the T-bird back. As I got out of the car, we split the tapes between us. I took two and Nan kept two, planning to listen to them in the privacy of our cars as we drove. I, for one, certainly would be keeping my windows rolled all the way up so no other drivers could hear.

As I started to close the door, Nan leaned over and looked at me through the open passenger door. "Hey, Bert?"

"What?"

"At least we know something now about that burglary at Stephanie's office," Nan said. "I'd say we can make a pretty good guess as to what the man in the suit and tie had been looking for."

I just looked at her. Then the name of the guy who'd broken into her office might just be written on one of the tapes we were about to listen to?

Just thinking such a thing made my stomach hurt.

Chapter 10

•

NAN

Listening to those tapes, I had one main thought. At least Stephanie sounded like she'd had a great time during her short life. It was the same way I'd felt when I'd heard the news about Princess Di—thank God she'd had a little wild and passionate fun if she was going to have to die that young.

At Lydia's, Bert pulled my Neon into the driveway and got out, her face looking a little rosy. Sometimes I cannot believe Bert and I were once the exact same thing—she was actually blushing. I got out and leaned against the T-bird, waiting for her to reach me. "Before we go back into that house to turn over the car keys," I said, when she was within earshot, "we really have to decide whether we should let Lydia know about Saint Stephanie's extra-heavenly pursuits," I said.

Bert's eyes widened. Apparently she hadn't thought about this little detail. "You mean, let Lydia actually listen to these tapes?" Her cheeks flamed. "You mean, the lady with all the church groups and the thinking that her daughter Stephanie was an angel? Listening to these tapes actually might kill her. Then we'd be responsible for the deaths of both the mother *and* the daughter."

I just looked at her. Really, Bert can be so dramatic

sometimes. "Bert, I really think Lydia could probably stand the shock. But it occurred to me that it really might be kinder just to keep this to ourselves, and not to—"

I was agreeing with Bert, for God's sake. Wouldn't you think she'd have been pleased? But no, she was frowning even before I finished speaking.

"But, Nan, what if one of these tapes has something to do with Stephanie's murder?" Bert said. "I mean, if these tapes were what the *GQ* Bandit was looking for, then his name could very well be on these tapes. And if he was the one who killed Stephanie—"

I interrupted. "We don't know that."

Bert was still frowning. "Well, no, we don't. But we don't know it isn't, either. Maybe we really should tell Lydia. And turn these tapes over to Hank, so that the police can look into this."

I rolled my eyes. "Oh, sure, I can just see all the cops standing around, snickering over Stephanie and her men friends and their version of dessert. That would really make Lydia happy."

"But one of these men on these tapes could be the intruder who ran into you on Saturday," Bert said. "Sure, it may be a little late now, but maybe you could still identify him."

"Bert, for one thing, none of this may have anything to do with Stephanie's murder. And you've got to admit, some of the things being said on the tape are not exactly flattering to Stephanie."

Bert nodded, her cheeks flushing again. "In fact, listening to them," she said, "you could actually get the idea that Stephanie was a tramp."

It was an effort not to roll my eyes again. "That's what

they'd called girls like her back in the fifties, Bert. These days they're called loving and giving human beings."

Bert didn't buy that one. Now *she* rolled her eyes.

"At any rate," I went on, "instead of telling Lydia, why don't we do this? We'll go visit each of these men and see if any of them rings a bell to me. That way we'll at least know if one of them is the burglar. If the tapes turn out to be relevant, we can turn them over to Lydia and the police then. That way, we don't ruin Stephanie's reputation in her mother's eyes or anyone else's for nothing."

What I didn't add was that we might also find out just exactly how responsible we were for this mess. I didn't exactly want to say it out loud, but I had to admit that one of the main reasons I wanted to look into all of this was that I wanted a little reassurance that our switch had not inadvertently resulted in Stephanie's murder.

Bert was still frowning, but she nodded anyway. "All right," Bert said. "I guess you're right. Lydia certainly wouldn't want Stephanie's private life exposed to strangers. Particularly the whipped-cream part. And it doesn't take a genius to figure out how happy our own mom would be with us if we did a smear campaign—no pun intended—on the recently deceased daughter of a close friend of hers."

"So you won't tell your boyfriend about the tapes yet?" I pressed the question. I wanted to hear it from Bert's own lips to make sure there was no misunderstanding.

Bert looked a little odd when I said the word *boyfriend*, but she went ahead and nodded. "All right, all right," she said. "At least not until we find out for sure that these tapes have something to do with Stephanie's murder. But we do need to find out right away. Which means that we need to talk to the men on these tapes very soon. Like, today."

"But we're going to talk to them together, OK?" I added. "Just in case one of the men we're talking to happens to be homicidal."

Bert shrugged and nodded, but I made her say it out loud. "We'll do it together," she repeated.

I smiled and checked my watch. "Right now, though, I've got a radio show to do."

Bert agreed to meet me after my air shift. We dropped the keys off to Mom (Lydia had finally taken her up on the idea of lying down for a nap), and I drove Bert downtown to where she'd left her own car last night and headed for WCKI.

All during my air shift, I had a hard time keeping my mind on Garth Brooks and Clint Black and Vince Gill— something that was usually quite easy—mainly because I was mulling over those tapes we'd found. The one reason for Stephanie to make those tapes that I didn't mention to Bert was, of course, blackmail. Blackmail happened to be an excellent reason for a woman to get herself murdered, too. Unfortunately, that would also mean that the guy I saw Saturday really might've been the person who murdered Stephanie, something I didn't even want to think about.

I remembered the posh River Road address for Stephanie that Lydia had given to the police. Could Stephanie have afforded such digs on her income as a mere divorce lawyer? Not unless she was making big bucks for her clients. Or unless she was raking in a few hundred thou on the side, dating prominent married men and making them pay for the privilege.

Bert was waiting for me outside when I walked out the door at WCKI. One look at her face, and I knew something was up. She was all but jumping up and down, and in her arms were several file folders. Her expression was glum.

"It's even worse than we thought," Bert said, as soon as I came up to her.

"What's even worse than we thought?" I asked. We moved off simultaneously, walking down the street toward my car.

"Those tapes. I went back to Stephanie's office while you were on the air. I thought I'd see if there were any other tapes there. Or anything that would give me a clue as to what Stephanie was doing when she made them."

"And you found something?" We reached my car, I unlocked the door, and we climbed in.

Bert gave me a dourful look. "I just knew those names sounded familiar."

She handed me the file folders, and I glanced at the label on top—"Mrs. Dalton Roark?"

"The Third. These women were all clients of Stephanie's," Bert said, not waiting for me to read the rest. "Every single one of them."

I lifted the top file and looked at the one underneath it. The file label read "Mrs. Horace Bledsoe." The others bore the names of the other two wives of the men on the tapes.

Bert went on, her tone dejected. "Stephanie represented all of these women in their divorces against their husbands."

I was still flipping through the file-folder contents. All of them seemed to hold about the same things—court documents, separation and property-settlement agreements

I looked at Bert. "Stephanie was dating the husbands of her clients? Isn't that kind of unethical?"

"To say the least," Bert said. "At the very best, it's not

a very nice thing to do. Oh, Nan, we can never tell Lydia what Stephanie was up to. Never."

I was still flipping through the files' contents. "Well, at least Stephanie knew the men were available."

Bert glared at me. "Oh, sure, make a joke. Stephanie may have broken up these men's marriages, then served as the divorce attorney to the wives. That's just terrible."

"It's one way to scare up business," I said. The files all held the final bills stapled to the front of the file folder on the left. All made out in amounts ranging from $25,000 to $50,000. For services rendered. All stamped paid in full. Wow. Maybe divorce lawyers made a tad more than I'd previously thought.

Looking at the addresses given in the files, we discovered that the nearest was that of the Reverend Burlington Loudon, whose address was on Lower River Road, not far in fact from where Stephanie lived. Without even discussing where we were going, I headed toward the river.

We pulled up in front of an absolutely gorgeous ultra-modern contemporary house—overlooking the Ohio River, no less. Glancing up at the imposing facade, Bert smoothed her short navy-linen skirt and straightened her pristine white-silk blouse and navy blazer. She looked over at me as we walked toward the front door. I was wearing my usual country-music uniform—blue jeans with holes in the knees, ragged denim jacket over a sleeveless black pullover, and cowboy boots so scuffed they really could've been worn in a rodeo. I, of course, could not help but notice Bert's disapproving look. "OK, Bert, just tell them I'm your clone, and something went horribly wrong during the procedure."

At our knock, the door was opened by a woman wearing the same kind of clothes as Bert, only about three times more expensive. The woman was about fifty, attractive, although with the deeply tanned, lined face of a woman who has logged too many hours under the sun lamp. Her short ash blond hair had the look of a salon rather than of a beauty parlor. "Yes?" she said, starting to smile at Bert until she caught sight of me and my attire. Her eyes widened, and her smile never quite became a smile.

I just stared right back at her. Great, another fashion critic.

"Is the Reverend Loudon at home?" Bert asked. Over her shoulder, I could see what looked like an original oil on the wall of the entry hall. A chandelier hung in the room beyond. Unless Mrs. Loudon was an heiress, it looked as if the religion biz had been quite the moneymaker for the Loudons.

"The Reverend Loudon doesn't live here anymore," the woman said. "Now if you'll excuse me—" She started to close the door in our faces.

I stepped forward and stuck my foot in the door—something radio announcers learn to do after going on a few client calls with sales reps—and asked, "Then you're Mrs. Loudon? Mrs. Eleanor Loudon?"

Her eyes narrowed as she studied me. "Yes, I'm Mrs. Loudon." She stared pointedly at my foot.

Hey, I took the hint. I removed it.

"Mrs. Loudon, could we speak to you for a moment?" I asked. "We're friends of your—"

"I know who you are," Mrs. Loudon interrupted. "I've seen your face on TV and I've heard you on the radio. I'm not about to talk to the media about all of this."

Oh, great, not just a fashion critic but a fan.

She tried to close the door again; and this time, I wasn't

so quick. However, Bert, having collected for about a million school drives for one thing or another, used a skill she'd perfected during those collections. She stuck her foot in the door, just like I had. Unfortunately, she was wearing summer pumps instead of boots.

Wincing, Bert asked, "Mrs. Loudon, we know you were represented by Stephanie Whitman in your divorce. I work in Miss Whitman's office and she—"

Mrs. Loudon interrupted again, her tone haughty. "Then you know that the good Reverend and I just completed the settlement phase of our soon-to-be-final divorce. If you wish more information, I suggest that you speak to your employer and my attorney."

"Actually, that's going to be a little difficult," I said. "Stephanie Whitman was found murdered yesterday."

"Stephanie was *murdered?*" she repeated. Mrs. Loudon's jaw dropped open, and she made gasping noises, a lot like a fish out of water. When she could finally speak, her tone was even colder. "If the *authorities* wish to talk to the Reverend Loudon," she said, "they should try his church, The Apostolic Church of the Evangelist. He lives above the chapel in a very tiny room there." She gave the tiniest flicker of a smile at this pronouncement, then she unceremoniously pushed Bert's foot aside with her own and closed the door. Firmly. The lock behind the closed door clicked. Twice.

"What a charmer," I said, walking back to our car.

"She really did seem to be surprised about Stephanie's death," Bert said. "I thought she would keel right over."

"Of course, she could've just been pretending not to know," I pointed out. "But if she didn't know Stephanie was dead, what was all that talk about not talking to the media? About what?"

"Divorcing her minister husband? It's got to be kind of traumatic for a minister to be getting a divorce. Not exactly the kind of example you want to set for the flock," Bert said. "Remember Tammy Faye and Jim?"

"There's a real difference here," I said. "She wasn't crying. In fact, that looked a lot like a smirk to me. Especially when she got to the part about her hubby living in a small room above the church."

We stopped at a phone booth on Ninth Street in downtown Louisville and asked Information for the number of the Apostolic Church of the Evangelist. Louisville Information used to give you addresses, too, but these days they prefer to keep that information to themselves. Instead, a little automated voice asks you what city and what number; and you never talk to a real person during the entire process. They call this progress.

In fact, the only way you get a real person is if you make a mistake in asking for the number. So, naturally, I asked for the number of the Apostolic Church of the What-sits; and a real person came on the line.

"We have no listing by that name. We do have the Apostolic Church of the Evangelist," the young woman said.

"Is that the one up on Market Street?" I asked.

"No, this is listed at 21513 Outer Loop."

"That's the one," I said. I took down the number and address and thanked her.

Wouldn't you know it? When we got to the church, the secretary there—an elderly woman sucking a Tootsie Roll pop and running church bulletins off on a copy machine—said the Reverend Loudon wasn't there. There'd been a recent death in the church, she said, and he wouldn't be in all day. He'd even canceled Wednesday night prayer meeting for the evening. She also said she didn't know the name of the parishioner who'd died. We left our names and work numbers with her, asking her to call us when the Reverend Loudon was in.

As we walked back to my car, Bert and I looked at each other. "Did she say a recent death—" Bert asked.

"—or a recent murder?" I finished for her.

Chapter 11

•

BERT

"So where to now?" Nan asked me, once we'd settled ourselves in her Neon.

I looked around. The horizon was brilliant with oranges, purples, and reds, one of your average gorgeous Louisville summer sunsets. "Well, it's going to be dark soon, and I really don't think we should be calling on anyone after seven."

Nan gave me a long-suffering look. "Please don't tell me that you're playing Miss Manners," she said, "when there's a possibility—remote, though it may be—that one of the people we're calling on is a murderer. Without a doubt, they're lechers."

Well, really. Playing Miss Manners hadn't occurred to me, but it did seem that we didn't have to stoop to being rude to these people. "No," I said slowly, "I'm not trying to be socially correct. Although I would point out that only the men involved here are lechers. The women may be very nice. I just don't think that visiting a murderer after dark is all that appealing."

I could tell Nan thought I had a point. I could tell because she nodded, started the car, and said, "You have a point."

"The nearest address now is Judge Horace Bledsoe—he's on Zorn Avenue."

Nan pulled out into traffic. "OK, here come de judge."

The house on Zorn Avenue was one of those gigantic multistoried brick houses with white columns in front that would make Tara in *Gone With the Wind* look like a cottage. A small sign on the mailbox at the bottom of the hill leading to the house proclaimed Twin Oaks. Naturally, there wasn't an oak in sight.

There was not just one front door, but two massive oak doors. Maybe these were the oaks referred to in the sign. An enormous ornate wreath, made of dried herbs and flowers, graced each door.

"Want to bet which one will be the one to open?" Nan whispered, as I rang the bell. A deep Westminster chime rang within.

I was almost expecting Mammy to answer the door, but the right-hand door was opened by a short, overweight woman with tightly curled bright red hair that had that overall garish shade that pretty much proclaimed that everyone *and* her hairdresser knew for sure. Tucked under her left arm was a tiny white fluffy dog that began yapping at the top of its canine lungs as soon as the woman opened the door. The little dog was wearing a rhinestone-studded satin collar, perfectly coordinating with the many rhinestone rings the woman wore on both hands.

I deduced that this woman could not be the help.

"Hush, Lacey-love, hush," the woman crooned to the barking dog. "Hush, now." Lacey-love ignored her, its barking raising a notch and now wiggling so violently that the woman also dropped her. Nan took a step backwards from Lacey-love's tiny white bared teeth.

"We're looking for Judge Bledsoe!" I yelled, in an attempt to be heard over the yapping dog. "Judge Horace Bledsoe?"

"What?" the woman yelled back. Lacey-love almost made it to the ground, but the woman managed to reel her in just in time. I hated to think what might happen if Lacey-love got loose. Those teeth really did look pretty sharp.

The woman grabbed the dog's snout, holding its mouth together like a muzzle. Lacey-love still managed to emit rather loud squeaks, but at least we could hear each other now.

"Judge Horace Bledsoe?" Nan asked. "Is he at home?"

The woman gave a nasty little chuckle. "Judge Bledsoe is at home, but that is certainly not here," she said. "I'm Barbara Bledsoe. His *ex*-wife. Can I help you?" Her eyes looked from Nan to me and back again. "Are you two twins?"

"Yes, ma'am," Nan said. "Do you know how we can reach Judge Bledsoe? We have a personal matter we would like to—"

"You're not one of the good judge's playmates, are you?" She looked us up and down, like we were something reptilian that had crawled up on her doorstep. "He always did go in for the oddities in that department."

I stared at her. "I beg your pardon?" She could not be saying what I thought she was saying. Could she?

Nan apparently did not have any question that she was. "Excuse me, lady, but whom are you calling oddities?" Nan asked. At that moment, Lacey-love jerked her head out of Mrs. Bledsoe's hand. The dog snarled and lunged for both Nan and me. I expected Mrs. Bledsoe to grab her, but she let the dog go. On purpose, it seemed.

Lacey-love hit the ground on all four painted-toe paws

and threw herself at its mistress's nearest visitor, who happened to be Nan. The little white dog lunged and leaped at least two feet off the ground. Nan put up both hands to fend off the tiny teeth. Instead of biting, though, little Lacey-love began to lick, licking Nan's hands, her wrists, my hands, my legs, our clothes, anything she could lay her little pink tongue on. As she carried on this lick-fest, Lacey-love made pleasurable little sounds to herself. Mrs. Bledsoe, on the other hand, merely looked extremely disgusted with her little dog.

I took a step forward. "Could you please just tell us where to find Judge Bledsoe?" I was pretty sure that my hands were going to be chapped soon, if this animal did not stop slobbering on them.

"As I said, he's not here. Nor is he expected to be. He's probably at the YMCA. Or maybe some pitiful hotel room. I really don't know, nor do I care. Where he goes and what he does is no longer my concern. Our divorce was final three days ago." Mrs. Bledsoe made it sound as if she were recounting a victory.

"Mrs. Bledsoe, I know all about the divorce. I work for Stephanie Whitman," I said. "I understand she was your attorney."

Mrs. Bledsoe's eyes widened. Then she squinted at me. "Stephanie Whitman is dead," she said. "I saw it on the news."

"We know that," Nan said. "That's one of the reasons we want to speak with the judge." She bent to scratch the dog behind the ears. Lacey-love gave an audible sigh of pleasure. "There are some things that might come out, now that Stephanie is dead, and we need to—"

"But you can't do that!" Mrs. Bledsoe's voice was shrill.

Nan looked up at her in surprise. Mrs. Bledsoe's eyes were fixed on Nan's denim jacket, its back now visible as Nan knelt down with the dog. The jacket back was emblazoned with the call letters of the radio station, WCKI-FM, embroidered in large white letters. Tiny letters are sewn on the pocket of Nan's jacket, too, but apparently it took great big ones for Mrs. Bledsoe finally to register their implication. Suddenly, Mrs. Bledsoe was rapidly surveying the porch, as if she were seeking some kind of help in the shadows of her portico. "You can't. You just can't! I won't allow it!"

Nan and I looked at each other. OK, this was an unexpected development. This crazy woman was almost acting like we were threatening her. But with what?

"We can't what?" we asked in unison.

"Now, look here. I had an agreement with Stephanie Whitman," Mrs. Bledsoe said, her tone back to huffy now. She'd obviously regained her composure. "Client-lawyer privilege, that's what it was. All that went on between us was confidential—even if she is dead now."

"She was murdered," Nan said, standing up.

"I know that, and I don't care," Mrs. Bledsoe said. "It doesn't change anything. You must know I have a standing in this community. I have my clubs and my charity work. If one iota of our agreement gets into the media, I will sue you. I will take every penny you have earned or ever will earn. You'll wish you'd never heard of Barbara Jane Bledsoe."

I already wished I'd never heard of her.

Then she stooped down to scoop up Lacey-love with a furious scowl. Lacey-love looked at us with complete adoration, her little pink tongue hanging out, until Mrs. Bledsoe slammed the door in our faces.

And locked it.

For a moment, Nan and I just stood there, staring at the door. "What in hell was that all about?" Nan asked.

I was looking for something to wipe dog spit off my hands. "I really have no idea. She actually acted as if we were trying to threaten her in some way."

"It all started when she saw my station jacket," Nan said. She casually wiped her hands on her jeans.

I stared at Nan. Yuck. I was not going to wipe it on my clothes.

"Right," I said. "When she realized you were from a radio station."

I pulled a flower from one of the wreaths on the front doors, and blotted my hand carefully with it. Then I stuck it back in, fluffing it and the surrounding dried herbs. It almost looked as pretty as the other one. The curtain at the front window moved as I finished fluffing. Well, she shouldn't let her dog slobber on people if she wanted to keep her wreath nice. Nan and I started back toward the car.

We climbed back into Nan's Neon, and she pulled out onto Zorn. "What is it that she doesn't want to get out?" Nan said. "Surely, she knows that the divorce is public record."

"Do you think she knows about Judge Bledsoe and Stephanie?" I asked. "And now, how in the world are we going to find Judge Bledsoe?"

Nan shrugged, pulling over into the left lane. "I guess we can always catch him at the courthouse."

"One thing, I'm beginning to wish I'd had Stephanie as my divorce attoney. Have you noticed? We've gone to the addresses listed for the men in the files, and all the ex-wives are there. They seem to have always gotten the house."

"And the furniture and cars. Not to mention the jewelry. Did you see the rings that woman had?"

"Those had to be rhinestones, don't you think? I mean, surely, she wouldn't put diamonds on a dog."

"Bert, I don't think those were rhinestones." Nan patted my hand indulgently

I hate it when she pats me. It's so condescending. "You really think they were diamonds?" The very idea actually made me feel a little sick. That woman was wealthy enough after a divorce to put diamonds on a dog? And a slobbering dog, at that?

Good Lord.

"Don't feel so bad," Nan said. "Jake wasn't exactly mega-bucks. These guys apparently were heavy-hitters. Major players. They probably had plenty to go around."

"Well, sure, but I don't know that that made a difference. I mean, Stephanie went up against a judge, for goodness sakes; and it looks like she won major bucks for her client. You'd think a judge, knowing the legal system the way he did, would have fared a lot better."

Nan blinked a couple times at that. "You know, you're right," she said. She made no move to pat me. "Barbara Bledsoe should be the one living at the Y, not the judge."

I took a deep breath, and tried not to feel depressed. "Even Lacey-love seemed to make out better in a divorce than I did." I smiled, of course, when I said it, but you know, it wasn't all that funny. When Jake and I had divorced, he'd walked away with the house I'd lived in ever since Brian was born, because there had simply been no way I could make the mortgage payments. Jake was still living there today.

So exactly what did these women know that I didn't?

Chapter 12

•

NAN

The next morning, Bert and I were on the road again, à la Willie Nelson, except we were still solvent. I figured we could visit one of the last two remaining men—if we finally got to talk to any of them—before Bert dropped me to go on the air at ten. This time, we were calling on Dalton Roark, the Third, no less. The man with the appetite for whipped cream.

Roark's address was way out on Brownsboro Road in one of those expensive real-estate developments that have sprung up east of Louisville. All of them have names like "The Something at Something Else." Such as The Copse at Hursthaven. Or The Clearings at Bellemeade. This one happened to be The Dells at Brownsboro. As I pulled in the huge mock-wood gates, I could see that most of these homes had those vinyl crisscross beams, fake thatch roofs, and faux leaded windows that are so expensive. God knows what the real ones must cost. The development was designed to look as if somehow English Tudor cottages, each with no less than six bedrooms, four baths, and a three-car garage, had been airlifted into suburban Louisville.

Bert looked around as we walked up the fake cobblestone walk past the perfectly manicured lawn to the front door. I stooped down to make sure the grass was real. It was. I could tell Bert was pretty impressed. OK, I was impressed, too. Mainly because of the yards.

English gardens were the style here, also. Fuchsia-colored gladiolas, mixed with red and white geraniums, were in full bloom; and an old man in grass-stained white overalls was on his knees, weeding the flower bed of petunias, daisies, and hyacinths that ran the length of the front of the house. The back of his overalls read "Jennings Nursery" in block letters.

"Wow," Bert breathed, looking at all the flowers. "They're gorgeous."

"Right," I said. "And expensive. I hate to guess how many dollars per petal."

The old man tipped the brim of his cap at us as we passed him. "Mornin'. Hope you all ain't here selling nothin'," he said. He glanced from Bert to me and then back again, his eyebrows furrowing. "And not collecting for some cause or 'nother."

"Good morning to you. Why not?" I asked.

"The lady of the house—she be having herself a hissy fit," he said. He checked Bert and me out again, taking off his cap and scratching his bald head. "You ain't twins, are you?"

Bert smiled at him. "Yes, we are."

He slapped his leg, chuckling and shaking his head. "Why, do tell. I knew it when I looked at you two—I says to myself, they's twins. But then I says, well, maybe no—they ain't dressed alike. But then I says, naw, they's gotta be twins." All the while, he was chuckling to himself, pleased to have realized that we were absolutely, no doubt about it, *twins.*

It continues to amaze me the reactions that people have

to twins. Especially twins as old as Bert and me. The reactions seem to come in two categories. Either other people are delighted with themselves for noticing they're in the presence of twins, or, when it finally occurs to them, they're irritated with us that we've been trying to pull a fast one on them. The old man was still watching us, grinning from ear to ear, shaking his head, as we rang the bell.

There was no answer.

"Did you notice he said lady of the house?" Bert said. "Don't tell me Roark has already remarried."

"He's got to have someone to keep track of his gladiolas," I said. "But I think this is the same song and dance as Mrs. Loudon and Mrs. Bledsoe. It's obvious Mrs. Roark got the house. And custody of the gardener."

We rang again. The door was finally opened by a tall woman, about forty-five or so, wearing glasses on a cord around her neck and carrying a cordless phone. She was wearing what used to be known as lounging pajamas—satin gold pajama bottoms with a short-sleeved white-satin top with braided frog closings at the neck. She wore gold high-heeled mules with marabou feathers on the toes. And I'd thought Joan Crawford was dead.

"Maybe you didn't understand me," the woman was yelling into the phone. "The dining-room suite I received yesterday has a scratch on the door of the hutch. It's junk. If I don't get a replacement today, just cancel the order. Take the whole set back. *Comprendez?* Got it? Do we understand each other now?" She looked at us and snapped. "Yeah? What?"

"Is Dalton Roark at home?" I asked.

The woman was not listening. She barked into the phone again. "That's right. Then what time will it be delivered?

All right, but five minutes later, you can just forget it!" She looked around the open doorway, obviously wanting to slam the phone down, but had to content herself with merely clicking the off button several times very, very hard. Then she barked at us again. "I said, what?"

Bert was just standing there, staring at the woman, no doubt amazed that one could be so rude to someone on the phone, a person whose voice was all you could hear. Bert has, of course, never worked in radio. I repeated myself. "Is Mr. Roark at home?"

"Hell, no, he isn't home," she snapped. "Why should he be?" She actually started to close the door in our faces. God, what was it with these dames? Did they just enjoy the sound of a door slamming or the sound of themselves being unbelievably nasty?

"Are you Mrs. Roark?" I asked.

"Of course not. I'm Sarah Roark. The *ex*–Mrs. Roark," she crowed. "What's it to you?"

"Were you represented by the attorney Stephanie Whitman in your divorce?" Bert asked.

Like a button had been pushed, Mrs. Roark's demeanor immediately changed. She blinked a couple of times and stared back and forth at Bert and me. "Yes, I was. Why do you ask?" She obviously seemed taken aback at the mere mention of Stephanie's name. "What is it you want from me?" she asked. "Are you twins?" All of these questions she delivered with the same trace of irritation.

"Yes, we are. May we come in and talk to you for a moment?" Bert answered in reverse order.

"What about?" she barked.

"I worked for Stephanie Whitman, and we're helping her

mother clear up some matters regarding her estate," Bert lied smoothly.

I turned to look at her in admiration. A well-turned lie actually deserves applause, but I held back for the moment. "We just needed to ask you a couple of questions about your legal dealings with Miss Whitman," I added. I did notice that use of the word "estate" didn't cause Mrs. Roark to blink an eye. Obviously, she'd already heard about Stephanie's death.

"I don't know what you need to talk to me for," Mrs. Roark said. She actually sounded even more nervous now. "But come on in."

We followed Mrs. Roark down a long entry hall in which one could easily bowl. We entered a basketball court–sized living room. She crossed the room—exercise in itself—and put the phone down on its base where it rested on a shoulder-high mahogany entertainment center. She opened a glass rectangular dish next to the phone, took out a cigarette, and tapped its end on her palm several times. She'd lit it and drawn a long puff before turning back around to us.

Mrs. Roark actually looked surprised that we were still standing. "Sit, sit," she said irritably, waving her free hand vaguely toward the furniture and looking more and more rattled. "You were saying something about Stephanie Whitman?"

Bert sat down on a damask-covered sofa while I took the matching chair. "I guess you've heard about the murder," Bert began.

Mrs. Roark remained standing, beginning to pace in front of us as she talked. "Yes. I heard it on the radio. And, to answer your question, yes, of course, Stephanie Whitman was my attorney—she was wonderful, too, just wonderful. The best. I'd trust her with my life."

That threw Bert, who stared at her. "She was? You would?" I know Bert had to be thinking of this woman's husband on the tape we'd found and his whipped cream chatter with Stephanie. I believe Bert's doubt might have come through in her tone.

"Why, yes," Mrs. Roark said, obviously puzzled. "You did work for her, didn't you? Hell, she was absolutely wonderful. Stephanie helped me tremendously—through a very difficult time. I really don't know what I would have done without her. That louse of a husband of mine actually had the nerve to tell me I wouldn't get a thing from the divorce— just because I had my own real-estate business—just like his—and owned a few minor pieces of property downtown. Pish-posh. But Stephanie put a stop to that nonsense."

"She did?" Bert asked.

Before we both began to look like double idiots, I thought I'd better jump in and ask something else. "Then your divorce is final now, and your husband no longer lives here?" I asked.

"Hell, no," Mrs. Roark said, "We've been divorced now for almost three months. Thanks to Stephanie. What a gal. What a loss." Then she did this unbelievable thing. She actually began to tear up. "I really can't tell you how much Stephanie meant to me. Her death is an absolute tragedy to all women everywhere," she said. She snatched a tissue from the porcelain box on the coffee table and took a long puff from her cigarette. "I certainly hope they catch the little prick that killed her; and, when they do, I hope they cut his cahoonas off very slowly—with a dull razor."

Bert's jaw dropped, but I merely stared back at the

woman. It was actually quite a sweet sentiment. She really must've liked Stephanie. I just wondered if she'd be saying the same thing if she knew about the tape of Stephanie with her husband, the dessert king.

"We're going to need to talk very briefly with your husband, too," I said.

"Whatever for? Stephanie was my attorney, not his." Mrs. Roark was nobody's fool. Slowly, her eyes widened, and she took a couple of quick puffs from her cigarette, blowing the smoke straight at us. "This isn't about Stephanie's business, is it? Jesus, you don't think he did it, do you?" she asked.

Then she did another unbelievable thing. She began to laugh. Loudly. Really cackling. "Oh, boy, can you imagine? Dalton gets taken to the cleaners, with me as the proprietor, and gets so steamed he actually loses it."

At least, she didn't mix her metaphors.

She could hardly contain her laughter enough to continue speaking. "Picture it. Dalton gets so pissed, he actually has to kill my attorney. Hah! I only wish it were true."

This time my jaw dropped.

"Oh, I don't mean that Stephanie would get killed. Just that Dalton would be made that mad. But, come on, he wouldn't have the guts."

"Well, could you give us his current address and phone number, just in case he happened to find his guts?" I asked.

She was still laughing as she wrote the information down—an apartment on Breckenridge Road—on a piece of stationery she pulled from the antique desk in the corner of the room. I was sure that was why her hand shook so much as she wrote down the address and phone where her ex-husband could currently be reached. "Tell the louse I said hi," she said as she handed over the paper.

Going back to the car, Bert said, "Goodness. What a really mean woman."

"Just your average pissed-off divorcee," I said. "And she appears to have won. I wonder what she'd have been like if she'd actually lost her house and all her stuff in the divorce."

"And they think a nuclear meltdown would be bad," Bert said.

I unlocked the car, and we climbed in. "You know, we still haven't talked to a single man on the tapes."

A faint smile crossed Bert's face. "They weren't at home." It was the smile of a divorcée who'd not made out quite so well. I guess there is a sisterhood among divorcées that at least celebrates the accomplishments of others who've been through the experience. Like survivors of a horrible disaster.

"There's one more address we haven't gone to"—she checked her list— "that of Dr. Bryce Hollister. Then we need to look up these other men."

"But, first, I gotta go to work," I said, getting behind the wheel.

Driving into Louisville to the radio station, I made Bert promise she would not go see any of the men before I was off at three.

"Sure," she said. "I know we need to go together. We don't know who we're dealing with. There's safety in numbers and all that."

I stared at her, feeling a tad uneasy at her ready agreement. "You mean it? You'll wait for me?"

"Why, yes," she said, a trace of irritation in her voice. "I said I would, didn't I? Why don't you believe me?"

The answer, "Thirty-nine years of twinship," leaped to mind, but I didn't say anything. I pulled up to the curb and got out as Bert came around from her side.

"See you at three," Bert said as she passed me. Then she got in my car, buckled up, and rolled down the window. She waved merrily at me, as I started down the street, heading for WCKI. I glanced back after I'd gone a few steps. Bert was still there at the curb, sitting at the wheel of my Neon, smiling and nodding and waving.

Right.

Yeah, she was going straight to Bryce Hollister's house.

Chapter 13

•

BERT

I did not go straight to Bryce Hollister's house.

I actually did try to think of something else I might do while Nan was on the air. But all I thought of was going back to Lydia's or going back to Stephanie's office. Since wandering around the lion's cage at the Louisville Zoo was more appealing than seeing Lydia again—at least until I knew if Nan and I really were responsible for her daughter's death—I settled for going over to the office to put back the files I'd taken and to record a message on Stephanie's answering machine.

At least, the office—crime scene that it was—had been released by the police now. I avoided looking into Stephanie's office to see if there was a chalk outline where her body had draped over the desk. I went instead to the answering machine on the credenza behind my desk. Then I sat there, trying to think of what to say. My message should've been along the line of "Because of Stephanie's horrible murder, you'd better get yourself another attorney," but that sounded kind of abrupt. I settled for "Due to the death of Stephanie Whitman the office is closed."

While I had the phone in my hand, I realized I hadn't promised Nan that I wouldn't at least call anybody. Which brought still another a thought. We could've just phoned the others.

It was just like Nan or me to realize at this late date that we could've saved ourselves a little time by letting our fingers do the walking. The bad thing about having the exact same genetic mix as the person with whom you hang around is that her foibles are your foibles. There's usually not a lot of offsetting or complementary characteristics. There's just identical characteristics. Which accounts for Nan and me often making the same mistake. Twice.

I looked up Judge Horace Bledsoe's work number in the phone book and quickly dialed his office number before I lost my nerve. An answering machine picked up. I left my name and work number and, just to be thorough, left Nan's name and work number, too. I did the same with Dalton Roark, only this time I got his private secretary at the real-estate-development office which he owned. I left the same information with her.

Finally, I looked up Dr. Hollister's phone number—nothing listed in the phone book. However, in his wife's divorce file was what I needed—at least, the file listed the address and phone of where he'd been served his divorce papers. Naturally, it was the same as his wife. I thought about that. All of these guys had been living at home when the divorce papers were filed. Now *that* little event must've made for a fun household.

I pictured the scenario. The Mrs. out in the kitchen cooking the dinner—or with these dames, supervising the people cooking the dinner; hubby sitting with his pipe and slippers reading the paper. The doorbell rings; the wife's ears perk, and the hubby answers. Wham-bam, here's an envelope, and next thing hubby knows, he's outta there.

Would the men go immediately to pack their stuff? Or would there be general yelling and screaming and gnashing of teeth, with the wives all wearing that same little gotcha smirk? With Jake and me, the actual divorce papers had been just a formality—we'd already been living apart by the time we both went to attorneys. Jake had moved out because he'd wanted to spend as much time as possible with his secretary and, let's face it, living with me kind of cramped his style. But, for these couples, the filing of the papers was just the beginning of the good-byes. It was the final decree that said, don't let the door hit you in the behind.

I dialed the doctor's home number in the file.

The ringing phone at the home of Dr. Bryce Hollister was—no surprise at all anymore—picked up by a woman. "Hello?" she asked.

"Is Dr. Bryce Hollister there?"

"No, he isn't—he doesn't live here anymore."

"Could you tell me to whom I'm speaking?"

"Why don't you tell me who you are first, sweetie?" The voice was friendly, but with an edge.

I told the woman my name and explained that I was trying to reach Dr. Hollister about a very important matter.

"Are you a patient of his?"

If I'd known what specialty Dr. Hollister practiced, I probably would've been offended, but instead I answered no and gave her the song and dance about working for Stephanie and clearing up her estate.

"Oh, then you don't want to talk to Bryce," the woman said. "Stephanie was *my* attorney. I'm his ex-wife, Cindy Hollister."

No kidding. So you lucked out with the house, too. I was

beginning to wish more and more I'd met Stephanie *before* my own divorce.

Mrs. Hollister agreed to talk with me, and as I was getting directions to her house on Lexington Avenue, it occurred to me that I'd promised Nan not to go without her.

Then, of course, I remembered that, technically, I'd only promised not to visit the *men*. I was smiling to myself as I drove over to Lexington Avenue. Isn't it grand what a little rationalization can do? And you can pretty much know you're rationalizing whenever you begin to use words like "technically."

Rationalizing or not, I drove over to the Lexington Avenue home of the former Mrs. Bryce Hollister. It was another one of those gorgeous, antebellum look-alikes sitting far back from Lexington Avenue in a grove of maple trees. A yard man was riding a lawn mower slowly around the expanse of yard as I pulled into the circular driveway. I was really glad I'd driven Nan's car. Her new Neon made a much better impression than my poor ancient Camry. As I got out of the car, I could see a chain-link fence surrounding a tennis court in the rear yard. It was a good thing that I hated any sport that could possibly result in perspiration, or I'd have been exceedingly jealous of—

"Mrs. Hollister?"

The woman who answered the door had the taut shiny skin of a face-lift and the toned shapely body of my daughter, Ellie. But, take away her perfectly coifed shoulder-length golden hair, her aquamarine contact lenses (nobody's eyes could be that color), and her energetic manner, and you've got your average-looking middle-aged woman. In other words, you've got me.

She was wearing one of those spandex bodysuits that

hugged every curve, running shoes, a sweatband, and a towel over one shoulder. "Are you Miss Tatum?" she asked, blotting nonexistent sweat off her forehead. "And, please, call me Cindy. Come on in—it's time for my health drink. Wink, wink." She laughed and motioned me to follow.

I followed her down the parquet wood entry hall, past several immense rooms, into her kitchen. Actually, it looked more like the kitchen for a gourmet restaurant than for a single household. I understood the wink, wink part when Cindy began mixing some tomato, V8, and other juices in a blender, splashing in a generous amount of vodka. She poured equal amounts into two large glasses and handed one to me.

"Here's to Stephanie," she said, holding her drink out for the toast. "What a loss. May she be filing interrogatories for the angels!" We clinked glasses, and I took a sip. Except for the strong taste of alcohol, it was really quite good. Cindy took a long gulp.

"So what do you think?" Cindy asked. "Did Stephanie do right by me, or did she do right?" Cindy gestured at her surroundings with her glass. "Believe me, it was not easy, either. As the wife—excuse me, *ex*-wife—of a prominent physician (he's a psychiatrist, really—do shrinks really count as physicians?) I'm continuing in the life to which I had so joyfully become accustomed. Filet mignon every night, a private trainer for my exercise, and, of course, this house. The prominent physician, on the other hand, is eating bologna, riding a stationary bike, and renting an apartment." She giggled merrily and took another drink.

I tried not to draw comparisons between myself and the prominent physician.

"How long has your divorce been final?" I asked.

"Let's see now"—she counted on her fingers—"nineteen months. Goodness, almost two years. I have a hefty allowance besides," Cindy added, her tone full of malicious glee. "Your boss was one vicious broad."

She must've noticed my look, because she stopped and stared at me. "You did work for Stephanie, didn't you? Surely you were aware of her methods. Really, it was only fair. I get mine, sweetie—just proper compensation for the years I served as gofer and secretary to that weasel of a husband of mine as he built his practice as physician to the wackos. Just your basic I-Win-You-Lose divorce." Cindy grinned again and took another long sip.

I remembered my cover story about clearing up Stephanie's estate. "So you would say Stephanie's services to you are now complete?" I asked.

"Complete?" Cindy chuckled, taking another drink as she perched on one of the oak stools at her breakfast bar. "And how. Stephanie did a stellar service for me—absolutely stellar. What a loss. I'd have recommended her to anyone— and I actually have—to all my buddies at the country club."

"Such as Mrs. Burlington Loudon, Mrs. Dalton Roark, Mrs. Horace Bledsoe?"

Cindy's eyes widened. "Yep, told them all. Except that Bledsoe gal. I don't think I know her. They all hired her, too. Stephanie was a real pro—computer expertise, all the latest equipment, everything state-of-the-art. But you should know. Even though she was originally from the south end, Stephanie was a class act."

I stared at her. I'd heard of this class distinction in Louisville before, but I'd never heard it expressed so blatantly. From what I'd heard, Louisville's east side was New Money, the Highlands and Cherokee Park was Old Money, and the south and west ends were No Money. This woman, for all her hearty friendliness, was a bigot.

"I grew up in Valley Station," I could not help saying, naming a suburb in the south end of the city.

Cindy didn't even blink. "Well, see what I mean? Stephanie hired her own kind—see how wonderful she was?"

"A saint," I murmured. "That's how she managed to win all her cases."

For some reason, Cindy thought that was the funniest comment. She roared, slapping her free hand on one perfectly toned thigh.

"That was a good one," she snorted when she could stop chortling. "I gotta admit. Stephanie was absolutely brilliant, too, setting up the good doctor the way she did. Frankly, her fee for services rendered was cheap, considering the service she performed." Cindy leaned close to me. "The very best part was the chance to beat my husband at his own game. Cheating the cheater—how sweet it is."

I blinked. "Cheating the cheater?"

"Well, yeah. Those tapes certainly did the trick. Let him explain his own voice on tape to his marriage-counseling group," Cindy didn't even notice that I hadn't understood. "Oh, sure, Dr. Hollister can help keep your marriage together, all the while he's picking up beautiful young blondes in bars during his own marital bliss."

I stared at her. What was it she was saying? It didn't take me long to put two and two together. Or more like one and one. One beautiful lady attorney and one stupid horny fool about to be taken on the divorce ride of his life. Apparently, Stephanie had hit upon the ideal way to win at the Divorce Game. She came armed with a tape of the man in the proceedings coming on to her, and she used it for leverage in her dealings for her client.

"Wow." It was all I could think of.

"Yeah, wow," Cindy said. "Stephanie was the ideal person to work the whole thing, too." She shook her head admiringly. "Any woman who's ever lost a lot in a divorce can kind of see the justice in it all."

She had a point. I thought of my own case. Of course, proving Jake's infidelity wouldn't have helped me. He'd have probably just been delighted that everyone knew he could get young girls. He would've only thought of a tape of him actually doing so as proof of his desirability, rather than of any wrongdoing. He'd have probably handed out dubs of the tape himself at the final court hearing.

That made me think of something. "There's one thing I've always wondered about the whole idea," I said. "Being able to prove your husband's infidelity shouldn't have helped you. I mean, Kentucky's a no-fault divorce state, anyway."

I'd always loved that phrase—no-fault divorce. It was kind of like no-fault auto insurance—when your marriage was a wreck, no one was to blame.

"Sure, Kentucky's a no-fault state," said Cindy. "But, the tape wasn't to get the divorce, silly. It was to soften up dear hubby for the settlement." She grinned and lifted her glass again, toasting her ceiling as if Stephanie were on the other side of her roof. "Stephanie was one sharp cookie. That tape had things on it Bryce might not want brought out— after all, he was married at the time. Like I said, he wouldn't want his patients to know what he'd suggested doing with Stephanie within the sanctity of his own marriage." She snorted and drained her glass. "Some sanctity."

I thought of the other men whose tapes Nan and I had

found. One a judge, another a minister, another a prominent businessman—oh, yeah, they might be persuaded to make good settlements just to keep this stuff from becoming fodder for any local reporter who thinks he's Geraldo.

I saw the big picture now. Stephanie had not dated her client's husbands. No, she'd taped these men's advances to her, then used the tape in the divorce proceedings against them.

"Stephanie's clientele was growing, too. By leaps and bounds. All by word of mouth," Cindy went on. "All of my friends who suspected their husbands of cheating on them, or anyone who had any reason to believe that her husband was getting ready to dump her, had found Stephanie's services well worth every penny."

Goodness, these women must've really hated their husbands. Their marriages made mine look like Shangri-la.

I must've had that disapproving look on my face again, because Cindy added "You know, sweetie, taping Bryce would've been totally harmless, or taping any of the other husbands, unless the men intended to cheat on what was then their wives. If they'd been good little boys, none of this nastiness would've happened. It's really their fault. That's what's so great about it. Besides, I got the impression that Stephanie kind of enjoyed double-crossing the men involved." Cindy actually laughed. "Hell, I certainly did."

I wondered how angry such a trick could make a man. "I don't believe Stephanie enjoyed getting murdered," I said.

Cindy blinked a couple of times, then shrugged. "Well, there's nothing to say that all this was connected to her murder," Cindy said. "I thought it was a burglar or something, according to the paper."

This time, I was the one who shrugged. "The police really don't know."

"Hm. I guess one of the men involved could've killed Stephanie—being double-crossed is a real bitch. Just ask Bryce. Personally, I hope it was my ex."

I stared at her. Hadn't Nan and I heard the same sentiment from Mrs. Bledsoe? What was it with these women?

"I'd really enjoy seeing him on death row," Cindy said with a wide grin. "That or skid row. Whichever. I'm not picky."

How should I respond to something like that? I just stared at her.

"I suppose you're in touch with the police, since you worked there and all," Cindy added, taking a pad and ball-point pen out of a nearby drawer and scribbling something. "So you may want to encourage the police to talk with Bryce."

She handed over a paper showing two phone numbers and an address. "That's where he can be reached now. Pitiful, isn't it?" I glanced at the address. An apartment complex on Fern Valley Road, in the south end, of course. "Poor boy. Do be sure to tell him I sicced the cops on him," she added gleefully.

"I will."

"Hell, maybe he did do it," Cindy said thoughtfully, tapping a forefinger against her lip. "I was at my bridge club the night Stephanie died—in full view, eight to midnight, of twenty or so of the better-dressed women in town. Although they're boring as hell. The point is, *I* can account for where I was." She gave that mean little grin again. "I'll bet you fifty bucks my dear sweet ex-hubby can't."

Chapter 14

NAN

This was beginning to be a habit.

I get off work and Bert's right there, waiting for me—jumping up and down in excitement. This time, though, she wasn't carrying file folders in her arms. She was alternately standing and sitting in the reception area, trying to make conversation with our receptionist Bambi.

With a name like Bambi, you'd expect the woman to be doe-eyed and petite, wearing lace dresses and talking in a breathy whisper. Other than the whisper part, WCKI's Bambi was as far from that whole picture as a woman could get—she weighed about two hundred pounds with a wardrobe of gray sweat suits.

Bambi was also in a snit today because the powers that be had actually asked her to answer the telephone, in addition to her duties as chair-warmer. So the conversation with Bert was pretty much one-sided. "—and we've talked to several of Stephanie's clients already," Bert was saying as I came out of the door.

"Do tell," Bambi responded listlessly, yawning and taking a long draw off of her cigarette. When Bert caught sight of me, she catapulted off her chair. Like yesterday, she seemed to be bursting with something to tell me. Or for someone to, at least, listen to her.

"Wait till you hear why Stephanie was making tapes of all those men," Bert said. She was literally bouncing up and down on her toes.

I eyed her critically. "You mean it was for something other than recording her memoirs?"

"Much, much more."

We took our leave of Bambi—who growled at us as she picked up the ringing phone and did the same to the caller— and Bert filled me in on what she learned from Cindy Hollister as we walked to my car. "Stephanie was, in effect, coming on to the husbands involved. And then zinging them in the divorce if they responded to her."

"Wha-a-at?" I stopped dead in my tracks on the sidewalk, alternating between outrage for the guys and outright admiration for the gals.

"Stephanie would tape the men's advances," Bert said. "Can you imagine? Now, if that's not a motive for murder, I've never heard one."

"Yeah, one of those guys might not have had a sense of humor," I said, which brought to mind another little detail. "Now let's see if I've got this straight," I said, heading toward my car again. "You went over to Dr. Hollister's house, after promising you wouldn't, and got this information. In other words, you lied to me. Have I got that right?"

Bert drew herself up with an injured air. "Technically, I promised not to visit Dr. Hollister. This was his ex-wife." She sounded as if she'd already practiced this response.

"Technically?" I asked. "So if something disastrous happened to you, then *technically*, you would still be OK?"

I could tell the conversation had taken an ugly turn,

because Bert changed the subject. "Ooh, look at your car," she said.

We were about half a block away from my Neon, where Bert had parked at the curb near Fifth and Muhammad Ali Blvd. A white slip of paper stuck in my windshield wiper seemed to wave at me, as it fluttered in the July breeze.

"Crap!" I said. "I've gotten another parking ticket. Make that you've gotten me another parking ticket." Ever since Louisville started to reopen the Fourth Street Walkway, the rules have changed regarding where people can park downtown. Or, rather, they seem to have changed. What was probably really happening was that enforcement of the old rules had become more stringent. At any rate, it appeared that we downtown workers may actually have to start following the law when it came to parking. How unfair.

"Oh, dear," Bert said, eyeing the guilty piece of paper. "I was sure I could park here." She got to the car first and pulled the paper out. Glancing at it, Bert turned white as a sheet. "Oh my God." Her hand shook as she handed it over.

"Come on, Bert, it's not that bad," I said, taking the paper from her. As I looked at it, I realized I was wrong. It was that bad. Very, very bad. The paper read, in large handprinted block letters, KEEP YOUR NOSE WHERE IT BELONGS OR YOU'LL END UP LIKE THAT WHORE.

"Someone is actually threatening you," Bert whispered.

"It does seem so," I said, reading the note again. The only whorelike person I could think of who had ended up in a way that I really wanted to avoid seemed to be Stephanie Whitman. "Someone who knows Stephanie Whitman, perhaps?"

"But who?" Bert asked.

"Offhand, I can think of only one. Reverend Burlington Loudon—he's the only person in this whole thing for whom we left a message with his secretary. He'd know where I could be reached."

Bert's face fell. "Better make that four," she said, shaking her head sadly. "While you were on the air, before I visited Cindy Hollister, I left messages on the answering machines for Loudon and Roark, giving them our work numbers. And after I left Cindy, I phoned her ex at his home, leaving a message on his answering machine, too." She gulped. "I told every one of them it was about Stephanie Whitman."

I turned to stare at her. "Well, at least you were thorough. Why on earth would you do that?"

"I just thought it would save us some time—they could call when we could come and talk, instead of our having to keep trying to catch them when they happened to be in."

"Bert, one of these guys could be a murderer—we're not exactly making a social appointment with these men."

"I know that. I just figured the guilty one wouldn't call back."

I stared at her some more. "No, Bert," I said slowly. "He wouldn't. He'd come by in person and put ugly threats on my car." I unlocked the passenger car door, and Bert climbed in.

When I got in on my side. Bert said, "I guess I really wasn't thinking. I've been under a lot of stress, you know."

I didn't trust myself to respond.

"We've got to tell Hank about this right away," Bert said. "There could be fingerprints on this note."

I turned around to look at her. "Bert, the only fingerprints on the note will be ours. Whoever wrote me this note is no dummy. He'll have been wearing gloves when he wrote it—just like he was wearing gloves when he killed Stephanie."

"But it's idiotic not to—"

I gave her The Look. The one Mom always gave us when she'd reached the limit of her patience. Then I counted to ten, and, keeping my voice steady, said, "Let's go see Bryce Hollister."

Bert took a deep breath and apparently resigned herself to my idiocy. "I don't think Hollister's at home—at least he wasn't a few minutes ago. Why don't we phone his office and see if he's in?"

"Right, we'll want to let him know we're coming so he can put fresh bullets in his gun."

Bert ignored me. It did make sense to at least see if the guy was there. We stopped at the first phone booth that passed Bert's inspection—meaning it appeared unlikely to get something icky on her shoes—and she made the call. While I waited with my motor running, she spent quite a bit of time in that booth, dialing numbers from a piece of paper she drew from her blazer pocket.

When she got back in the car, Bert said, "Dr. Hollister wasn't in his office, but"—she paused here—"I made an appointment with his receptionist for us to see him tomorrow right after Stephanie's funeral. The Reverend Loudon still isn't in, and his secretary wouldn't make an appointment for him."

"It's beginning to appear as if the men in this thing are lying low," I said. "Don't I wish we were."

Bert ignored me. "But," she went on, and from the sound of her voice, I could tell this was a big but. "Dalton Roark, the Third, is in his office even as we speak. I sort of led his secretary to believe we were interested in buying some property he was advertising in the paper right now. And Roark can meet with us, before his next appointment, if we can get there in fifteen minutes."

I got there in twelve. Roark's real-estate office—a four-story modern monstrosity in St. Matthews—was located on Shelbyville Road. His secretary, her long blond hair held back in a blue ribbon à la Alice in Wonderland, was wearing a navy plaid jumper, the skirt at mid-thigh, a white blouse with a large bow tied at the neck, the whole getup looking a lot like a private school uniform. Bert and I exchanged looks. Child labor?

As we got closer to her, though, the woman was easily in her early thirties, her ample chest filling the top part of the schoolgirl jumper. We exchanged the usual pleasantries with the woman, and she ushered us into Roark's office, giving her boss an adoring look. She threw us a hands-off glower just before she closed the door behind her. I surmised that she was, no doubt, doing the schoolgirl bit to please her boss.

Mr. Reddi Whip was obviously a man who could be easily pleased that way, too. He winked at his secretary before she closed the door, then turned toward us.

Oh, yeah, Roark was definitely slime. And rich slime, a combination you don't see all that often. Generally speaking, I would expect one's sliminess to impair his ability to make money. But not in Roark's case. Apparently, even his costly settlement with his wife hadn't stopped him from owning expensive suits that Rick Pitino, UK's spiffy ex-coach, would envy.

One thing for sure, Roark wasn't the guy who'd tossed me on my backside on Saturday. If this guy had touched me, I'd have still been in the shower trying to get clean.

Roark had what sex-harassment lawyers call "roving eyes." As we took our seats, his eyes roved all over Bert and me, lingering on the good parts, before he finally made it up to our faces. Then he blinked a couple of times. "Twins, huh?" were the first pearls from his lips, which he proceeded to lick a couple of times.

Bert looked like she might throw up, as she began to button all four buttons of her linen blazer, so I dived right in. "Why, yes, we are twins. And thank you for meeting with us on such short notice."

"Hey, sweetheart," he said, leering at us in the most annoying way, "anything for a chance to do business with a couple of gorgeous twins—right, am I right?" He looked back and forth from Bert to me and back again. "Wow, the soldiers from Fort Knox will love you two," he said.

I stared at him, feeling Bert next to me doing the same. What was that he said about soldiers?

"So what is it you're going for here?" he asked, gesturing at my T-shirt and torn jeans and Bert's navy suit. "Good girl, bad girl? Wow. Great, just great." He beamed at us both, admiringly. "You two've got it made."

We both stared at him. If I was interpreting this twerp right, we'd just been insulted. I glanced at Bert, who was busy pulling her skirt down over her knees. What on earth had she told this pervert's secretary to get this appointment?

"Look here, Roark—" I began, but he cut me off.

"You know what? I've got a great name for your new place—I can see it on the sign now. 'Double Your Pleasure'—what do you think?"

"How about Double Your Broken Bones?" I asked.

He blinked at me, then laughed a little nervously. "Ha-ha. Right, I get it. Down to business." He pulled forward a large black photograph binder, opened it to a particular page, and turned the binder around toward us. "You said you were interested in the property I was advertising right now. I've got several pieces of property with a downtown location—any of these should be just right for your new business." The page he showed us held four or five glossy photos of buildings with captions beneath each picture. Oh, great, he was launching into his real-estate sales spiel now. "So what kind of square footage did you need—for just retail sales or a live show, too?" Roark was asking.

"What we really wanted was to ask—"

Bert nudged me with her elbow, hard, and I looked over at her. Bert's eyes were about twice their normal size and glued to the binder. I glanced at the pictures. The photos were of real-estate property, all right, but were punctuated with words like "GIRLS, GIRLS, GIRLS" and "XXXX-RATED" on the marquees that decorated their entrances. A couple of the photos were just of storefronts, their windows covered in brown paper, with "NO ONE UNDER 21 ALLOWED INSIDE" printed in Magic Marker on the outside of the paper. "For Sale" signs, giving this slimebag's phone number, were in the corner of the buildings' glass doors.

Now I understood how Roark had become rich slime. This man dealt in the sale of real-estate property for sex shops and strip joints. Bert had actually made us an appointment with a porn king. And he believed we were ready to do business. I had to try very, very hard to keep a straight face.

"Actually," I said slowly, when I had myself under control, "Mr. Roark, we were more interested in learning more about Stephanie Whitman. And her relationship with you."

Roark's eyes bugged a little, but he recovered rather quickly. "What do you mean?" he asked. "I hardly knew Miss Whitman. She was my wife's bitch of an attorney in our divorce proceedings."

"The bitch of an attorney has been murdered," I said.

"No kidding. I was sorry to hear about that," Roark said. "But, like I said, I hardly knew her. Now, if you two aren't interested in any of these—" He snapped the binder shut and stood up.

Bert finally had caught her breath. "Well, if you didn't know Stephanie Whitman, then why is there a tape of you and her, making a date at The Cat's Meow?"

Roark began to look a little hot under the collar at this point. "You shut up," he hissed at us. He came around his desk and walked right past us, checking that his office door was firmly closed. Which, to me, pretty much confirmed what we already knew, that he was doing the secretary. Probably while he was making dates with Stephanie for whipped cream and thou.

When he turned back to us, Roark's face was crimson with fury. "Did my ex-wife tell you about that tape?" He spoke quietly but his voice shook with anger.

Bert blurted, "No, Mrs. Roark didn't. Really, she didn't."

"I don't believe you. You tell that first-class bitch that our settlement agreement stated that she was not to mention that tape to anybody, and if she doesn't keep her ugly pie hole shut, our agreement is void. You got that? And you tell her she doesn't want to find out what void means."

I personally did not like his tone.

Bert's eyes were more huge than when she'd seen the pictures of the porn shops. She stood up, looking him in the eye, so I stood with her. We both faced the angry little twerp. "I've told you already." Bert said, her voice cold. "Your ex-wife didn't tell us about the tape. She really didn't. I promise. I worked for Stephanie Whitman. That's how we knew about the tape."

I knew what Bert was doing. If this jerkwad was the one who'd murdered Stephanie, she sure didn't want us throwing him back on his ex-wife. Even if he happened to be right about her being a first-class bitch.

He actually smiled at Bert then. Not a pretty sight. "If that's true, then, you two had better keep your pretty mouths shut about that cassette tape, too, hadn't you? I won't be having that little indiscretion hurt my reputation."

I stared at him. His reputation as what? A dealer in porn real estate? Or as faithful boyfriend to Little Miss Muffet out there? Probably the latter. He came toward us, then, and took us both by the elbows.

Then he unceremoniously threw us out.

Chapter 15

•

BERT

"One thing for sure, I've never seen that little prick before in my life," Nan said, as we walked away from Roark's office. "And, personally, I wish I never had. Of course, pervert that he is, being called a prick is probably a compliment to him. Dickhead probably makes him really proud. And Jerk-off—"

"You don't think he'll actually hurt his ex-wife, do you?" I interrupted. "Because I really didn't like that thing he said about voiding their agreement." I shivered, remembering Roark's ugly expression.

"Oh, his bark is probably worse than his bite," Nan said. But she didn't sound all that convinced as we got into her car.

"We need to turn those tapes over to the police," I said, buckling my seat belt.

I'd expected Nan to disagree, but she merely nodded as she started the car. "You've got a date with Goetzmann tonight, right?"

"Oh my goodness, that's right," I said, surprised. "I'd almost forgotten." That surprised me even more. Usually, I was very aware of when Hank and I would see each other again. But I hadn't even talked to him very much since the murder—much less seen him.

"Maybe," Nan went on, starting her car, "if you give the tapes directly to your lover boy, he can keep the whole thing as quiet as possible," Nan said. "I'd really hate to see Lydia hurt any more than she has been."

I ignored the lover-boy reference. Actually, the term made me uncomfortable. Because I still wasn't absolutely sure he ever would be. I'd made tonight's date with him before Stephanie's murder. I found myself hoping he'd be too busy and stand me up.

We drove back to WCKI, and Nan made dubs of all of the Screw-tapes, as Nan called them. Screw-tapes, she said, because on them, someone was definitely getting screwed, and it wasn't the woman.

Nan pulled the last one out of the tape deck. "OK, we'll have copies now. Just in case," Nan said, putting a label on the cassette. I knew what she meant. After I handed them over, Nan didn't quite trust Hank to ever let us get our hot little paws on these tapes again.

Before we left the radio station, Nan and I tried to call the other men involved, to see if they were back at their homes or their offices. Still, no luck.

We got back home, with just enough time for me to run in my apartment, put on fresh lipstick, and run a brush through my hair. I noticed the run in my hose just as I was changing my shoes to black high-heel pumps

I searched through my bureau drawer, looking for a new pair. I really hoped Hank wasn't expecting to be invited to stay overnight. Because I still hadn't made up my mind whether going to bed with Hank was something I wanted to do. There was no doubt that I was attracted to the man, maybe even falling in love with him—but being a Nan rerun was still really getting to me.

I pulled a crumpled pair of hose from the far corner of the drawer, stretching out the legs on my hands to hunt for telltale ladders in the legs. At least, I'd be making Hank happy in one way tonight. He'd be very pleased to learn about the tapes Nan and I had found. Those tapes would be finally something pertinent to go on, in investigating Stephanie's murder. My doorbell rang just as I was wiggling out of my old pair. Goodness.

As usual, Hank was punctual in picking me up. Usually, I loved that in a man. During our marriage, Jake's version of being on time was that he arrived on the right day.

I yanked the new hose up my legs, slipping into my high heels as I went down the stairs toward my front door. I was a little breathless as I opened the door.

Hank was standing, his back to me, his huge shoulders filling out a very nice loden green blazer. Tan slacks, an off-white button-down-collar shirt, and a tie that picked up the green highlights in his hazel eyes. He turned around at the sound of the door opening, and his tough-guy face softened into a smile.

"Hi."

"Hi," I said, turning back into the room. "I'm running late, of course, but I'll just get my purse and my—"

Before I knew what was happening, Hank had stepped into the living room and closed the door behind him with one hand, taking my arm and pulling me toward him with the other. Then he was kissing me.

A long, slow, very warm, very wonderful kiss, pressing my body against his with his beautiful big hands against my back. I felt that old inevitable pull toward him, that melting-butter kind of feeling that I get these days whenever he kisses me. My heart started to pound, and I slipped my arms up and around his neck, pulling his mouth even closer to mine.

After a very long time, he pulled his head back and looked down at me, his arms still around me, his hazel eyes studying my face. "I've missed you. Are you OK?"

"Yes," I whispered. "I am now."

He smiled. "Because you've had one hell of a week. Why don't I take you out and buy you the best meal in Louisville?"

"Sounds great. Let me get my things."

Hank followed me around, as I retrieved my purse and keys and turned off lights and checked the stove and the curling iron—all the things that a paranoid woman does before leaving her home.

"I know I said this before, Bert, but I'm really sorry about your boss," Hank said. "Finding her body had to be just horrible for you. Even worse since you know her mother."

That reminded me.

"I've got something for you." I got the package of tapes from the dining-room table where Nan had left them and handed them to Hank with a little flourish. "You're going to be so pleased."

Hank peered into the manila envelope, his eyebrows going up as he looked inside. "What's this?"

As he pulled the four cassettes out, I explained what Nan and I had learned about Stephanie's little technique for winning her divorce cases. I guess I should've picked up on the fact that Hank's eyebrows were no longer up and questioning but generally crashing together about halfway through my story.

I was so pleased with myself for being able to help him out that I didn't notice that his mouth was a grim line as he sat down at the dining-room table. He drew out his little notebook and made notes of the men's names and of their ex-wives, Stephanie's clients—even though I'd already listed the names on a piece of paper stuck in with the tapes—as I talked.

When I finished, I smiled brightly at Hank, waiting for the praise that I knew he was about to heap upon me.

"You got these tapes yesterday morning?" was the first thing he asked. I nodded and felt the smile begin to freeze on my face.

"You waited until now to hand these tapes over?" Hank continued. "A full day and a half later?"

I nodded again. I began to feel that I was being questioned by a policeman. I didn't particularly care for the sensation.

Hank stood up. "I take it that you've never heard of things like concealing evidence or obstruction of justice. For your information, those are crimes, Bert."

Now I didn't particularly care for his tone. I stood up, too, feeling the color rising in my face. "And I take it you've never heard of things like 'thank you' and 'I appreciate your help.' For your information, those are good manners, Hank."

Hank, for some odd reason, began to sputter and stomp around the room. For a guy his size, that was a lot of stomping. "I can't believe you wouldn't turn these tapes over right away, Bert. Didn't it occur to you that these tapes give someone a motive for murder? Didn't it?"

All right, so he had a point. And I actually opened my mouth to tell him so, that he was right. After all, I had thought of turning the tapes over sooner, but I'd let Nan talk me out of it. Not that I felt like humbling myself and eating crow with a guy I still hadn't decided if I was in love with yet. A guy who'd had the nerve to talk to me this way when he'd dated my twin sister before me. A guy who was trying to get me to go to bed with him, just like he'd done with my twin sister. So he could make comparisons and find me lacking. Like I said, I opened my mouth to tell him he was right.

What came out was something different. "I'll have you know that if you and your cop buddies didn't have the reputation of snickering over every seamy little detail when it comes to evidence involving women, then maybe law-abiding citizens like me would hand over evidence a whole lot sooner." I got up in his face and poked my forefinger into his chest to punctuate every third word or so.

"Maybe if I'd known for sure," I went on, "that you cops know the meaning of privacy, I'd have felt like I could hand those tapes over. And if I'd known that these tapes were related to Stephanie's murder—which I still don't—I might've turned them over sooner. But, like you yourself just said, Stephanie's mother is going through a lot, and she doesn't exactly need to hear her daughter's name dragged through the mud by the police force of Louisville." I poked him again.

"You're saying that it's my fault?" Hank said right back and, unlike mine, his voice was raised. "My fault?" He ran one hand through his hair. "Look. This is crazy. You're a civilian, Bert. You don't know what you're letting yourself in for, poking around where you don't belong. You don't realize you could get hurt—"

"Don't be so patronizing. Of course, I realize," I interrupted. "Nan has already been threatened—just today." I clapped my hands over my mouth, but it was too late.

"Wh-a-a-a-a-at?" Hank bellowed. So then I had to tell him all about the note on Nan's car.

"I am telling you for once and for all, you had better stay out of this—you hear me?" Hank yelled at me. "For safety's sake. You had better let the professionals do their job. Or, so help me, Bert, I'll throw you and Nan into jail for obstruction of justice—just to protect your pretty little behinds."

"Well, you should know!"

Hank drew himself up, blinking at me. "I should know what?"

"Exactly how pretty it is!" I spit back.

He stared at me, his face turning red. "Is that what this is really about? My dating Nan before you? Is it?"

I stared at him. I really didn't know what to say.

Hank blinked at me a couple of times. Then he picked up the package of tapes, marched to my front door, threw it open, and would've slammed out; but my son Brian was standing in my doorway, the key I'd given him so he could come and go as he pleased still poised to insert into the keyhole.

Brian looked up at Hank and then at me and then back at Hank. "Hey ya, Hank. Have I come at a bad time?" He glanced back at me. "Mom? I thought you said you were going to be out—I was going to set up that modem and the new software for you on your home computer. Remember?"

I nodded, as Hank glanced back at me. "Good-bye, Bert," he said. Then he was gone.

I thought about running after Hank. I really did. For about a split second. When I thought about his toe-curling kiss earlier. But then I thought about his having dated Nan. What in the world did I think I was doing with this man?

Besides, my son was here. I really didn't feel like acting

like a lovesick teenager in front of my own perpetually love-sick teenager. When I turned back toward Brian, he was busy in the living room at my rolltop desk, already plugging wires into the back of my computer.

I could tell Brian knew exactly what had gone on here. Brian was smiling to himself.

Chapter 16

•

NAN

I *hate* funerals.

Of course, I'm not sure anyone likes them—except maybe funeral directors and those crazy old ladies you read about every once in a while who attend services for total strangers for the fun of it.

Some fun. I had to take off half a vacation day from work because this wasn't the death of a near relative, so I couldn't take a bereavement day. I also had to listen to my program director Charlie Belcher bemoaning the sad effect on my ratings by my being off so much this week. As if my listeners would've actually noticed. We've had announcers who've quit and moved out of state, and listeners have called WCKI looking for them for a full two years afterward. To hear Charlie tell it, listeners were hanging on every word, and the second I wasn't there to deliver it, they punched in the numbers of a competitor on their radio dials. As if my listeners would use the energy needed to reset their radios. Believe me, I wasn't worried.

I swung by home to pick up Bert and noted that she, too, had the funeral-day blues. She climbed into my Neon without speaking. I also noticed she'd managed to find something nice in her closet that was all black—a linen suit with a small black bow at the neck. The only all-black outfit I owned was a cocktail dress, cut to *there*, and I sure couldn't wear that. For one thing, Mama and Dad would be there.

I'd opted for a black T-shirt, black jeans and boots, and a black-denim jacket. At least the jeans didn't have any holes in them, although I could try out for one of Johnny Cash's backup singers in this getup.

I drove for about fifteen minutes before I finally realized that Bert wasn't just down about Stephanie's funeral. I realized this because, to break the silence, I asked, "So what did Hank say about the tapes?"

"Nothing much," came the clipped response. And then Bert's eyes welled up with tears.

"Want to talk about it?"

"Nope."

In a flash of twin vibes, I intuited that Bert and Hank were no longer an item. I also intuited that a Twinquisition of the whys and wherefores of what had happened was probably not exactly appropriate right now. Or Bert would be a basket case by the time we got through the funeral. She didn't speak again all the way there.

Stephanie's services were being held at Lydia's church, the Evangelical Church of the Living Son, one of those non-denominational churches that welcome just about anybody, this one located out Fern Valley Road. What struck me first as I pulled in was that the parking lot was crowded. I mean, really crowded, with the cars still coming in.

I circled the lot twice and finally had to park out on the road. Bert and I walked in with a group of three other women, one already holding a hankie to her eyes. The woman noticed me notice her, and murmured, "I can't believe she's gone. Stephanie was an absolute godsend." Around us, the other two women nodded agreement.

Bert gave me a look that asked, Had these women met Stephanie?

She and I slipped into a pew in the back, and I looked around. I spotted Mama up front with Lydia, with Dad seated next to her. Mama was patting Lydia's hand; and Dad was mostly looking uncomfortable. Probably because he was wearing a suit.

Dad's attire since retirement from General Electric has been a lot like mine—jeans and cotton shirts in the summer, jeans and flannel shirts in the winter. He kept glancing around and tugging at his collar like it was too tight. I finally caught his eye, and he rolled his eyes at me. Very un-Dad-like. Especially in church.

Bert nudged me. "Do you notice something odd about this group?" she whispered.

I looked around. It took me a second for it to hit me. The room was packed almost entirely with women—of all ages, black, white, Asian, whatever, some dressed elegantly, some not so elegant. It looked like a meeting of the National Organization of Women. No wonder Dad looked so uncomfortable. His kind was way outnumbered. I understood now. These women had all come here to mourn Stephanie. Or, more likely, the loss of her services.

I noticed Sarah Roark, her lips pursed in a disapproving line—death was probably something her social class really doesn't do. Although being married to porn kings was.

Along the far wall, I spotted Eleanor Loudon and Barbara Bledsoe seated together, Eleanor's ash blond head and Barbara's bright red head bent together in conversation.

Apparently, Eleanor and Barbara were friends. Barbara had fortunately left Lacey-love at home.

A young man with a Beatles haircut began to speak up front, and I at first thought he was a choirboy or something. "We are here to say good-bye to Steffie Elaine Whitman," he droned. "Taken from us in such a sudden, sinful way. How can we find comfort through this terrible loss?" That's when I realized he must be the minister. He droned, "How can we make sense of it all? What can we say about Steffie?"

A young woman in the congregation with a Mohawk haircut yelled back, "We can start by calling her by the right name."

The young man gulped a couple of times and glanced at his notes. When he spoke again, he got the name right, going on and on about Stephanie's virtues. He kept glancing nervously at the congregation before him like a country-music singer booked into a punk-rock concert. The poor guy seemed a little taken aback at the crowd of somewhat hostile women in front of him. After all, he represented the enemy. He looked nervously around until he spotted Dad in the front row. From then on, he spoke only to Dad. I noticed Dad tried to do his part by nodding attentively, but I could tell his heart really wasn't in it. I could tell because Dad began to nod about halfway through, and Mama gave him a nudge with her elbow.

At the close of the service, Dad and the rest of us were invited to come up and say "so long for now" to the body in the casket—a grotesque ritual, as far as I'm concerned, since the person we're good-bying is already gone. But apparently it was something everyone in the church except Dad wanted to do. Women from all corners of the room filed up to the front, hankies to their eyes.

Bert and I looked at each other. I knew that she was thinking what I was. If we didn't go up, it would certainly be noticed. By Mama, if not by Lydia. "All right, all right, let's go tell Stephanie's body good-bye," I said.

Lydia stood beside the casket, listening to the remarks the women made, as we got our turn. The sixtyish woman in front of me, wearing no less than five diamond rings and a mink coat in the summer, murmured that Stephanie had been a blessing to her. And that Stephanie looked like she was sleeping, she was so beautiful. "She reminds me of Sleeping Beauty waiting for her prince," she said, patting Lydia's hand.

Personally, I thought Stephanie just looked dead.

Lydia patted her eyes with a lace-trimmed handkerchief. "Except that Stephanie's prince never came."

"What do you mean by that?" a male voice asked from behind me.

Lydia looked up, and her face changed like a chameleon. From sadness to surprise to irritation to outright anger, in a split second. "Stephen, what are you doing here?"

Stephen? Then it hit me. Stephen Varner, Stephanie's ex. He moved toward Lydia, cutting ahead in line, to the disapproving murmur of the crowd. He really was great-looking. Slim, medium height with dark black eyes like David Duchovny of *X-Files*, his hair in a Bill Clinton coif, his jacket and slacks looking brand-new and very Ralph Lauren.

Surprisingly, Stephen actually seemed upset, his eyes straying to Stephanie's body, his lips white, a muscle jumping in his jaw. I think he might've wanted to cry; but, instead, he picked a fight with his ex–mother-in-law.

"I wanted to pay my last respects," Stephen answered Lydia's question. "I've been back in Louisville for a couple of months, just visiting my parents. I'm sort of between jobs right now," he said. (Translation: He was fired and he's mooching off Mommy and Daddy.) "And I resent your saying that her prince didn't come," Stephen went on. "Not to speak ill of the dead, but Stephanie wasn't exactly a princess either. She never really loved me. Certainly not enough. And I tried to make that marriage work, Lydia—you know that I did."

Lydia's eyes blazed. "I know no such thing. How dare you come here and talk about Stephanie, behind her back."

Not exactly, but the general meaning was there.

"I have a right to be here," Stephen spit back. "I was her husband. Obviously Stephanie felt that she'd been in the wrong in our marriage, too, because she visited me over at Mom's recently. For closure, she said. I always hoped that Stephanie and I could be friends, once she realized that the problems in our marriage had been her fault—"

"You little weasel!" Lydia yelled at him. "The only problem in your marriage was you wouldn't get a job. You lived off of Stephanie, and she loved you so much, she let you."

"I was looking for the right gig," Stephen yelled back. "Stephanie understood that I had to—"

"She didn't understand anything except that she adored you since high school! And you took advantage of her from day one. She built up her law practice while you sat on your rump and did nothing!"

"I was looking for the right opportunity, how many times do I have to tell you?"

But Lydia was on a roll. "So the right opportunity was to get half her business, when she finally had the sense to divorce you?"

Stephen sniffed importantly. "I was there when she started the practice. I contributed a lot—"

"You contributed zilch! You contributed nothing! She loved you, do you hear me? And you treated her like a meal ticket! You—you—"

"Gigolo!" a woman in line behind us offered.

"Parasite!" another woman hollered.

"Asshole!" came from in back of the line.

"Shithead!"

"Creep!"

For some reason, old Stephen began to sense the crowd around him wasn't exactly seeing it his way. He began moving toward the door. Lydia followed right after him, yelling. "But not at the last! Stephanie was finally getting over you! She'd seemed happier just lately! More content than she'd been in years! She was happy, you hear me?"

"No wonder," I whispered to Bert. "Stephanie had been finally getting some of her own back."

Stephen was already out the door, almost running toward his car as the women followed him.

"She didn't love you anymore, Stephen!" Lydia hollered after him. "She didn't love you!" As he pulled away in what was probably his parents' car, Lydia turned back toward the vestibule. "Just when it looked like Stephanie was going to be happy," Lydia murmured to no one in particular.

Her shoulders started shaking, and I realized she was crying. Mama appeared from nowhere at her side and took her by the arm, and Dad on the other side helped her back inside the church to a pew. They sat with her while Lydia cried, and the rest of the women filed out.

Bert and I sat in the next pew on the other side of the

aisle, giving Lydia a little privacy for her grief. "Goodness, I really wish I'd liked Stephanie more," Bert said.

We sat there, waiting for the moment when we'd all drive out to the cemetery for the graveside services. The church slowly emptied, but near the back of the church on the other side, I noticed a man about our age sitting alone. He was handsome, distinguished really, with dark hair and graying temples, in a dark suit, tie, and horn-rimmed glasses. Tom Selleck-ish, the way Tom had looked on the TV show *Friends*, but without a mustache. The man sat alone, the muscle in his jaw jumping as he stared at Stephanie's casket. When he noticed me watching him, he rose and headed for the door.

Bert leaned across the aisle. "Mom, Lydia, do you know that man?" Bert asked.

Mom shook her head, and Lydia did the same. The man nodded at Lydia and almost ran out the door.

When the pallbearers went by, with Stephanie's casket, we all rose to follow. At the front double doors, Bert slowed her pace.

I turned to look over at her and then at where she was looking. Hank Goetzmann stood in the vestibule, his eyes on Bert.

"You doing OK?" he whispered to her, when she was walking past him. Which, to me, seemed a rather nice thing to do.

Bert looked as if he'd spit on her. "Peachy," she snapped. And then she swept on by him, without a backward glance.

"Take care of her, Nan," Goetzmann said to me. "She's been kind of upset."

No kidding.

Chapter 17

●

BERT

I could tell that Nan was just busting for me to tell her all the gory details about Hank's and my fight. I could tell because she kept looking over at me and lifting her eyebrows as we left the gravesite. But, to tell the truth, I just didn't have it in me. I really didn't want to relive every horrible second as I filled Nan in. Suffice it to say, whatever Hank and I had had was over. I knew I'd tell Nan all about it sooner or later, but right this minute, it was later.

Nan kept glancing over at me, her eyes worried, as we drove over to the office of Dr. Bryce Hollister, Cindy's ex. I ignored her, staring out the window, engrossed by road signs, and was relieved when we finally pulled up in front of Dr. Hollister's office. To hear Cindy tell it, after she and Stephanie finished with him, Dr. Hollister should be eating out of garbage cans with all his worldly possessions in a shoe box. But it turned out that he still had a very nice office on Broadway, near a lot of the other medical office buildings in Louisville.

The woman behind the little sliding-glass window in the reception area had a voice so soft, I could hardly hear her ask us for our names. "You're twins?" she murmured, her eyes darting back and forth from me to Nan. "Both of you

are here to see Dr. Hollister? *Together?*" She seemed to be
a little startled at the whole idea, giving us sideways little
glances as she checked her book of appointments.

I guess she spoke so low so as not to push any of Dr. H's
patients into an ugly relapse; and she no doubt thought that
Nan and I were there for treatment of identical psychotic
tendencies.

"We're here for couples therapy," Nan said, and the woman's eyes widened even more. She turned her back on us to
thumb through her book of appointments.

"His ex-wife actually asked if I were a patient of his
when I called for him at his house," I told Nan.

"I guess only crazy people call doctors at their homes
anymore," Nan said.

The receptionist turned back around, murmured something inaudible, and abruptly left. Nan and I exchanged
looks. Then we took a seat and waited. Nan started giving
me those questioning glances again. Just as I was expecting
Nan to finally break down and ask me directly about Hank,
she said, "I guess you're expecting me to finally break down
and ask you directly about Hank. I certainly don't want to
disappoint you. So what happened?"

"I don't want to talk about it," I said.

"So I gathered," Nan said. "Was it something he said?
Or did?"

I ignored her.

"A combination of both?" Nan asked.

I flipped through a dog-eared copy of *Psychiatry
Tomorrow*.

In frustration, Nan grabbed another copy and flipped
through it. "Hah!" she said, pointing to a page and then
sticking it under my nose. The article that had caught her

eye dealt with the higher percentage of brain damage occurring in the firstborn of identical twins, resulting from that first twin's being smooshed up in the birth canal. Smooshed up was a technical term.

Being the first twin, a whole ten minutes older, I have to admit I experienced a trace of irritation. Nan leaned toward me. "This explains a lot," she said. I continued to ignore her.

"You know, picking a fight with Hank keeps you from having to decide whether to sleep with him or not," Nan went on.

I turned to stare at her. "Exactly what do you mean by that remark?" I said.

Nan shrugged. "I'm just saying that—"

"Dr. Hollister will see you ... two ... now," the receptionist whispered, appearing suddenly at the door. I actually jumped at the sound. I don't care if the receptionist did move so quietly so as not to push some manic-depressive over the edge—she could really get on my nerves.

We were ushered into Dr. Hollister's office, and, believe it or not, there was no couch in there. Maybe shrinks don't use couches anymore, but I really was a little disappointed. Instead, there were just several wing chairs, upholstered in a velvety pine green, a round maple coffee table, and subdued lighting. And walls painted a soft green. Even a Kleenex box on the coffee table in a green porcelain container—just in case one of his patients breaks down. The whole effect was very soothing.

Until I saw Dr. Hollister.

He was handsome, distinguished really, with dark hair and graying temples, dimples, in a dark suit, tie, and horn-rimmed glasses. Tom Selleck, the way he looked on the

TV show *Friends*, only without a mustache. "You were at Stephanie's funeral," I blurted.

He didn't seem surprised at all to see us. Apparently, it wasn't exactly a reach to assume the twins at Stephanie's funeral were going to be the twins he'd be meeting with now.

Dr. Hollister shrugged. "I just wanted to pay my respects. Of course, I hardly knew the woman—Miss Whitman was my ex-wife's attorney—but when I read in the paper how she died, it seemed so horrible for the family. I felt like I had to go."

I remembered his nod to Lydia. OK, so maybe he was drumming up business. Or maybe he was making sure Stephanie was really and truly dead. He gestured toward the wing-chair grouping and waited until we took a seat before he took his. Quite the gentleman.

"If you didn't know her very well," Nan asked bluntly, "how come there's this tape going around of you and her where you two are arranging a date, if that's what you'd call it, in a local bar?"

A man who can listen to the sex fantasies of his patients without appearing judgmental has a certain amount of self-control. He didn't blink an eye. Dr. Hollister smiled, looked a little sheepish, and said, "I suppose my wife told you about the tape. You've already talked to her, I assume?"

I nodded. "Yes, we've talked to her."

"Well, it's true, I admit it," Dr. Hollister said. "Miss Whitman and my ex-wife really put one over on me." He shrugged and smiled, almost bashfully. "And what a trick, too. But, let's be honest here, I had it coming. I wasn't exactly being the devoted husband to my wife. They caught me with my pants down, so to speak, and I deserved it."

"You don't mind that they'd tricked you?" I asked.

"That they double-crossed you?" Nan added, clearly disbelieving.

Dr. Hollister shook his head. "Of course not. Actually, I could afford to be magnanimous. I've got a very profitable practice here. And I'd been very unhappy with my wife for quite a long time. That tape and the fact that she would even think of doing such a thing just proved to me I was making the right decision in breaking off the marriage. The whole tape idea was Cindy's, you know," he said. "And just the kind of thing I would expect her to think of, too." He shook his head, still smiling. "I assume it was just the kind of thing that Miss Whitman would go for, too."

"She's done it several times since," I told him, immediately surprised that I was sharing that information. The man had an air about him that made you feel as if you could open up to him.

Dr. Hollister shrugged. "Well, I certainly didn't mind making a generous settlement with Cindy, although she may think of it differently. Cindy was always into the I-Win-You-Lose kind of contractual agreements in her relationships with other people. She would have to believe she beat me to feel good about herself."

Nan shifted uncomfortably in her chair. I was sure she expected Dr. Hollister to start into a lot of psychological mumbo jumbo. He didn't disappoint her.

"Cindy's behavior was classic, really, based on the kind of upbringing she had. Her own parents were at each other's throats from the day she opened her eyes. She learned to do battle at her mother's knee. I would assume Miss Whitman had some kind of traumatic experience that led her to behave as she did, also."

Did she ever, I thought. His name was Stephen.

Dr. Hollister nodded. "Personally, I prefer the I-Win-You-Win scenario. I got what I wanted, and Cindy got what she wanted. I got my freedom and Cindy got a lot of expensive possessions. Actually, I sort of admired the way they did it. They were really kind of clever, the little scam they pulled. Can you imagine? Wearing a wire for an encounter in a bar? It was just like some kind of television show. For my part, I certainly bear no hard feelings to either one of them. And I'm truly sorry about Miss Whitman's death."

I stared at him. His manner was subdued, almost wistful, as if he were recounting some fond memory. Goodness, maybe the life of a psychiatrist, listening to everyone's personal secrets, wasn't as interesting as you might think. Maybe Stephanie and Cindy's nasty little trick was one of the more novel things that had happened to this guy.

"Do you have any insights on the person who killed her?" Nan asked.

I looked at her. Actually, that was a great question. Particularly, if the killer was actually Dr. Hollister.

He stared off into space for a moment. When he turned back, it almost seemed as if those eyes behind the horn-rims were misted. He blinked rapidly, taking his glasses off to shine them with a Kleenex from the box on the coffee table.

"Dr. Hollister?"

He looked apologetic. "I'm sorry. I really can hardly stand to think about any person who would kill another human being. But, to answer your question, I would guess he would have to be very angry, very troubled. Someone who cannot stand losing control of a situation. I would assume that murder was the only way he felt he had left to gain that control again."

"Someone who might leave threatening notes on a person's car perhaps?"

Dr. Hollister stared at Nan. "You've been threatened?"

Nan nodded. "Of course, I don't think it really meant anything," she said.

Dr. Hollister shook his head, his expression grave. "I would take that threat very seriously. Very seriously, indeed. He must see you as a threat himself. Please realize that this person has killed before. He's already given himself permission to do such a terrible thing. He would not hesitate to do it again."

Beside me, Nan stiffened under his gaze. I stared at him. The room seemed suddenly much colder. The sinister way in which Dr. Hollister spoke almost seemed as if he himself were threatening Nan.

"Dr. Hollister?"

I jumped as the receptionist appeared from nowhere and whispered to the doctor. That woman had actually managed to open the door without making a sound. "You wanted me to tell you when your four o'clock was here."

Dr. Hollister nodded at her and smiled at us. "Well, I've got someone waiting. She's a little paranoid, so I'd better not let her stew too long." He stood up and shook each of our hands, his grip warm and filled with sincerity. I noticed Nan pulled her hand away quickly. Dr. Hollister noticed, too.

"I hope I haven't said anything that would upset you." He pulled out a pad of paper from a drawer in the coffee table and scribbled something on it. "I'd really like to talk to Mrs. Whitman, if she'd let me." He offered the paper to Nan, who didn't take it, then finally handed the slip of paper to me.

"This is my home phone number," he said. "It's unlisted now, and I've just moved a couple of weeks ago, so the phone book would be wrong either way. If there's anything I can do to help Mrs. Whitman, I hope you'll let me know."

Oh, great. Had I been right? Was he really scaring up business when he attended Stephanie's funeral? I slipped the paper into my purse.

"Well, I hope I've helped you," he went on. "I'm still not sure what you wanted to talk to me about—"

Nan turned to go. "Just checking to see if you killed her, Doc."

We left Dr. Hollister and his nurse openmouthed.

When we got into the car, Nan glanced over at me. "I probably shouldn't have said that thing about his being a suspect. It's just that it made me so angry when it seemed he was almost threatening me himself. And then to want to gain Lydia as a patient. Doesn't that seem kind of ghoulish to you?"

"On the other hand, maybe he really was trying to be helpful," I said. "Dr. Hollister actually seemed like a nice guy."

Nan snorted, a really disgusting sound, as she started the car. "Let's face it, you'd like any man who admitted he was in the wrong."

She had a point.

Nan went on. "It could be that he just does a great nice-guy impression." She turned left on Broadway. "His apologetic air could be just a ploy to hide the fact that, once upon a time, he got so angry at his ex-wife and her lady lawyer, he committed murder."

Chapter 18

•

NAN

"OK. So where to now?" I asked.

Bert thought about it for a split second. I was really hoping she would begin to mention the prospect of visiting Mickey D's for something to eat; but, unfortunately, that was not her first thought. "Well, since we're already downtown, why don't we go see if the judge is in his office."

I sighed, turning the car toward Jefferson Street.

Judge Horace Bledsoe, ex-husband of Barbara Bledsoe, the lady with Lacey-love, the dog you love to hate, was a hard man to find. His secretary or court clerk or whatever she was—a harried young woman who didn't even look up from her typing when we came into Judge Bledsoe's office on West Jefferson Street—just mumbled, "He's in court," even before we asked. She pointed out the window in the vague direction of the Jefferson County Courthouse.

The courthouse in Louisville, an imposing-looking building where every crime is disposed of, from murder to inflated property taxes—is located at Court Place (appropriately named) near Sixth and Jefferson Street. After Louisville had a few shoot-outs between defendants and judges, the powers that be finally decided everyone going to court should be checked for Uzis, so entering the courthouse these days is a lot like going through security in an airport.

When we got our purses out of X-ray, we asked directions from the gum-smacking security guard running the machine. She told us that Judge Bledsoe was holding session in the first courtroom down the hall on the left. We caught up with the judge just as he was leaving by a side door, probably headed for his car and home. Or, if those tapes were an accurate portrayal of his usual behavior, for a tryst with one of his defendants.

At least, we figured the guy who exited from the door next to the courtroom had to be Judge Bledsoe—he was the one wearing black robes, its long skirt ruffling around his trouser legs. I don't care what anyone says—men look ridiculous wearing dresses. And I'd say the same thing to any priest or Scottish bagpipe player.

"Judge Bledsoe?" Bert asked, when we reached the man.

"Horace Bledsoe?" I added.

The man in the dress stopped and turned around. Although I had certainly heard of him, I'd never actually laid eyes on the guy. Looking at him now, I realized I'd certainly not seen him breaking into Stephanie's office either. If this guy had knocked me down, I would've been out like a light. Bledsoe was exactly what you'd never expect a judge to look like. Actually, he looked more like a heavyweight wrestler—reddish hair, long bushy mustache, about six-six with a bulky muscular build—Hulk Hogan in a black robe.

"Yes?" he asked. He made a point of pulling up his black sleeve and looking at his watch. "Is this about one of my cases? Make it snappy," he said, "because I'm really in a hurry here—I've got an early racquetball time."

This joker played racquetball? I'd bet he was wheezing like an asthmatic about two minutes into play. Of course, maybe he played like John Candy did in the movie *Splash*— smoking a cigarette and drinking a beer.

About this time, Bledsoe started doing that tennis-match thing where his gaze bounced from Bert to me and back again. "You gals twins?" he asked, looking delighted. His expression changed from mild irritation to smarmy interest.

"Yes, sir," Bert answered.

I looked at her. *Sir?* This was the guy we'd heard tell Stephanie on tape that he liked to walk around naked when he had a few friends "of the feminine persuasion" over, and she was calling him *sir?*

"We were wondering how well you knew Stephanie Whitman," I said.

His smarmy little eyes turned into hostile daggers. They narrowed as he took in the WCKI call letters on the pocket of my denim jacket. "You're that radio announcer, aren't you?" he asked. "Look, I don't have anything to say to the press. All I know about the Whitman woman is that she represented my wife in our divorce. That's it. Now, if you'll excuse—"

"So how did your voice get on a tape with Stephanie in a bar talking about the joy of nudity?" I asked.

The judge's eyes bulged like they'd been inflated from within. He hastily looked over his shoulder, noticing the other people also leaving the courthouse all around us. He smiled and nodded at one man in a gray-linen suit, and then grabbed us both by the arms and pulled us around the corner. Bert and I shook off his hands simultaneously and turned to glare at him.

"Now look here, Miss"—he realized he still did not know

our names—"Whoever-It-Is-You-Two Are, the matter of Miss Whitman's death does not concern me." Judge Bledsoe's voice was taking on the tone of a member of the bar. "I am not involved. I don't know anything about a tape. Any insinuations to the contrary I must take as a slander of my good name. Naturally, I'd be glad to tell the peace officers investigating this crime all that I do know, but, as I said, I don't know anything." He nodded gravely as if that statement should satisfy us.

"So you'd be glad to tell the cops about that tape of you and the murdered woman?" I asked.

He began to bluster. I really had never before seen what the act of blustering involved, until Judge Bledsoe did it— sort of huffing and puffing and snorting before he spoke. Quite a show.

"You people should know that I am still a practicing attorney and quite familiar with the laws of slander and libel. As well as those of contractual obligation. There are ways I can deal with you in court. I'll have you know that I will not stand for being double-crossed a second time."

Bert and I just looked at him. What in hell did he mean— double-crossed a second time?

The judge apparently picked up on the fact that we didn't understand his threat. It really hurts your ability to be threatening if the person being threatened doesn't understand what's going on.

"I have a signed agreement," he huffed, "—an executed legal document—with my ex-wife regarding this Stephanie person and her defaming tape recording. To bring it up again in any form constitutes a breach of contract. If you so much as leak an iota of that tape to anything as little as a high-school bulletin, I'll see you and my ex-wife in court."

"But then we'd have to play the tape in open court," Bert said, "to see if it really did defame you." Yeah, that went over well.

Judge Bledsoe pulled himself up to his full height. Wow, he was big. He really could look kind of menacing. "Well, I think you have a lawsuit on your hands. My wife agreed in writing not to ever even speak of that tape again, and now she's told you all about—"

"Judge, your ex-wife didn't tell us about the tape," Bert interrupted. It was reminiscent of her trying to convince Dalton Roark that his wife hadn't told tales on that worm either. This guy, though, for all his black robes, seemed even more volatile than Roark had been. A sleeping volcano waiting for a reason to erupt.

"Then from whom did you hear it?" The judge thundered. "Don't tell me it was Lacey-love?" His sarcasm was a little forced.

"No," I said. "We heard it from you. We heard the tape."

If I'd thought that the huffing and puffing before was blustering, I'd apparently been mistaken. Judge Bledsoe began puffing like a steam engine, exhaling so powerfully, it made the ends of his mustache stand straight out.

"I want that tape, and I want it now," he said through his teeth, putting out his hand, shaking the arm of his black robe to get the sleeve off his hand. "Do you hear me? Right now."

"Sorry, bub," I told him, "you'll need to get it from those peace officers you were talking about. They're probably making dubs and sending them around to play at city-government office parties right now." We turned to go. But then I stopped and turned around. "Oh, and Judge? Don't ever manhandle me or my sister again? Or you'll be looking at a court from the other side. Now, do you hear me?"

Bert and I turned and walked away. I was hoping that the fact that my knees were shaking wasn't all that apparent. Bledsoe probably tried to live up to his name—by the time he got through with the people who opposed him, they would have definitely bled so. It wouldn't surprise me a bit if it turned out that he was the one who killed Stephanie.

Bert seemed a little shaken when we got into my car for what seemed to be the twentieth time today. I was really getting tired of talking to these angry men.

"Well," Bert said, when I stepped on the gas and peeled past Judge Bledsoe, who now stood at the curb glaring at us. "Apparently, Bledsoe's agreement with his ex-wife was much like the one Dalton Roark had with his ex."

"It looks like it," I said. "Just like the gays in the military. Don't ask, don't tell. I'll bet Stephanie drew up the agreement herself. Apparently, both of these men paid off their ex-wives with handsome settlements for the privilege of never hearing anything more about Stephanie Whitman. Ever again."

"Bledsoe certainly didn't want anyone to know he'd been caught that way," Bert said. "But apparently the women involved told other women, so the word was going around regardless. Cindy Hollister concocted the idea of taping the men; and after she did it, she told Eleanor Loudon and Sarah Roark about Stephanie's willingness to help."

"And then Eleanor Loudon told Barbara Bledsoe," Bert said. "No telling who else Eleanor told. Or who Barbara told. I mean, Stephanie's referrals for her taping skills were by word of mouth only. She couldn't exactly advertise what she did in the newspapers or on television. I just wonder what Bledsoe will do now that he's found out that the word is out about his taped escapades in bars?" Bert said.

I glanced over at Bert. "Maybe he's already done it."

Chapter 19

•

BERT

Thank God Nan insisted that we stop and get something to eat before heading back to the house. As far as I was concerned, I was ready to start gnawing on my purse. And maybe my belt, as an appetizer.

Nan immediately headed for the nearest Mickey D's without even asking if that's what I wanted. It wasn't hard to find one. I could see a pair of yellow arches up Market Street.

We decided to just go through the drive-through and eat in the car. This time we tried a change of menu, too—a Big Mac instead of a Quarter Pounder with cheese.

This is one of the great things about running around with a person who has the same body as yours—she gets hungry when you get hungry, she needs a bathroom break when you do, and she's thirsty when you are. You never have to make an accommodation for someone else, because the person you're with is you.

On the other hand, Jake and I had never been on the same wavelength on anything during the entire duration of our nineteen years of marriage, up to and including whom he might date. Like a lot of women, I spent a lot of time eating when I didn't want to or stopping when we were

traveling when I'd just as soon continue or readjusting the
furnace thermostat after he'd left for work. The single life—
or even life with your twin sister—certainly had its advan-
tages. Unbidden, the thought of Hank Goetzmann popped
into my mind. I pushed it away.

Nan finished the last bite of her Big Mac and crumpled
up the wrapper, stuffing it into the bag. "It's getting pretty
late—why don't we pop in on the Reverend Loudon and see
if he's finally crawled home," she said.

It took us a little over ten minutes to get to the Outer
Loop from downtown Louisville. It would've taken us even
longer except traffic had thinned out considerably on I-65.
And Nan drove like a bat out of hell, a thing which seemed
singularly appropriate considering where we were headed.

At this time of night, the Apostolic Church of the Evangelist on Outer Loop looked very dark and very uninviting.
It was one of those terribly modern churches that are being
built so often now. Red brick with a sharply angled roofline,
it looked more like a school than anything else. In fact, the
only thing that gave it away as a house of worship was the
enormous cross on the front of the building. The church
was in the middle of nowhere—or at the very least, we'd
certainly passed nowhere on the drive out here—and the
expanse of parking lot around the church was empty and
unlit.

As we got out of her car, Nan pointed at a small lamp
shining in a window above the main chapel. Next to the
window was the entrance, a wooden door facing a metal
landing. An exterior black-metal fire escape led up the side
of the building to the door. Wow. Eleanor Loudon—with
the help of Stephanie, of course—had turned the not-so-
good Reverend into a *West Side Story* reject.

Nan didn't even pause. She pocketed her car keys, slung her purse over her shoulder, and started to climb up the fire escape. She was almost all the way up when apparently she realized that the only sound of shoes on metal that she could hear were her own. I was not behind her.

Oh, yes, I most certainly was not.

From her lofty perch above me, Nan frowned. "What's keeping you, Bert?" she said. "Get a move on."

What can I say? That kind of encouragement was hard to resist. Somehow, however, I managed. Still standing firmly on the pavement, I shook my head. "Oh no."

Nan's frown deepened. "What do you mean, oh no?"

Her voice was sort of loud to be speaking so close to the lighted window. I tried to whisper when I answered. "I mean, oh no, I am not climbing that thing."

"And why not?" Nan asked, her voice irritated.

I crossed my arms over my chest, peering up at her. Oh, yes, break my heart. Be irritated with me, OK? More power to you. However, I will still continue to have every one of my bones all in one piece, thank you very much.

"I don't want to," I said.

"And why not?" Nan asked again, her voice a little more irritated this time.

I gave Nan a disgusted look. So much for twins' reading each other's mind. "Are you kidding?" I said. "It's too high!"

"Don't be ridiculous—you've climbed higher than this."

I shook my head again. "No, *you've* climbed higher," I said. Nan, on occasion, had actually sat up on a billboard as part of a promotion for WCKI. Except for the throwing-up episode, she'd sailed through the entire ordeal without a hitch. In comparison, this fire escape probably seemed about as high as an anthill. "But not me. I've climbed nothing. Not to mention, that contraption looks as if it's going to fall apart any second." I rubbed a finger along the rung at waist level. "Look at all this rust."

"Don't be silly, Bert. It's fine," Nan said.

I was still shaking my head. "No, it's not fine. Besides, I have heels on."

"Oh great, you're going to send me up here all alone because I'm wearing the right footwear? Listen to me, Bert, it's fine," she repeated. "Look, it's very safe. Very secure. Sturdy as a telephone pole." As if to show me, she actually gripped the metal handrails by both hands and shook the whole structure. It gave a sickening lurch, rattling like the chains of Marley's ghost, followed by an ugly creaking noise. Louder than I would've thought possible. It sounded as if the metal of the stairs were finally giving way. Nan, no doubt consumed with certainty about how exceedingly safe the thing really was, scrambled up the rest of the way to the metal landing, moving as fast as I've ever seen her move.

The noise must've been heard by whoever was inside, because almost as soon as her foot touched the landing, the wooden door swung open.

"Who's out there?" a deep male voice asked. The door had opened just in front of Nan, but I could see pretty clearly. I glimpsed a dark head with the door and metal grid only partially obstructing my view. Because Nan was behind the door, and the landing was very tiny, the guy didn't seem to see her.

"Reverend Loudon?" I called.

He looked down.

Through the metal grid of the landing, I could see Nan on the other side of the door, looking down at me. I could also see the man in the doorway, his eyes on me. I wiggled my fingers at him in a hello wave.

"Hello, Reverend," I called.

The man's reaction was instantaneous. "You!" he bellowed.

He grabbed for something that jangled from just inside the door—probably his car keys—slammed the door behind him and ran for the stairs of the fire escape, swinging his legs over and around to start the climb down.

He noticed Nan a second too late. At least, it was certainly too late from my point of view. And Nan's, too.

His shoulders as he swung his body around to the fire escape bumped heavily against Nan.

I believe I mentioned that the landing was very, very small.

Nan teetered, pinwheeling her arms in an effort to maintain her balance.

Then, as I watched in horror, she fell over the edge.

Chapter 20

●

NAN

As my feet went out from under me, and I slipped over the edge of the fire escape, I believe I showed admirable restraint when all I yelled was "Shit!" at the top of my lungs.

From down below, I could hear Bert give a short, terrified shriek. I don't think she actually screamed a word, or anything. She just shrieked, a short, piercing sound that pretty much let me know that I was in deep, dark what-it-was-that-I'd-just-yelled.

I might've yelled a few, even more eloquent four-letter words, except that I didn't really have much time to yell anything. As I pitched over the side, more or less plummeting to the concrete below, I was kind of busy, flailing wildly, trying to grab hold of one of the metal rods supporting the handrail that had given way.

My hand slammed into the metal rod, I grabbed hold, and then a ripple of pain pretty much shot up my arm. Right after that, the sudden jolt to my arm, as it took the full weight of my body, was excruciating enough to make me grit my teeth.

Dangling there, holding on by just one hand, I would've screamed again, except that I couldn't quite get enough breath to make a sound. My legs were swinging way out as if I were doing some kind of acrobatic stunt. I started to look down, but I knew if I actually saw how far up I was, I might get so scared I could possibly let go just from fear. I tried not to look at anything that wasn't at eye level.

I frantically twisted my body back toward the landing, reaching with my free hand. After a couple of tries, I managed to grip another metal rail with my right hand. Now I was hanging there, like a trapeze artist. A terrified, weak-limbed trapeze artist.

Below me, I could hear Bert screaming again. The sound of the fear in a voice so much like mine made me even more frightened than I had been already. My stomach lurched as I hung there by both hands. *Oh God, oh God, oh God.*

Please, dear God, don't let me lose my grip. I promise I'll never say another curse word again. Then, in the interest of being totally honest with Him, I added that, of course, He realized there was no way in hell I wouldn't slip up once in a while. Make that no way in heaven. But please, dear God, help me anyway.

Below me, Bert continued to scream. Her panicky screams almost covered the fading clatter of the man's shoes as he hurried down the fire escape. The thought of him getting away made me realize something else. That son of a bitch had just left me up here, hanging out to dry. He hadn't even stopped to haul me back up. He intended to get away, and if I fell to my death, well, that was just too damn bad.

Now, that really pissed me off. He was going to be sorry, so help me. All I had to do was get myself out of this. Come on, it couldn't be that hard. After all, I'd seen this kind of thing in the movies—all you do is just pull yourself back up with your arms. It had to be relatively easy. Sylvester Stallone did it all the time.

Right. Of course, Stallone has arms the size of country hams. I don't know if I've ever confessed to anyone how really out of shape I am—and let's be honest here, a diet of Big Macs and Quarter Pounders is not exactly muscle food—but the idea of smacking the pavement below like a bug on a windshield really can add strength to one's grip.

I started the agonizing process of pulling myself back up on the landing. It's times like these that make you really regret any extra weight you've put on, say, eating a couple of chocolate donuts in the morning. I concentrated on putting every bit of my rather pitiful strength into my left arm and leg, swinging my body ever so slowly until it gained momentum. I pulled with my arm and finally managed to swing my left foot up level with the landing. Sweat streamed down my face as I hooked my heel on its metal rim.

Below me, I suddenly heard the sound of whap! Whap! WHAP!

For a second there, I thought maybe Bert was heading up the stairs to help me. But the sound didn't seem to be getting any closer.

Oh my God, was the creep hitting Bert? *Beating* her? I had to help her. I slowly pulled my body up, using my arms and the one leg I'd hooked onto the landing. It took what seemed like an interminable amount of time, but finally, I tumbled onto the metal grating, my arms and leg burning with pain.

I got to my feet as quickly as a body can, when it's going through racking, searing pain. Then I raced down the fire escape. OK, not raced. Limped. I limped as fast as I could, but when I got near the bottom rungs and saw what was happening, I stopped trying to hurry.

Oh, yeah, someone was hitting someone, all right. But it wasn't exactly the way I'd thought.

The man who'd left me dangling was doubled up on the ground, writhing, clutching his private parts; and Bert was standing over him, her purse over her shoulder, held like a limp bat. As the man tried to struggle to his feet, grabbing at Bert, she swung low and belted him in the crotch with her purse. He dropped like he'd been poleaxed. "How dare you!" she hollered. "How dare you not help Nan! And how dare you keep me from helping her! You terrible, terrible, horrible, horrible man!"

My, my. Hell hath no fury like a Bert when she's scared.

Apparently this guy was a slow learner. He kept trying to get up, and Bert kept hitting him. Considering what Bert's purse weighs, it must've felt a lot like getting an anvil in the pelvis. There was a good chance this yo-yo was going to be singing soprano in the church choir for a long time.

When I limped up to Bert, she stopped with the purse abuse, and threw her arms around me. I noticed, however, that she still managed to keep a wary eye on the squirming man on the ground. "Are you OK, Nan?" she asked, "Are you? I was coming up to help you, but this asshole wouldn't let me get by. He was so busy trying to get away to notice all I wanted was to get up those darn steps! When he came toward me, I hit him with my purse. Then he just kept grabbing at me—" She paused for breath, her eyes filling. "Oh Nan, I really couldn't bear it if . . ." She couldn't finish. Tears were streaming down her cheeks.

It didn't take twin vibes to understand her perfectly. "I'm fine—really. I'm just fine," I said, staring at the writhing man on the ground. His eyes opened wide when he saw us both.

"Oh dear God in heaven," he muttered. "Two of you?"

I studied him more closely. "Bert, do you know who this is?"

Bert looked at him like he was a zoo exhibit. He'd stopped writhing, and started to stand up again. This time, when Bert raised her purse, he quickly stopped moving. He just lay there on his back on the pavement, holding his crotch and groaning. And glaring at us. "Well, I assume this is the Reverend Loudon," Bert said.

"I certainly am the Reverend Burlington Loudon," the man on the ground said, actually managing to put some authority into his quavering voice. "I'm pastor of this church, and I'm going to have you both thrown into jail for—"

I interrupted the creep. "He's not wearing a three-piece suit, but this really is him."

Bert's eyes widened as she realized what I was saying. "You mean—"

"This is the guy who's been making a habit of knocking me down," I went on. "He was at Stephanie's office that day; he's the one who tried to burglarize her law office."

At this news flash, Loudon actually managed to struggle to his feet to run, but before Bert took a swing at him, I decided it was time I got to knock him over, like he'd been doing to me. I stuck out a foot and he tripped over it, then Bert and I both jumped on him.

It felt just like the playground in grade school when Scotty Dameron stole our jacks ball. Just like we'd done to Scotty, we both sat on Loudon, holding him down. All the while, he raved about having us arrested, but we pretty much ignored him. Then we hog-tied him, hands and feet together in back, improvising a rope. I hate to admit it, but this is something that Bert and I have actually done before.

Bert wanted to go behind some shrubs in front of the church to take her panty hose off, but since she was needed to help sit on the creep, I just held my hands over his eyes, at her insistence, while she squirmed out of the hose. Bert said she didn't want to give the guy a free show. Right, as if his gonads didn't hurt so much, he'd actually be interested.

Except for their slightly springy quality, the panty hose made dandy ropes. "What were you looking for in Stephanie's office?" I asked Loudon, while we tied him up.

"I wasn't even there!" he bellowed.

"Could it be the tape Stephanie made of you and her in that bar?" Bert asked, wrapping one sandalfoot of the panty hose around his wrists.

"That little Jezebel! Working with my wife to bring down a man of the cloth!" Then he seemed to realize he'd said too much. "How did you know about that tape?" Loudon thundered. I could see how this guy might be able to reach even the back pews with that voice.

"Is that why you killed Stephanie?" I asked. "To get the tape?"

"I didn't kill her!" Loudon yelled, his voice probably carrying into the church nursery this time.

Once we had Loudon securely panty-hosed, I dialed 911 at the phone booth on the corner. When the officers arrived, Bert and I explained who Loudon was and why the police might want to talk to him.

Bert positively identified the creep, as the man who broke into Stephanie Whitman's office on Saturday. Just like I would have. Loudon didn't even seem to notice that we'd made a switch since our conversation with him. Hey, what can I say; sometimes people meeting us for the first time get a little confused.

The Reverend Burlington Loudon was then taken into custody to be questioned regarding the recent break-in at the office of Stephanie Whitman, deceased. As well as to answer questions regarding the break-in and its connection to her murder.

Don't you just love it when, not only are you not killed, but the creep who almost managed to do it to you ends up in deep, dark what-you-yelled?

I know I sure do.

Chapter 21

•

BERT

Sitting in Nan's apartment, I watched her unwrap my Quarter Pounder, hand me my package of fries and my supersize Coke, and I have to admit it. I was pretty impressed. Judging from the way she was acting, you'd have never guessed that an hour or so earlier she was hanging by her arms from a fire escape.

I was still a little shaky myself, just at the thought that Nan was almost killed. But Nan? It had been her idea to get something more to eat. As if facing imminent death had really whetted the old appetite.

I mean, what can I say, but: whattawoman.

Of course, as soon as Nan had mentioned it, I had been suddenly aware that I was indeed starving. "You know," I told her as we ate, "physical assault can really make you hungry."

Nan grinned. "Especially when you're the one doing the assaulting," she said.

I took another bite, feeling a real sense of satisfaction. I thought of clouting Loudon with my purse and the satisfying thud the impact made as my purse struck him you-know-where. I chewed slowly, as something else occurred to me.

"Nan? You know what? I've never seen Loudon before in my life."

Nan looked up from taking a long sip from her Coke. "Good grief, Bert, you're not worrying about identifying him for the police, are you? It's no time to nitpick. You'll just say you recognize him, if they call you to testify, and that's all there is to it. I mean, *I* recognize him, and that ought to be good enough."

"No, no, no," I said, shaking my head. "It's not that. What I meant is, Loudon wasn't at the police station when I was there. Loudon is definitely *not* one of the criminals who walked by me there on Monday. Don't you see? I didn't let a murderer go. The man they'd arrested must've been just one of your regular run-of-the-mill criminals."

Nan just looked at me. "Thank God," she said. "Just your regular run-of-the-mill, ordinary-type criminal. Wow. That's a load off my mind."

I ignored her sarcasm, I was so relieved. I took a pleased bite of a french fry. "So. Do you think the preacher did it?"

"He sure ran like he did," Nan answered. "But, to be honest, he didn't really seem any more angry about the whole taping business than Roark did. Or Bledsoe. They all seem to be about the same level of pissed. The only man who actually seemed OK with the whole thing is Bryce Hollister."

"Yeah, he just seemed sad," I said. I chewed on that idea, along with another mouthful of Quarter Pounder. "Come to think of it, Nan, Hollister was the only one of those four men who attended Stephanie's funeral. Don't you think that's kind of odd?"

Nan met my eyes. She took another long sip of Coke, then she set the Coke back down on the table, still thinking.

Finally, she got up and went over to the phone. Without her saying a word, I knew what Nan was going to do—dial Directory Assistance for Hollister's number.

"Wait a minute," I said, getting up. "You're just going to get one of those unlisted number messages. Hollister had his phone changed, remember?" I went to my purse, pulled out a small piece of paper, and handed it to her. "Here you go."

Nan dialed the number and handed the paper back to me. She held the phone out from her ear a little so I could hear, too.

Dr. Bryce Hollister answered almost immediately. The sadness in his voice came through, even on the phone. When Nan asked if we could come see him, he gave a little sigh before speaking. "It is kind of late ..." he began, then seemed to change his mind. "Oh, what the hell. What have I got to lose? Sure," he said, "sure. I'd like to talk to you. Come ahead." With that, he gave Nan directions to his apartment on Fern Valley Road.

Driving over, I wondered aloud to Nan about Dr. Hollister. "Despite what he said, that divorce of his must've knocked him flat. He must be one of the saddest men I've ever met."

Nan nodded. "I wonder if he's always been like this," she said, "or if something happened recently that has caused him a lot of pain."

I looked over at her. "Maybe he feels guilty."

Dr. Bryce Hollister's apartment complex had a run-down, dilapidated look that would've warmed Cindy Hollister's heart. A couple of the shutters were missing off of windows, and the eight-plex brick building itself could've used some paint on the doors and trim. Once inside, though, we found the wood floors clean, with freshly polished wood-work smelling of lemon polish. Hollister's was Apartment D, the one farthest from the front door on the first floor.

He answered the door at our first knock and invited us in.

Hollister's apartment reminded me of Hank's—furnished in what Nan has always called Early Divorce, that is, pieces of mismatched furniture that he'd been granted custody of after the marriage ended. Unlike Hank, though, Hollister had a few beautiful antique pieces, too, a mahogany dining-room suite and a walnut coffee table that must've belonged to his family before his marriage. Or, no doubt, Cindy would be mixing her health drink on these right now.

Hollister gestured toward an antique settee and took a seat himself on a matching chair. He was as handsome as ever, but a little more haggard-looking. He gave us that Tom Selleck, self-effacing look as he took a seat opposite us. Then he sat and looked at his hands.

"Dr. Hollister, we want to know why you went to Stephanie's funeral," I began.

"—and don't tell us you wanted to help her mother," Nan added.

Hollister looked up at Nan. "That thing you said really got to me."

Nan stared at him. I pretty much knew what he was talking about, but I let Nan ask it anyway. "What thing was that?"

"About whether I killed Stephanie. I could never have killed her—or hurt her in any way. I just couldn't. I can hardly bear it now without her."

Nan and I exchanged looks. Was this guy saying what we thought he was saying?

"I take it you two were—?" Nan began.

"We were lovers," Hollister said. He put his hands over his eyes. "No, we were more than lovers. We were soul mates."

I stared at him. How on earth could he and the woman I knew have become lovers? Let alone soul mates? The way I remembered it, she'd double-crossed him. It wasn't generally the kind of thing one soul mate did to another. Of course, maybe he'd known her earlier. "You knew Stephanie before she represented your ex-wife?" I asked.

He looked over at me, those large eyes filled with sadness. "No, I didn't. We first met when she taped me that time in the bar."

I just looked at him. All right, that could've made for a cute how-they-met story for the grandkids.

"When Stephanie contacted me about making a settlement with Cindy," Hollister went on, "and she told me about the tape, we naturally got to talking. I could tell there was a lot going on with her."

Hate and the need for revenge came to mind.

"Stephanie had endured a really hard time with her own marriage," Hollister said. "Naturally, she had a lot of issues. She really had a lot of unresolved anger."

And how.

Nan was nodding. "Naturally," she said.

"So I could certainly understand why she was doing this—taping me and then those other men. And I've already told you about Cindy. Naturally, I understood both of their motivations."

"Naturally," I said.

"Anyway, to make a long story short—after the divorce was final, I called her. And Stephanie agreed to meet me to

talk about her feelings and try to work out some of her
hostility and feelings of worthlessness and rejection. At first,
I told myself I just wanted a professional relationship with
her, I just wanted to help her through her anger and resent-
ment against men. But I soon stopped lying to myself. I
knew I was violating patient-doctor ethics—that's why I
didn't tell you about us at first. But I was so hopelessly in
love with her, I couldn't help myself. She was just so damn
beautiful. And so sad."

Tears welled in his eyes.

Bert and I exchanged looks.

"Everything was going so well," Hollister went on. "We'd
had quite a breakthrough just recently when Stephanie realized that she loved me, too. That she could actually trust a
man again. She even went to see that jerk of an ex-husband
of hers to get closure on that episode of her life. So she could
finally be free of all that baggage and let herself be happy."

Nan glanced at me. Stephen had mentioned seeing
Stephanie recently. So that was why Stephanie had gone to
see him.

Hollister was now looking at his hands again, and tears
were running down his cheeks. My eyes actually began to
burn a little. And, my goodness, I hadn't even *liked* Stephanie.

"The last time I was with Stephanie, we were talking
about marriage." Hollister looked up and almost smiled.
"That was where she was that last weekend—she and I had
gone away to a little bed-and-breakfast in Vermont. No
phones, no television, no newspapers—just us and the beginning of the rest of our lives together."

I could feel the lump forming in my throat. I remembered
Lydia telling Stephen at Stephanie's funeral that Stephanie

had been happier just recently than she'd been in years. At the time, I'd thought Lydia was just saying that to get Stephen's goat, but now I realized Lydia had really meant it.

More tears were welling in Hollister's eyes. "The rest of our lives," he repeated. He tried to smile at Bert and me, but he didn't quite make it. "Oh, well, at least, I'll always have Vermont."

Hey, it wasn't Bogart and Bergman, but it still broke my heart.

Chapter 22

•

NAN

"What a load of crap," I said, starting my Neon and pulling out of the apartment-complex parking lot. "Hollister expects us to believe that Stephanie Whitman, the woman who helped his ex-wife take him to the cleaners, was the love of his life? I suppose Paula Jones is President Clinton's true love, too."

To my surprise, Bert turned to me, her eyes wide. "You didn't believe Dr. Hollister? But he's a psychiatrist, Nan. He's used to understanding why people do what they do. And the man is obviously suffering."

I pulled out onto I-65, heading north and toward home. "Yeah, murdering someone can do that to you. This *Love Story* he's telling, where she's Ali McGraw and quite dead now, and he's Ryan O'Neal bravely going on, makes a perfect cover for murder."

Bert shook her head. "I really don't think he did it. He's so sad."

"So are the Menendez brothers." I eased into the middle lane and accelerated. "OK, granted, the guy does seem pretty upset. Personally, I'd put my money on the preacher-man. One thing for sure, though, if Hollister is telling the truth, he didn't fall in love because he's so understanding.

He fell in love with Stephanie because she was gorgeous. Pure and simple. I mean, he's a man, isn't he?"

"That's beside the point," Bert said. "I believe him. Besides, that was the saddest thing I've ever heard. I really don't think I'm going to be able to sleep tonight after hearing that."

"Bert, you hated Stephanie, remember?" I pulled up behind an eighteen-wheeler with a bumper sticker that read, "GOD IS MY CO-PILOT." He and God pulled away from me, doing about ninety.

"I didn't actually hate her," Bert said, this from the woman who'd gone to great lengths, up to and including lying to the police, to find a new boss. "I just didn't like her very much. Obviously that poor, poor man was able to see something in Stephanie that I couldn't."

"Yeah, like a sex partner," I suggested.

"It does makes you wonder . . ." Bert said, tapping a forefinger against her upper lip. She pulled a small piece of paper from her purse and then another one, looking at them thoughtfully.

"What's that?"

"Dr. Hollister's phone number," she said, frowning.

I pulled into the lane to take the Watterson Expressway east toward home, when Bert said, "No, wait. I really can't sleep just now anyway. Just take me back to Stephanie's office—I want to look at something."

I turned to stare at her. "Bert, it's nearly midnight."

"I know, I know," Bert said. "But I'm wide-awake. You can just leave me there. I really need to look at something."

"Just leave you there? Where there's been a murder? At *midnight?*"

"OK, come with me. It'll only take a minute," Bert said,

smiling. That smile of hers made it obvious that my coming along with her had been the plan all along.

Bert unlocked the door to Stephanie's office, switched on the lights, and headed straight for her own desk. She sat down and switched on her computer. The hum it made as it powered up sounded like an angry bee loose in the empty building.

"I just want to take a look at that file Stephanie was working on when she was killed." Bert glanced at the screen and started punching keys.

I stared at Bert. Was I missing something here? "Don't you have to get into Stephanie's office to do that? She was working on her own computer at the time she was killed."

Bert was already shaking her head, her eyes on the screen. "Uh-uh. Stephanie had installed one of those automatic file-transfer programs. Whenever she saved anything she was typing, it went automatically to any other computer connected to hers. That would be mine. I think she didn't want me to miss a second of work time."

Now that sounded like the Stephanie someone might want to kill.

Bert was frowning now, punching more keys. Then she frowned some more and punched some more. "It's not here," she finally said.

"What's not here?" I asked.

"The file."

"The file?"

"The *file*. The one Hank said Stephanie was working on when she died. The one that she last saved at 9:12. You know, the file."

I came around the desk and stared at the screen. As if I actually knew what I was looking at. The screen showed two columns, the left one headed with "File Name," the right column headed "Last Modified." Names of various files were in the left column with their corresponding dates and times in the right column. The files appeared to be listed with the most recent one at the top.

"See?" Bert said, pointing at the screen. "It should be the first file in the list. I don't see any file that was last saved on the day Stephanie died at 9:12 P.M."

"Maybe the program didn't work that transferred the file," I said, peering at the screen. As a radio person, I was very familiar with computer programs that screwed up royally.

Bert was already getting up and going to her handbag. She pulled out her ring of keys and went over to Stephanie's door. Inserting a key into Stephanie's lock, she said, "Sit right there, OK? Just watch the screen on my computer and tell me what happens."

I sat at Bert's desk obediently, looking at the screen. From inside Stephanie's office, I could hear the hum of that bee again and then the computer in front of me hummed, too. "It's humming," I called to her.

"Just watch the screen," Bert called back.

I watched.

"OK," she called. "I've found the file that Hank was talking about. It reads 9:12 P.M., just like he said. It's just some stupid file containing a list of Stephanie's travel expenses. That's all it is."

I started to get up to go see, but Bert must've heard me. She called out to me. "Are you watching the screen?" I sat down again.

After about three minutes, the computer in front of me hummed. And, at the top of the list of files, a new name suddenly appeared. The right-hand column that was headed "Last Modified" showed today's date, and 12:34 A.M.

"It changed," I called. "It has the current date and time, and the new file's name is "Letter to Plaintiff." But by this time Bert was behind me, peering at the screen.

"OK, the program is working," Bert said. "All I did was open that file, type a couple of words, and hit the keys to save the changes. And, *voilà!* here it is."

I stared at her, still completely in the dark. It was hard to believe that Bert had suddenly become some kind of computer whiz. "So what exactly does this mean?"

Bert shrugged. "It means, someone deleted the travel file on my computer."

"But why on earth would anyone do that?" I asked. "The file is still on Stephanie's computer. Why delete it on yours?"

Bert was shaking her head again, her eyes on the screen. "I have no earthly idea." She turned to me, brightening. "But I know who could help."

She picked up the phone, and I watched her punch in some familiar numbers. "You're calling home?"

Bert nodded. "I'm calling Brian. He was coming over again tonight, to finish up setting up my home computer with a modem. Brian showed me how Stephanie had linked the two office computers together to transfer files automatically in the first place."

That explained it. Bert wasn't the computer whiz—Brian was.

"Brian can help us figure this thing out," Bert said. After a few minutes, she made a disgusted sound, then dialed her home again. "Darn, it's still busy. Not only has Brian set my new modem up, he's probably using it."

I nodded. *"Dial-a-Trollop* is probably doing big business at your house," I said.

Bert made an even more disgusted sound and dialed again. She played Listen-to-the-Busy-Signal for a couple of more times before finally giving up.

"Can you go get Brian, Nan?" Bert asked, turning to me. "He's obviously still there, running up massive phone bills. While you're gone, I want to read that travel-expense file. After all, that was where Stephanie was that last weekend— traveling. Maybe there's something there that Hank and his crew missed."

"She was traveling with Dr. Bryce Hollister, don't forget," I said, as I went out the door. "The oh-so-sad man who makes the real *Love Story* seem like a comedy."

Bert gave me The Look and headed back inside Stephanie's office.

Chapter 23

●

BERT

I hardly heard Nan leave as I read over the file of Stephanie's travel expenses. Surely, there'd be something in the file that would explain why it had been deleted. Unfortunately, the file was about as fascinating as those brochures in doctors' offices. When I finished, I just shook my head in frustration.

There was nothing there. Just a very boring list of Stephanie's cases and the mileage she'd used running around Louisville for her clients. Nothing about personal travel at all. And no mention of Dr. Bryce Hollister. No mention, in fact, of any of the men she'd double-crossed.

So why on earth would anyone want to delete this file from my computer?

I went back into my office and looked at my computer screen again. It was as puzzling as it had been a few minutes ago.

When Brian had helped me with the computer before—that time I'd accidentally deleted all those files—he'd left me a computer diskette with a program on it that could restore deleted files.

"For you to use when you do it again, Mom," he'd said. At the time, I'd been annoyed at his use of the word "when" rather than "if." And even more annoyed that he'd left the diskette behind for me in the first place. Now, it seemed that little diskette could be put to good use.

I found the diskette in my desk drawer under the stack of business envelopes where I'd hidden it. I certainly hadn't wanted Stephanie to discover that I had this little problem keeping her files where they belonged—in her computers. And I figured this hiding place would be ideal—she'd never stoop to addressing an envelope all by herself

I slipped the diskette into my computer's disk drive and watched the program show up on the screen. It started out asking me if I really wanted to load this program. Yes or no? That was a good sign. That meant this was one of those programs that assume you don't know anything. Something you could pretty much expect from a program that is to be used for the purpose this one was used for. It seemed to say, if you're stupid enough to delete a file, it stands to reason you're going to need to be bottle-fed this program.

I typed in Y, then punched the key the screen told me and started following the rest of the instructions that appeared on the screen. Apparently, deleted files aren't actually deleted—they're just in hiding. And the place in which they're hiding out is the computer's hard drive. From what I understand, the hard drive was actually located somewhere in the computer, and this little program could race through the hard drive, looking for any file you named.

I punched some more keys, still following the simple instructions, and actually managed to load the program. When it asked me what I was looking for, I wanted to type "Stephanie's murderer." Or even, "true love." If this program could find either of those, I'd sell the darn things myself.

Instead, I typed the name of the travel-expense file and

hit the return key. Almost immediately, the screen indicated that it had located the file and even told me that the chances of restoring it was 100%. Obviously, it didn't know me.

The screen then asked me if I wanted to restore the file. Since "Are you kidding?" wasn't one of the choices, I typed Y for yes. The travel-expense file itself suddenly appeared on the screen. I hit a couple of keys and then started skimming through it realizing immediately it was exactly the same boring file that I'd just read on Stephanie's computer.

I was so disappointed.

I don't know what I was expecting. A secret code that listed the name of the murderer would've been nice. Or even the murderer's name in plain English. I closed the file, stared at the screen, and gritted my teeth.

That's when I saw it.

The list of files had changed. Oh, sure, the travel expense file was there all right, and it was now second from the top of the list, right after the file "Letter to Plaintiff." That would mean it had been saved before the file I'd sent while Nan was here.

But the time listed as the last time the travel expense file was modified read *7:12* P.M., not 9:12. Unlike Stephanie's computer, the file was now an entire two hours earlier.

I stared at the thing, trying to comprehend why on earth it read a different time. Could this mean that Stephanie had not been killed at 9:12, after all? Could she have been killed at 7:12, two hours before?

My God.

I heard Nan coming in behind me, and I didn't even turn around as I skimmed through the list of the rest of the files to see if any other changes had taken place. "I don't even think I'm going to need help after all," I said over my shoulder. "You're going to be so proud of me. I restored the file, all by myself, and you'll never believe it—it was last saved at 7:12. Not 9:12. Do you realize what that means?"

"Why don't you tell me?" The voice was female, cold, and definitely not Nan's.

I swiveled around in my chair, and Cindy Hollister stood there in the open doorway. As she moved quickly toward me, I noticed three things. One, she looked very angry. Two, she looked a little crazy. And, three—and, most importantly—she was holding in her right hand a gun that was probably small in the general range of gun sizes, but it certainly looked like a bazooka to me. The bazooka was pointed straight at me.

"Why, Cindy!" I said, trying to keep my voice light. No use panicking a crazy lady with a gun. "What are you doing here?" I figured mentioning the gun at this point might encourage her to use it.

"It appears I'm here for the same reason you are," she said. "That damn file."

"File? What file?" It's always amazed me how very stupid I can act at a moment's notice. "What on earth are you talking about?"

She made an exasperated noise. "The file you just restored—the file that shows everyone that my alibi is worthless. The file that'll help put me in the electric chair."

For a crazy person, old Cindy made a lot of sense. Of course, I believe a gun will add authenticity to just about anything.

I held my hands out, trying to show her how sympathetic I was. I also started talking a mile a minute, something I frequently do when I'm more than a little rattled. "Cindy, I won't tell anyone about the time on the file. I really won't.

And you and I can permanently delete the file—in fact, we can do it together. Because I know how you feel. I've been divorced for two years now myself. Goodness knows, for a while there, I would've liked to kill the woman who stole Jake away. Of course, now, I don't hold any animosity toward Jake's secretary anymore. I don't quite understand really why women blame the other woman. After all, she never made a promise to *me* to forsake all others, you know, for better or worse, and all that. Only Jake had done that. But I certainly can't blame anybody who does. Blame the other woman. I mean."

Cindy just stared at me as if I were the one who'd lost my mind. However, she had not shot me yet, so I took that as encouragement to go on.

"What I mean is," I hurried on, "even though I now blame Jake, I can certainly understand your blaming Stephanie. After all, she was your lawyer. You paid her to be on your side. And I can certainly understand your killing Stephanie for stealing your husband away from you."

"She did NOT do any such thing!" Cindy yelled. "I never wanted him, anyway. All I wanted to do was to win. *That's* what I wanted. I couldn't stand for Bryce to think that he'd actually bested me. The nerve of him!"

I was confused. Actually more frightened than confused, but I knew I had to keep her talking. After all, Nan and Brian should be here any minute. And maybe they could sneak up on her and overpower her, before Cindy had made up her mind to send a bullet my way.

"But, Cindy, my goodness, if you didn't want him," I asked, "why did you kill Stephanie?"

Cindy snorted. "I just told you. Weren't you listening? Bryce would have won." She said this last very slowly as if maybe she'd decided I wasn't all that bright. This from a woman who'd decided the best solution was to kill people. Talk about nerve. "I never realized that Bryce wouldn't care if I took all his furniture and his possessions," Cindy went on, "including his precious golf clubs, and I made him pay me alimony, and I got the house and both cars. After all I'd done for him, Bryce was willing to let me have those things. Can you believe it?"

"The cad?" I said. It would probably have helped if I could've sounded more convincing.

"After I slaved to build his practice, doing his typing, his billing, his recordkeeping," Cindy raved on. "I did it all. And he repaid me by giving me everything he had and still managing to be happy."

"What a terrible, terrible man," I said. I looked around the top of my desk, searching for something I could protect myself with. All I saw were paper clips, a stapler, a calendar, and a stack of files.

"Well, I showed him in the divorce exactly whom he was dealing with," Cindy went on. "But I thought I was getting all those things because of that tape with Stephanie. I didn't know then that Bryce didn't even *care* about those things."

"The swine," I said, shaking my head sympathetically. My mind was racing. If Nan and Brian came walking up behind her, Cindy would still be able to fire the gun. They might overpower her, but she would still have beaten me. Which was probably all she wanted. I could be leaping to conclusions here, but I was pretty sure I would not be able to convince her that I wouldn't mind getting killed.

"Even so, I'd have still beaten Bryce, too," Cindy raved on, "if that bitch hadn't double-crossed me. I could've made his life miserable. I was always calling him, showing up unannounced, making scenes at his apartment and his office. It was wonderful. No matter what he did, I would still manage to get his phone number and find out where he moved, no matter how hard he tried to hide it from me."

"I noticed you gave me the same number that Dr. Hollister did—his new unlisted phone number. You got the number from Stephanie's Newton, didn't you? When you killed her?"

Cindy threw me a victory smile. "Well, my dear, it was right there for the taking—I couldn't let a chance like that go by. I had to keep following him, seeing what he was up to. That's how I found out about him and Stephanie in the first place. Just keeping tabs on dear Bryce."

"Well, of course you did," I said. "You had to keep tabs on the man." The word "stalker" leaped to mind, but I certainly didn't say it.

"But Stephanie actually fell in love with that loser, can you imagine?" Cindy asked. "They actually went away together over the weekend."

"How awful," I said. I could hardly believe my ears. I'd thought Jake and I had a bad marriage, but apparently Cindy Hollister was going for the double whammy of a bad marriage and an even worse divorce.

I stared at her. The more Cindy talked, the more breathless she became. Her eyes were flashing, and her nostrils were flaring as she seemed to be working herself up into a real snit. Angrier and angrier and angrier. I wondered if that's what had happened to Stephanie, that Cindy had finally gotten so mad she just came around the desk and shot her. That, of course, was what she was going to do to me. I'd be found just like Stephanie, sitting at my desk, a bullet in my head.

Then, I'd say, people would be able to tell Nan and me apart.

I was feeling a little sick to my stomach.

Cindy was ranting now. "I even tried to talk sense to Stephanie that last night, but I could tell she wasn't really listening. She was going to marry Bryce. Marry him. Make him happy. She really left me no choice then. If Bryce had ended up with that beautiful young girl, he might've wound up actually winning. Well I certainly couldn't have that."

"Of course not," I agreed. I looked around the desk more frantically now.

"Now I've got you to deal with. You had to come snooping around, putting things together, figuring it out. I was safe, and I'd already won—Bryce was miserable, and he didn't even suspect me."

"I'm not going to tell anyone, Cindy, I promise," I said, but I don't even think she heard me.

"I warned you, you know I did," she said, her voice rising. "I put that note on your car. You can't say I didn't warn you."

I stared at her. Apparently, Cindy thought I was Nan. I'd been driving her car the day I'd gone to see her. I looked down at the desk. What could I use?

"But did you listen? Did you? No, you're just like Stephanie, selfish and thoughtless. You deserve what you get, you—"

I glanced up just as Cindy raised the gun.

Chapter 24

●

NAN

"Brian's on his way up—he's parking the car," I said, opening the office door and walking right in. "Bert, you really should keep this door locked." It was then, of course, that I noticed the woman standing a few feet in front of Bert's desk, her back to me. "Who's this?"

The woman's head swiveled in my direction. "You? You?" was all she said. "You?"

I didn't want to be cruel or anything, but this broad actually looked a little crazy. Once she got a load of me, she sort of stumbled a little to one side, her head continuing to swivel back and forth while her eyes bounced from me to Bert and back again, like a couple of mad Ping-Pong balls.

If I'd thought before that the woman was pretty much certifiable, Bert then did something even more crazy. She suddenly grabbed up the heavy metal stapler off the desk, and threw it with all her strength at the woman, hitting her hard in the back of the head, just as she was swiveling one more time in my direction. The woman didn't make a sound. She just dropped like a rock.

That's when I noticed the gun. It, too, dropped out of the woman's hand onto the carpet. Thank goodness it did not go off.

"Bert, what is this?" I was still staring, mouth open now, at the woman on the floor. "What's going on? Bert? Bert?"

I looked over at Bert, who was at that moment slowly backing up until she ran smack up against the far wall. After that she just sort of leaned against the wall, her eyes fixed on the gun.

"Bert?" I said again.

For an answer, Bert pointed wordlessly at the gun. I didn't really want to touch the thing, so I gave it a kick so that it was no longer within reach of the madwoman on the floor. Then, because Bert was looking strangely white, I ran around the back of the desk to her side.

As it turned out, I could've stayed where I was. Bert took a long shaky breath, tilted her head to one side, and then slowly dropped to the floor, sliding down the wall like a melting snowman. After which she just sat there, her eyes closed.

Through the open doorway, Brian came slouching in, chewing on an apple. Like a good son, he noticed his mother first. He took a bite of the apple. "Anything wrong with Mom?"

"No," I said, patting Bert's hand. "She's just fainted."

Bert was pretty much OK after the cops were called and the crazy woman revived and hauled away in handcuffs. Bert continued to sit on one of the office chairs, her head back, a damp washcloth over her eyes, but I knew she was all right. Brian had pulled up a chair to sit close beside his mother, while Hank Goetzmann hovered as close as he could without doing a Rhett Butler imitation and sweeping her into his arms.

Goetzmann had come in right after the other cops responded to our 911 call; and, naturally, Bert had immediately retreated under the washcloth the minute she spotted him. I think she would've fainted again if she could have.

Personally, I kind of felt sorry for the guy. Goetzmann kept stealing looks over at Bert during the whole time he was arranging for that madwoman to be taken into custody.

There's nothing quite like imminent death to make a guy think you're kind of special.

And, goodness knows, Bert was.

Someone else in this whole mess was special, too. Dr. Bryce Hollister. He'd actually been tormented by his ex-wife during their marriage and after, and yet, he'd still managed to fall in love again. And I had not been any too nice to him. Of course, remembering Stephanie, that could be the kind of woman he liked. Maybe I'd look him up in the not-too-distant future and, at the very least, apologize.

Chapter 25

•

BERT

I still couldn't bring myself to look at Hank. After all, he'd been right. I had involved myself in this murder, and Cindy Hollister had almost made me her second victim. I just couldn't look him in the eyes. Luckily, I didn't have to. I had a washcloth over my eyes. I lifted one corner.

Hank was over talking to Nan and Brian, no doubt avoiding looking at me, too. "I can't understand how this Hollister woman managed to change the time on that file of the victim, and give herself an alibi," Hank said.

"Actually, it's pretty simple," Brian said, using the kind of tact teenage boys are known for. "That lady just set the clock on the computer a couple of hours ahead. Then she saved the file and the computer logged the new time on the file. Then all she had to do then was just change the computer's clock back to the real time. No one would be the wiser."

Nan nodded. "She was banking on Stephanie's body not being found until the next morning; and she was right. It wasn't. Mrs. Hollister must've panicked just as she was leaving—when she realized Stephanie's computer was sending her doctored file to Bert's computer."

"Mom's computer would show the correct time for the file. And the lady would've noticed it was being sent right away, too," Brian said. "Because that weird screen saver on Mom's computer would go away and her computer would start humming. I guess the lady didn't have time to do it all again on both computers."

"I'll bet Cindy hardly had time to delete the file off Bert's computer and still make her bridge party on time," Nan added. She glanced over at me and saw that I'd lifted my washcloth off my eyes. She smiled at me and tapped Brian on the shoulder. "Come on, kiddo, it's late. Let's get outta here."

Brian looked at her. "But what about Mom?"

Nan actually glanced over at me, then at Hank. Pointedly. She was about as subtle as an avalanche. "I think she's got a ride."

After they left, I sat where I was, feeling dumb. Hank still stood across the room. I looked over at him. "I've been really stupid," I said.

He quickly crossed the room and knelt in front of me, taking my face in his hands and turning it up to his. "I won't stand for anyone calling you stupid," he said. "Even you. I don't know what I'd do if anything happened to you." Then he lowered his face to mine and kissed me—one of those gentle, sweet kisses that begin soft and quickly grow into something wild and uncontrolled. His big hands moved around me and then lifted me and pressed me tight against his body. I should have been thinking only of him. But, instead, I thought of the oddest thing while he kissed me.

When Cindy had been holding the gun on me, and I was sure I only had a few minutes to live, it had flashed through my mind all the things I would never have the time to do. And how very much I regretted not spending those precious minutes doing them.

I slipped my arms up and around Hank's neck and kissed him back with as much passion as he'd shown me. When I caught my breath, I whispered, "Let's go home."

He pulled his face back and looked into my eyes. "Home?"

"*Your* home."

I kissed him lightly on the lips, as he began to smile. It was about time.

Please read on

for a preview of

the next Bert and Nan Tatum mystery

DOUBLE DEALER

by Barbara Taylor McCafferty

and Beverly Taylor Herald

available now wherever hardcovers are sold.

BERT

Nan looked like she was having a cow. Come to think of it, Nan looked like she was having a whole herd as she barreled past me into my apartment.

She headed straight past me into the living room, flopped down on my sofa next to my daughter Ellie, and then just sat there, saying nothing, with a big frown on her face.

I hate this game.

It's a game I played far too often with Jake during the twenty-plus years that he and I were married: *Guess What The Problem Is. Guess* is sort of like *Twenty Questions* in that you keep asking questions, trying to guess what is making the other player look so miserable. Unlike *Twenty Questions*, though, if you haven't guessed the answer after asking twenty questions, you don't get to give up. You're still supposed to keep guessing. It is for this reason that this game could also be called *Twenty Billion Questions*. Also unlike *Twenty Questions*, there are no winners. Everybody loses—you lose time, you lose patience, and if the game keeps going on and on, you lose your temper.

I followed Nan into my living room, and sat down in the Queen Anne chair flanking my couch. I have mentioned to Nan several times exactly how much I loathe playing *Guess*, and how much I prefer people—when they're upset about something—to just spit it out. Having made myself abundantly clear, I would not have asked Nan what the problem was if she'd held a gun to my head.

My daughter, Emily Eleanor, on the other hand, at the ripe old age of twenty, apparently has not played *Guess* anywhere near as often as I have. Or it could be that my daughter just likes games better than I do. After all, Ellie had been totally absorbed in playing the computer game *Myst* on her Apple laptop when Nan came in. I'd actually tried a couple of times to start up a conversation with Ellie, but each time she'd answered me with monosyllables and turned back to her game. It was only when Nan sat down next to her, frowning, that Ellie finally stopped playing and turned to stare at her aunt.

After a minute or so, Ellie was still staring.

Nan was still frowning.

And I was wondering if I should start a load of laundry.

Ellie was spending the summer sharing her time between me and her dad, before returning to the University of Kentucky in the fall. She'd just spent a week with Jake, staying in his guest bedroom, and had arrived on my doorstep only a couple of days ago. She'd arrived—no surprise—with several bags of laundry, and had immediately laid claim to my washing machine.

That is one nice thing about college—if your children don't learn anything else, they do learn to appreciate appliances. Ellie had been appreciating my washer almost non-stop ever since she walked in my front door. So much so that I had not had a chance to run even a small load of my own things.

I'd just about made up my mind that I might as well use

this spare time to get a wash load out of the way when Ellie finally said, "OK, Aunt Nan, who died?"

Ellie actually asked that, right out loud and everything, and I didn't have even the slightest hint of a premonition. Which, I do believe, pretty much blows the theory that twins have more ESP than other people.

"Who died?" Nan was asking. "What do you mean, *who died?*" She continued to frown.

I almost smiled. You have to admire a really skilled *Guess* player. Answering a question with a question was a time-honored ploy.

Ellie ran her hand through her bangs. Up until this summer, she'd had gorgeous, wavy, long blond hair. I used to brush it for her, one hundred strokes every night, when she'd been in elementary school. A few weeks ago, though, Ellie had declared, "The only woman in Kentucky who still wears her hair long is Loretta Lynn, so unless I want to take up the guitar, I think I need a haircut."

Ellie's hair was now a very short bob, straight as a poker, with bangs to her eyebrows in the front and tapered into a sort of wedge in the back. Ellie insisted that it was the very latest look, and I'd had to bite my tongue to keep from telling her that it bore a remarkable resemblance to the haircut Dorothy Hamill had made famous during the 1976 Winter Olympics.

"What I mean is," Ellie was now saying to Nan, in a tone of infinite patience, "what's the matter?"

Nan's answer was quick, if not informative. "What makes you think there's anything the matter?"

I got to my feet. *Twenty Billion Questions* could take some time.

Seeing that I was about to walk out in the middle of her

game, Nan hurried to add, "We're just going to have to reinstate Twinstant Replay, that's all."

That stopped me in my tracks. "Twinstant Replay" was what Nan and I had at one time called our getting together at the end of each and every day and replaying everything we'd done during the day. Nan and I hadn't done Twinstant Replays since college. Back then we'd spent almost an hour every evening going over everything significant that had happened when we weren't together. *Everything significant that had happened* back in college, of course, had mainly translated to: *any guys we'd met.*

Nan had come up with Twinstant Replay after I'd snubbed some guy she'd been cultivating for months. It had not been my fault. To me, the guy had not been the least bit attractive. Far from it, to be blunt. During our freshman year, Nan had gone for artistic types, with long hair, dirty jeans, and moody stares. Me, I'd preferred men who, on occasion, bathed.

"Twinstant Replay?" Ellie echoed, looking first at Nan and then over at me. "What in the world is that?"

As she explained it all to Ellie, Nan started frowning all over again. "It seems to me that we're going to have to start doing Twinstant Replays again," she finished, "particularly if *some people*"—here Nan put an extra emphasis on those last two words and glanced over at me; the woman was as subtle as a train wreck—"are going to run around, calling other people names, and getting me in a lot of trouble. I mean," Nan went on, sounding injured, "if there's even the slightest chance I might run into people who are going to jump all over me, in public, where other people can hear, I think I deserve to be warned that these people should be avoided."

I took a deep breath and sat down again. Ellie seemed to be having trouble figuring out who all these people were that Nan was mentioning. Ellie's big blue eyes definitely looked confused. It no doubt helped to be working with the same brain as Nan. I knew exactly who Nan was talking about. Actually, it wasn't all that hard to figure out. How many people had I called names recently? Let me see, adding them all up, counting every single person, the sum total would be: one. I took a deep breath. "How was I supposed to know that you were going to the flea market?" I said. "You never go to flea markets!"

Nan glared at me. "I certainly won't be going back to this one. Not if that guy is going to yell at me again!" she said. "In public! Right in front of everybody!" She went on, giving us a play-by-play account of her encounter with that awful man at the Gigantic Flea Market.

Halfway through Nan's story, Ellie was not looking confused anymore. She was looking angry.

When Ellie gets angry, she always reminds me of her father. Just like Jake, her blue eyes always go a shade darker, and her face goes several shades of pink. Ellie is like Jake in another way, too. She can lose her temper in a split second—one minute she's honey-sweet; the next minute she's ready to go for somebody's throat.

She seemed to be leaning toward this last now. "I can't believe that jerk was yelling at you! He's got some nerve," Ellie said. "Franklin Haggerty is the one who should be yelled at! He's nothing but a crook!"

Nan shrugged. "I don't know about the guy being a crook, but he sure is a first-class jerk—"

Ellie interrupted. "Oh, he's a crook, all right. He's a fucking swindler—that's what he is!"

Ellie's eyes had darted quickly toward me right after she said the F-word. I kept my face perfectly still, registering no reaction at all. Ellie knows how I feel about her using language like this. It just sounds so vulgar—certainly not the way a young lady should talk. The last time I said something about it, though, Ellie had seemed delighted to tell me at length how she was all grown up now, and how these days she could decide for herself what was right for her. She certainly didn't need her "Mommy" telling her how to talk.

Oh brother.

As a mother, you expect that one day your child will be cutting the old apron strings. I'd just never realized that she'd be saying a few four-letter words when she did it.

Here lately, I've also begun to suspect that Ellie is talking like this just to watch the blood drain from my face. The language she'd used to that awful man—even if he had deserved it—had been enough to scorch your ears. I was pretty sure that Ellie would not have used those particular words if I had not been there. I really think that here lately she's been deliberately trying to shock me. That, of course, was why I didn't react this time.

I refused to be shocked.

Nan—whose own language every once in a while is only slightly saltier than a sailor's—didn't even seem to notice what Ellie had just said. "Swindler?" Nan repeated. "You mean, like he's pulling some sort of scam?" Her tone was skeptical.

"Aunt Nan, he's selling vintage Barbie dolls in new boxes!" Ellie said this the way anybody else might say, *He's been robbing banks!*

Nan looked disappointed. "New doll boxes?" She glanced

over at me and then back at Ellie. "And the problem with selling new stuff would be . . . ?"

Ellie rolled her eyes. "They're the boxes that came with the 1994 Thirty-fifth Anniversary reproductions of Barbie! They look just like the original boxed dolls. Haggerty is claiming that his dolls are totally original, box included, and he's asking hundreds, even thousands for some of his so-called vintage Barbies. According to my friend Chris, Number One Barbies can bring up to ten thousand dollars in the original box."

Ellie said it like everyone in the world knew that. Apparently, Nan didn't. She gaped. "Ten THOUSAND bucks? For a *doll?*"

I'd heard all this before, when we were standing in front of Haggerty and Ellie was—to use one of Ellie's own phrases—reaming him out. "Some rare dolls are even more expensive than that," I put in.

Nan shook her head. "I cannot believe it. All that money for a Barbie—"

Ellie nodded. "Mom didn't believe it either. In fact, she took up for the asshole at first, until I showed her that one line on every single box had been smudged so that you couldn't read it. It just happened to be the line that said that the boxes were reproductions. The fat turd had scratched over it to make it illegible. What a shithead!"

OK, I couldn't stand it. Maybe I could put up with *fat turd,* but *shithead* was too much. "The guy's name is Haggerty, I believe. Franklin Haggerty," I said.

Ellie just looked at me. Her eyes clearly said, *And your point?*

I ignored her. "And I wasn't defending Mr. Haggerty back at the flea market. I just like to give people the benefit of the doubt, that's all. He could've just made an honest mistake, and not even known that the boxes he was selling were new." Of course, once I saw the way he'd deliberately doctored the boxes, and heard the way he yelled when somebody pointed it out, I realized that Ellie had been right on the money. The guy was a crook, all right. A crook with a mouth almost as foul as my daughter's.

Ellie turned back to Nan. "Haggerty didn't just sell fake vintage doll boxes, either. Chris said that Haggerty put a Twist & Turn Barbie head on a Talking Barbie's body, redid her hair, and called it 'all original' on the tag. Haggerty labeled a Casey doll a Twiggy, and it's not. And he painted over the green ears on a Bubblecut Barbie, which you could only tell if you held it in the light just right. *And* he put a really cheesy wig on a fifties' Toni doll and said it was all original. The man is nothing but a criminal!"

Nan first nodded, and then looked puzzled. "Since when did you become a doll collector, Ellie? Next, you'll be standing in line to buy the latest Beanie Babies."

Ellie crossed her arms over her chest. "Chris says Beanie Babies are probably just a fad. Remember Cabbage Patch dolls? Remember Tickle Me Elmo?"

Nan was still looking at her blankly.

"OK, remember Pet Rocks?"

Nan momentarily brightened.

"Well, Chris says people were buying all those things like crazy and now, where are they?" Ellie went on. *"Never buy anything that someone manufactures as a collectible.* That's what Chris says."

"Who *is* this Chris?" Nan asked.

Ellie looked down at her laptop, turning the thing off. "Chris Mulholland. He's a dealer at the flea market, selling old toys and collectibles. I met him at UK. He was in one of my classes."

Nan looked as if she was about to say something more, but Ellie didn't give her the chance. She hurried on. "Poor Chris has had a pretty hard time, but you'd never know it to talk to him. Just a few months ago, both his parents were killed in a car accident—and then, after the estate was settled, he was left with nothing." Ellie's voice was filled with sympathy. "But Chris is determined to finish college. Being a dealer at the flea market is how he's earning money for tuition and books. Chris really liked the business. Until he noticed that some of the dealers were selling bogus items and undercutting his business. He's even complained to the people running the flea market, but they won't do anything. Chris says that most dealers are honest, but some are simply scam artists. The bad thing is, nobody seems to care, as long as they're making a buck. The crooked dealers just stick out signs that say, 'Items sold as is' and *'Caveat emptor.'* "

Ellie was winding up now. "It's honest people like Chris who pay the price for the crooked dealers because Chris can't match the cheaper deals."

"Well, well, well," Nan said. "Chris Mulholland." Her frown had totally vanished. "So, Ellie, tell me, is this Mr. Right? Or Mr. Right Now?"

I shifted position in my Queen Anne chair. Nan makes me so mad sometimes. She actually seems to think that a woman can't just be friends with a guy—that there is always something else going on. It was the dawn of the new millennium for God's sake, as Ellie was always reminding me. Men and women could just be pals, couldn't they?

Not to mention, I'd asked Ellie a similar question, and her answer had been a little indignant. "Mom," she'd said,

"Chris and I are just buds." I remembered her response quite clearly, because it had taken me a moment to realize that *buds* was short for *buddies*.

Ellie did not look indignant, however, at Nan's question. Instead, she smiled. "Chris and I are friends. That's all."

Nan returned Ellie's smile. "Yeah, right, you two are just friends. And Bert and I are just sisters. So what happened to Ted?"

Ted? I blinked and turned to look at Ellie. Who was Ted? I hadn't heard anything about a Ted.

Ellie shrugged. "Turned out Ted was just making me the lucky-duck offer."

"Oh," Nan said, sympathetically.

OK, now I was totally confused. I must've looked it, because Nan turned to me. "You know: *You lucky duck, I'm willing to sleep with you tonight.*"

I blinked, and turned to look at Ellie. *What?* Some guy was trying to get *my baby* to go to bed with him?

What I was thinking must've shown in my face because both Ellie and Nan started talking at once. "Don't worry, Mom," Ellie put in. "I'm not an idiot."

"Don't worry, Bert," Nan said. "Ellie's not an idiot."

I tried to smile, but let's face it, my head was spinning. I couldn't decide which was the most upsetting—my baby being propositioned, or my baby obviously confiding in Nan more than she did me. I'd known, of course, that Ellie thought that Nan was cool—and that Ellie thought I was, well, her mother. A thing which, I believe, is inherently un- cool. It had never occurred to me, though, that Ellie would be telling Nan things she didn't tell me.

"Boy, Aunt Nan," Ellie said, "you should've seen Mom

go after Franklin Haggerty. She practically leapt down his throat after he started yelling at me!"

What Ellie was doing was so transparent, I would've had to be comatose not to pick up on it. Obviously, Ellie wanted to change the subject bad. And she wanted to make me feel better, so I'd stop looking as if I'd been poleaxed.

"She was just great!" Ellie went on. "Mom actually told the guy to drop dead. Right in front of everybody!"

"Wow," Nan said. "You told him to drop dead, huh?"

I gave them both a faint smile. Oh, yeah, I'm hell, all right. God's gift to assertiveness training.

The two of them continued to smile at me for the rest of the evening. Nan stayed for dinner, Ellie insisted on cleaning up afterward, and throughout it all, they kept smiling at me and telling me how great it was that I'd told somebody I'd just met that I wanted his life to end immediately.

Of course, the next morning they had a slightly different opinion.

NAN

I suppose when most people see a cop at their front door, they feel a little apprehensive. Visions of unpaid parking tickets dance in their heads. Or they instantly recall how they cut that guy off in traffic the other day without using an appropriate hand signal. Or worse, they recall that they had indeed used a hand signal—one that had been all too appropriate—and that was the problem.

When I answered Bert's doorbell and found Detective Hank Goetzmann standing on her porch on Sunday morning, I didn't feel the least bit apprehensive. Not even a twinge. Of course, when your twin sister is dating a cop, it's not exactly a big deal to have him show up once in a while.

I barely gave Hank a glance as I left Bert's front door open and hurried back to her blue chintz sofa and *Cathy* in the Sunday comics. "Bert's in the kitchen," I threw over my shoulder at him. I sat down, retrieved my glass of Coke from the end table where I'd left it, took a sip, and turned the page to *Rex Morgan, MD*.

"Bert is *baking*," I added, without looking up. I couldn't help the note of amazement that crept into my voice. Bert's domestic leanings have always been a mystery to me. I don't know where she gets it. Bert and I are supposed to be

working with the same brain cells, and yet, believe me, my
brain cells do not make any sense out of baking. I mean,
sure, if you're on a covered wagon, headed west, maybe you
might feel a little inclined to whip something up. Particularly
if you're one of the Donner party. Barring that, however, it
seems like a colossal waste of time. Not to mention, you can
work all day, and the only thing you'll have to show for your
efforts is a mountain of dirty dishes. If you're really good,
you'll have the privilege of living with a lot of overweight
people. Nope, the way I see it, if there's anything even
remotely like a Winn Dixie or a Kroger or a Super Wal-
Mart within an hour's drive—or even a day's drive if you're
on the aforementioned covered wagon—all I can say is,
"Better Betty Crocker than me."

I was on the last frame of *Rex Morgan* when I realized
that Goetzmann had made no move whatsoever to go into
the kitchen. I glanced over at him again.

And saw something I didn't recognize in his expression.
What was this? Embarrassment? Discomfort? I was surprised to see something else, too.

Make that someone else.

A man was standing right behind Goetzmann. A Mount
Rushmore of a guy, Goetzmann could easily eclipse the sun,
so my not having spotted the other guy who'd come in right
behind him was not exactly a surprise. What was surprising
was that the other guy was Goetzmann's partner, Barry
Krahzinsky.

At six inches shorter than Hank's six-three and about
one-sixty to Hank's two-thirty, Barry always looks to me
like a teenager pretending to be a cop. Traces of acne on
his cheeks, his flattop haircut and his baggy clothes add to

the illusion. I'd been shocked when Hank told me that Barry was almost thirty-five.

What I gathered in an instant from the presence of Barry, though, was that this was no social call. The last time I'd seen Barry, there'd been a corpse on the premises. That could lead a person to believe that he and Goetzmann had to be on Police Business. Capital P, capital B.

Uh-oh.

About the time that little revelation hit me, Bert wandered out of the kitchen, wearing an oven mitt on her left hand, and holding a pan of steaming cinnamon raisin muffins. A rich aroma of cinnamon and vanilla came in with her. "Why, Hank!" she said, smiling. "I didn't hear you come in. What a nice surprise!" She headed straight for him, her mouth already puckering up for a little welcoming smooch.

Goetzmann began to back away. He could not have looked more horrified if Bert's smile had revealed newly sprouted fangs.

Bert looked puzzled, until Goetzmann did this little side-step so that Bert could see Barry. Bert took one look and froze for a moment. It was kind of funny. I sat there on the couch and watched Bert run through the same deductions that I had just made in exactly the same amount of time. She glanced uneasily at me, and then back at Goetzmann. "Why, what's wrong?"

Barry stepped forward. "Nice to see you again, ladies. We're just here on a routine inquiry. Just routine."

"Routine," Bert repeated after him, her voice distracted.

"So, Bert," Barry asked, "do you happen to know a Franklin Haggerty?"

I shifted uneasily on the couch. It wasn't the question that concerned me. It was the questioner. Goetzmann, the

Senior Control Freak of North America, was letting Barry conduct the interrogation? What on earth was going on?

Bert noticed who was taking the lead, too. She raised her eyebrows at Goetzmann. He just looked at her, his face betraying nothing, until Bert turned back to Barry. "Well, sure," she said. "Franklin Haggerty is that horrible, horrible man at the flea market."

"Nan?" Barry turned to me. "Do you know him?"

"Yeah. He's that horrible, horrible man at the flea market," I said. "What's this about?"

"How well do you two know him?" Barry asked.

"Not very well," Bert answered, gesturing toward the two blue chintz wing chairs flanking her sofa. "Would you two like to sit down?"

After both men took their seats, looking uncomfortable, and Bert sat down next to me on the couch, Barry cleared his throat. Not a pretty sound. One, in fact, that made you very glad there wasn't a spittoon anywhere handy. "So you two both knew Haggerty pretty well?" he said.

Bert and I both began shaking our heads in unison. "Oh no," Bert said. "My goodness, we didn't know him well. Oh my no. Not at all." Her tone implied that if either of us had known him well, we should be ashamed.

"We pretty much had a screaming relationship with him," I said. "What's this about?"

Bert must've thought I was being too blunt. She frowned, and then asked, "Can I get you gentlemen any coffee?" Turning to me, she added, "More Coke, Nan?" As she said this last, Bert evidently noticed that she was still holding the muffin pan. She held it out toward the men. "Muffins?"

I just looked at her. Bert and Martha Stewart could be best friends. Apparently, we were the target of some kind of police investigation, and Bert's chief concern appeared to be that she might not be considered a good hostess. I could just see her and Martha putting their heads together. Now what would be the perfect thing to serve during an interrogation? Something light, not too spicy, and definitely not too filling, in case one of us ends up taking a trip downtown in the back of a police car.

Bert noticed my look and glared back at me. Unfortunately, as her twin, I know her so well I could practically hear what she was thinking. *Look, Nan, just because we're the object of a dragnet is no reason we have to be rude.*

I swear, if Bert didn't look exactly like me, I'd be certain she was switched at birth.

After everyone had declined Bert's offer of baked goods and beverages, I tried again. "So what's this about?"

"When did you see Franklin Haggerty last, Bert?" Barry asked, ignoring me.

Bert obligingly filled him in on the yelling match she and Ellie had enjoyed with Haggerty the day before. "He was terribly rude," she added. "He used the F-word, the S-word, the B-word—"

Turning back to Bert, Barry said, "Tell me, Bert. Was it your daughter Ellie or you who told Haggerty to—and I quote—drop dead?"

Uh-oh. I glanced over at Goetzmann. I didn't really need to ask what was going on anymore. I was pretty sure I knew.

Bert was looking uncomfortable. Apparently, good hostesses do not tell people to drop dead. "Well, yes, I did say that," she said, looking down at the muffins she was still holding. "But Mr. Haggerty was very rude first. Why, some of the things he said were—" She broke off as something occurred to her. "Did he file a complaint or something? Because he really has some nerve, what with the yelling and screaming he did. He was awful!" She turned to Goetzmann. "Hank, you should've been there—you would've wanted to hit him. He said the most vile things just because Ellie pointed out the scam he was pulling!" Bert was now gesturing with the muffin pan, punctuating her every word. "That horrible, horrible man really has some nerve to file—"

Bert was really getting agitated. I reached over and touched her on the arm. "Bert," I interrupted. "Haggerty hasn't filed a complaint—"

She stopped her harangue and looked at me. "How do you know?"

I shrugged. "Hank and Barry are homicide cops." I looked over at the two of them. "So this has got to be a homicide we're talking about. Someone's killed the S.O.B., right?"

For only the second time since he sat down, Goetzmann spoke. "Early this morning, as Haggerty was arriving at the Fairgrounds for the last day of the flea market, some person or persons unknown met him in the parking lot. When Haggerty was finally missed at his booth, some of the flea-market directors went looking for him. They found him right next to his van, with a single bullet wound to the chest."

Barry continued. "Unfortunately, that one bullet severed the guy's aorta. He was probably dead before he hit the ground. We think the murder weapon was the handgun found next to his body. Haggerty's own .38, missing one round."

Goetzmann went on. "We think the individual or individuals who killed him probably didn't go there to murder him. But the argument escalated—and probably Haggerty pulled his gun. The individual got it away from him and shot him. Now we really need to find that individual."

I just looked at him. "Do you really think that individual was Bert or me? Are you kidding?"

Goetzmann sighed. "We're talking to everyone who had a recent argument with the guy. Your names came up."

"It's just routine," Barry added, smiling. I hated to break it to him, but hearing that wasn't exactly a comfort. A few thousand volts in an electric chair are just routine.

"If there's anything we can do to help, Hank," Bert said, "just let us know."

Goetzmann, instead of answering her, looked at his shoes. Uh-oh.

"Well, there *is* something," Barry said.

Bert looked at him expectantly. "Yes?"

"Can you tell us where we might find your daughter?"

Seated next to her, I could feel Bert suddenly tense. I looked over at her and saw the line of her jaw harden. Gripping the muffin pan tighter, she leaned forward and spoke only one word.

"Ellie?"

Oh yeah. I could swear there was smoke coming out of her ears.